ONYEKA

AND THE ACADEMY
OF THE SUN

TỌLÁ OKOGWU

SIMON & SCHUSTER

First published in Great Britain in 2022 by Simon & Schuster UK Ltd

3 5 7 9 10 8 6 4 2

Simon & Schuster UK Ltd
1st Floor, 222 Gray's Inn Road
London
WC1X 8HB

www.simonandschuster.co.uk
www.simonandschuster.com.au
www.simonandschuster.co.in

Simon & Schuster Australia, Sydney
Simon & Schuster India, New Delhi

A CIP catalogue record for this book
is available from the British Library.

PB ISBN 978-1-3985-0508-7
eBook ISBN 978-1-3985-0509-4
eAudio ISBN 978-1-3985-0510-0

Typeset in the UK by M Rules
Printed and bound by CPI Group (UK) Ltd, Croydon, CR0 4YY

MIX
Paper | Supporting
responsible forestry
FSC® C171272

CHAPTER ONE

'Onyeka!'

I flinch, a prickle spreading across my scalp as Cheyenne's impatient voice cuts through the panic rising in me.

'Come *on*, fam! While it's still 2025.'

The already stuffy heat of the changing room grows hotter and the sharp smell of chlorine stings my nose. I feel like throwing up.

'I'm not coming out,' I mutter at the thick, wooden door separating us.

A quick shuffle of feet, followed by a sharp knock. 'The pool's gonna close at this rate,' Cheyenne replies without any sympathy. 'Have you got it on?'

I stare at the swimming cap Mum insisted I wear, resting on the floor where I threw it. I knew it was going to cause me problems.

'It won't fit,' I say. 'I tried already. My hair's too big.'

Cheyenne makes a noise that sounds both like a sigh and grunt . . . a *srunt*. 'Can't you just ditch it?'

I snort back. 'You know what Mum will do if my hair gets loose or wet.'

'She won't find out,' Cheyenne replies. But we both hear the lie in her voice. Mum always finds out. It's her superpower.

'I'm not coming out,' I repeat, but there's a wobble in my voice that gives me away. I'm no match for Cheyenne.

She knows it too and pounces immediately, like a cheetah from one of the wildlife documentaries Mum loves. We watch them together the rare times she isn't working.

'Open up,' Cheyenne hollers, and the whole changing room grows silent around us.

My belly tightens. I hate it when Cheyenne does that. Just because she loves attention, doesn't mean I do too. The already tiny space of the cubicle closes in around me and my chest tightens, making it difficult to breathe. Energy surges across my skin, but I force it back down. I can't get upset. I am absolutely not allowed to lose control. It's Mum's number one rule.

I remember the first time I felt like this. Mum and I were waiting hand in hand at a bus stop and a group of kids started making fun of my hair. Mum ignored them, then bent down to me, as if she knew I was about to lose it. Her smile was gentle as she told me that I needed to control my emotions because bad things would happen if I ever set them free.

This was before she taught me the Fibonacci numbers that help keep my emotions in check. Apparently, it's some mathematical sequence from ancient India, but someone decided to name it after an Italian guy. It works though. It's hard to lose your temper when you're trying to remember what the next number is.

I close my eyes now and start counting, running through the numbers as I try to calm down.

Zero ...

One ...

With each number, I trace the shape in my mind, giving it a colour, texture and taste.

Zero is a rough-edged blue and tastes like waffles, no syrup.

One I give a shiny orange with the sharp tang of vinegar.

Bit by bit, the prickle under my skin goes away, but I continue to count, just to be safe.

I'm back to number *one* again. This time it's brown and squishy, but with the rich flavour of the doughnuts Mum never lets me have.

Two is a hazy, dull grey. Completely boring and *normal*.

I stop counting as number *two* does the trick and my racing heart begins to slow. The door handle rattles and I jump. I'd forgotten about Cheyenne. I unlock the heavy door and she slips in wearing a blue swimsuit. Her face is shiny, and I can smell the coconut oil wafting from it. She always uses too much. Even in her hair. Today, she's pulled it into a short Afro puff, held in place by a red, stretchy headband.

It's weird seeing her without the furry cosplay fox ears that usually rest on her head. Cheyenne is obsessed with Amaya, her favourite anime character, and she likes to dress up as her. I'm used to it, but I always catch people giving her funny looks. Not that Cheyenne cares what anyone thinks. Sometimes I think she likes standing out because it makes everyone pay attention, as if she's daring them to say something about her fashion sense. I prefer going unnoticed.

Cheyenne's got Turner's syndrome, and she has to take special hormones to help her grow properly. Her mouth is plenty big though. I once watched her shut down a Year Eleven girl with just one sentence. The g irl w as c hatting about my hair, so I guess she deserved it.

'Okay, where is it then?' Cheyenne's dark eyes scan the small room until she spots the swimming cap. 'Well, of course it won't fit,' she says. 'It's on the floor, you doughnut.'

Cheyenne is older than me, but she likes to act as if it's by years not months. She picks up the cap and her eyes widen in understanding. 'Rah, is your mum having a laugh?'

'I wish,' I reply. 'She thinks it's cute.' I flatten the *u* into an *oo* sound in imitation of Mum's strong Nigerian accent. Cheyenne smiles in instant recognition, her downturned eyes sparkling with glee.

I don't smile back. My eyes are fixed on the shiny swimming cap dangling from Cheyenne's middle finger. The bright white latex is covered in fire-engine-red spots.

Cheyenne's face is twitching, like she's trying to keep it straight. 'You know what you're gonna look like with all your hair crammed into that, don't ya?'

'Shut up,' I groan. Of course I know. It's all I've been thinking about today. I'm going to look like Toad from that classic Super Mario Bros game.

Her eyes shift to my head and the tangle of curls, coils and kinks sitting on top. It springs straight out of my head in an impressive riot that Mum finds overwhelming, so I rarely leave it loose. My hair has broken more combs, trashed more hairdryers and made more hairstylists cry than I can count ... so maybe Mum has a point.

Straightening it doesn't work, braids won't stay in for long and the only time Mum cut it, the strands grew back bigger and thicker. Now the longest bits that don't stick straight up or out, hang down my back almost to my bum. It always feels dry, no matter what I put in it, which doesn't help. The colour is cool though. A black so deep that when the light hits my hair just right, you can see bolts of blue fire shooting through it.

Cheyenne is proper laughing now. 'It's a-me, Mario!' she hollers with glee.

I wish I could laugh back, but I'm too stressed. It was

hard enough getting permission to even come swimming in the first place. Now that it's the school holidays, I'm either at Cheyenne's house or I have to stay at the salon so Mum can keep an eye on me. I left it until the last possible minute and waited until she was distracted with one of her clients before asking.

'Mum, can I leave early today please?' I asked.

Her hands stilled and silence descended on the salon. All conversation stopped as eager ears waited to hear Mum's reply.

'Why?' she finally said.

'Chey's having a pool party for her birthday,' I replied, not bothering to mention it was a party of two. At the sound of Cheyenne's name, Mum smiled, and I tried not to get my hopes up. 'Please, Mum,' I begged in a loud voice. 'You never let me go anywhere.'

'There you go again, always exaggerating,' Mum replied. 'Don't you go to school? Am I imagining your presence beside me at church on Sundays?'

I've learned not to answer questions like that. There *is* no right answer, so I remained silent.

'Why do you two want to go swimming anyway when Cheyenne gets all those ear infections?' she continued. 'You can't even swim very well.'

I ignored the bit about my rubbish swimming skills because she was right and I'd already told Cheyenne as much.

Mum was also right about the ear infections. Cheyenne gets them a lot because of the Turner's syndrome.

'It's been ages since Chey had one,' I replied instead. 'Besides, her mum said it was okay.'

Mum kissed her teeth at me. 'I do not want you out and about with so many strangers. You're not like everyone else.'

Not this again!

'Doesn't seem to bother you when I'm at the salon,' I muttered under my breath. 'There are always random people here!'

'What was that, Onyekachi?'

I plastered an innocent smile on my face. Mum is the only person who uses my full name and it's usually when I'm in trouble.

'Come on, Tópé, let the child have some fun,' Mrs Mataka said as she passed us on her way to the sink.

Hushed whispers spread across the salon and an annoyed look settled on Mum's face. She hates standing out almost as much as she hates me standing out. Then her face evened out suddenly, just before she gave in to the peer pressure she's always warning me about.

'Fine,' Mum finally said, and stunned relief filled me. I was fully ready for her to say no.

'But you must wear a swimming cap,' she added, and the relief melted away. 'I don't have time to wash and blow dry your hair today.'

Then Mum fully pulled out a swimming cap from one of her styling drawers. *Who has a swimming cap just hanging around?*

So here I am, trying to fit the ugly thing over my hair, and all Cheyenne can do is laugh. She finally stops spluttering long enough for me to get a word in.

'What am I going to do?' I ask.

'Sorry, fam, but you're gonna have to pack it up ... '

My mouth twists and her voice trails off. Cheyenne meets my gaze again, but there's no curiosity or pity. Not like I get from others. To Cheyenne, my hair is just another part of me, like the gap between my front teeth and my massive size-eight feet. The same way I see her love of furry fox ears and marmite. It's the way I wish the world would see both of us, instead of only focusing on the things that make us different. It's what drew Cheyenne and me together in the first place.

That, and the fact she's the only other Nigerian I know. Mum never talks about Nigeria or why we left, so the little I know about how it became so rich and powerful comes from history class. It's been this way for as long as I can remember.

Before she found work in the salon, Mum cleaned toilets in one of the local primary schools. She was so thin then, her second-hand clothes hanging off her. She doesn't think I remember, but I do. I also remember how long it took for her to find a salon willing to ignore the fact she doesn't have a British passport and also willing to pay in cash.

'Everyone is going to be looking at me,' I tell Cheyenne with a sigh.

Cheyenne shrugs. 'Does it matter?'

She's right, it shouldn't. But it does to me.

I grab the swimming cap from her roughly and scrunch it up into a ball.

'Yes,' I reply.

Cheyenne hesitates for a moment, then pulls it from my clenched fist. 'I don't know why you let what other people think bother you so much,' she says, smoothing it out. She reaches towards me, the cap resting between her small fingers. 'We don't need to fit in.'

But I do, I want to scream. *I need to feel like I belong somewhere.*

I don't though. Instead, I push the frustration back down to join all the other feelings I'm not allowed to have, like curiosity about my father and happiness at school. And the scariest one of all … hope that things will be different.

'Look,' says Cheyenne after a short pause. 'It's my birthday and your mum finally let you do something other than go to church. I'm not letting you waste it by acting moist in here.'

My eyebrows lift at her tone, but she's right, and I don't want to mess up her special day. I snatch the ugly cap from her.

'You're the one who's moist,' I reply with a small smile.

'Sorry,' Cheyenne shoots right back. 'I can't hear you past your mushroom head.'

CHAPTER
TWO

We quickly make our way poolside – a brightly lit, rectangular space that is even warmer than the changing room. The swimming cap tightens even more around my head.

In the middle of the space sits a large pool with people scattered everywhere. It's mostly kids, enjoying their summer holidays. Some are in the water, playing in lazy boredom, while the better swimmers zoom past them. The rest hang around the edge of the pool, chatting in small groups.

I feel the eyes and hear the sniggers following my bulbous head as we pass. A girl nudges past me with a wide-eyed look of wonder and I grit my teeth so I don't react. It's always the same and I've heard *all* the jokes. From how I look like a yeti to the *hilarious* one about using a rake to comb my hair.

Even adults, who should know better, can't help themselves. Every time we go to the hair shop to get products, Mum is always surrounded by people offering to do my hair, like it's so unbelievable that I would *choose* to walk around looking the way I do.

The worst part is watching Mum try to ignore them, her worry a constant blanket surrounding both of us. Mum says I shouldn't get angry or let it bother me when people chat rubbish. But when I see how sad it makes her and think about how she has to deal with it alone, I can't help but get angry. That's always when I wish my father was around. Mum says he felt things too deeply and his emotions would take over, just like mine. It's why he came up with the Fibonacci number sequence Mum then taught me – to stop his feelings overwhelming him.

Last year, Megan Gold said I tripped her on purpose. I didn't. The Velcro on her bag got caught in my hair. Ms Mason, our head teacher, didn't believe me and I got so upset I almost forgot to use my numbers. By the time I remembered, the prickles had spread from my scalp to my neck.

I wish my father were here so I could ask him how he dealt with his feelings. I'm sure Mum would be happier if he were here. I clutch the necklace round my neck. A single, white cowrie shell hanging from a thin, leather cord. It belonged to my father and it's the only physical connection I have to him.

Cheyenne coughs loudly, pulling me from my thoughts.

'Let's go,' she calls. 'My birthday only lasts for a day.'

I follow, silently. There are too many people and not

enough places to hide. Cheyenne and I usually just hang out in one of our bedrooms, watching our favourite anime. I love all the characters. In that world, being different is cool.

'There's a spot over there,' Cheyenne says, pointing to an empty space near the shallow end.

'Chey, I'm not sure about this,' I say, but she's already moving off and I rush to keep up.

'Ugh, will you just chill, Yeka,' she calls back, shortening my name, even though she knows I don't like it. 'You'll be fine once you get in.'

I catch up with her just as she reaches the edge of the water. 'But we're rubbish at swimming.'

'Shut up, I can totally swim,' Cheyenne says with a grin.

Cheyenne only just got her five-metre certificate. I know she's super proud and stuff, but I still don't understand why she thinks a pool party is a good idea.

Before I can say anything more, she steps into the pool and pushes forward until her body is fully submerged. *She makes it look so easy.*

I touch my head with nervous fingers and the stiff latex of the cap greets me. At least Mum will be happy. Then, with a deep breath, I follow Cheyenne into the pool.

The cold water is a shock, and my breath leaves my body in a sharp rush. How come no one else looks like they're swimming in a bowl of ice? I wade forward with gritted teeth until I'm waist deep in the water.

Cheyenne pulls an evil smile that proves she didn't warn me on purpose. The need for revenge takes over and, with a laugh, I splash towards her, giving her a shove.

Cheyenne stumbles backwards, surprised.

'I'm gonna get you for that,' she crows gleefully.

Before I know it, I'm fully underwater, Cheyenne's hands resting heavily on my shoulders. I struggle against her hold, pushing upwards until my head clears the surface.

Cheyenne gasps and her expression freezes. 'Rah, Yeka, I'm really sorry.'

Thick strands of hair now rest heavily on my shoulders, the ends swirling in the water around me. *So that's why the tight feeling around my head is missing.*

My chest pounds as heads turn in my direction while I search frantically for my swimming cap. By the time I spot it, it's well on its way to the deep end, weaving an impressive path between the thrashing bodies.

My eyes move back to Cheyenne's guilty-looking face, and I know she's seen it too. An uncomfortable silence stretches between us like a worn elastic band. Then something in Cheyenne's face changes and I see her eyes flick towards my cap.

'Chey, wait,' I call.

But I'm too late. Before I can stop her, Cheyenne turns, pushing towards it. Her body moves awkwardly through the water. But she can't keep up, and for every stroke she takes towards the cap, the swell of the moving water pushes it further away.

I want to yell at her to stop, to come back, but the thought of drawing more attention to myself freezes the words in my throat.

Then Cheyenne does stop, and a long shudder runs through her body. She starts flapping her arms frantically, as if she's in trouble. I swivel around to see if anyone else has noticed, but the world is still moving, totally oblivious. I turn back to Cheyenne in time to see her jerk once, before silently slipping under the water. The ripples go still. A second passes, then another, as my heart pounds a frantic rhythm in my chest.

Come on, Chey. Where are you?

Then something floats to the surface of the water. Something thin and red. Cheyenne's headband bobs up and down and I realize this is really happening.

'No, no, no,' I breathe out as panic snakes through me.

A part of me wants to run and hide, yet at the same time I know I need to call for a lifeguard. But fear has taken my voice. My gaze returns to Cheyenne's headband and my body makes the decision for me. I push forward, instinct taking over. My legs kick through the water in a clumsy rhythm, as if they have a mind of their own. *Maybe they do.* Maybe they somehow know that they need to get to Cheyenne.

When I reach the headband, I take a deep breath, then plunge downwards. Dark hair billows around me, dancing through the water, like swirling strings of blue-black ink. As my vision goes blurry, an eerie silence takes over and shafts of light stream into the water. I peer through it, searching for Cheyenne. I don't see anything at first, but then a dark blob at the bottom catches my eye.

I push downwards and wrap an arm around her small body before kicking out, trying to propel us upwards. But I'm too tired, and with the added weight of Cheyenne, it's even harder to move. My body seems to have finally remembered that I can't actually swim that well.

A prickle begins in my head, and my grip on Cheyenne loosens. We're going to die here, at the bottom of a swimming pool, in the middle of Woolwich. Panic fills my chest as prickling pain spreads through my body, and I try to calm down enough to think.

Zero . . . I count in my head.

I work to find a colour and texture, but all I can see is blue and all I feel is wet.

One . . . I try again, but I just can't hold onto it.

Anger courses through me. *I don't want to die. I don't want to leave Mum on her own!*

I kick out hard and try to swim to the surface, but my arms and legs aren't listening. My entire body is burning for oxygen. Then, suddenly, a sharp pain covers my entire scalp. The world around me transforms as my hair curves into a protective bubble, quickly surrounding us. My mouth opens, unable to believe my eyes, and water rushes in like a tidal wave.

Just as the water starts to slide down my throat, the bubble solidifies around Cheyenne and me, like a giant shield. For a moment, everything is still and strange and beautiful. Then, without warning, we start moving quickly towards the surface, pushed by the shield of hair. As my head clears the water, my hair melts away behind me like a dream, and an arm yanks us up. I gasp in some much-needed air, my chest heaving with the effort, and water streams from my eyes and nose as we are hauled to the side of the pool.

'Oh my God, what happened?'

Through my coughing and spluttering, the frantic voice of a lifeguard above me barely registers. I look over at Cheyenne.

'Chey?' I whisper.

She doesn't move.

'Chey!'

It's a scream this time, one that crawls from somewhere deep inside my belly. Heads turn in our direction, and a deafening silence falls as all activity seems to stop. Like hungry kids outside a chip shop, a crowd gathers around us. There are other lifeguards now, and I watch, numb with fear, as Cheyenne is swallowed by all the bodies. I lose sight of her and the pounding in my chest begins again, but there's also a new queasy tightness in my stomach. A steady beat and a rolling clench that combine into a painful rhythm.

'Are you okay?' I turn to find the lifeguard staring at me in a strange way. 'You all right?' he asks again.

I want to scream at the stupid question. 'Where are they taking her?' I ask instead, my voice hoarse.

He frowns, his eyes glued to my hair.

What's his deal?

'How did you manage to get her out?' he finally asks, ignoring my question.

There's a worrying note of suspicion in his voice, and I swallow hard. I don't know how to answer him because I don't know myself. One minute Cheyenne and I were done for, then suddenly there was all this hair.

My hair!

My stomach tightens and I reach up with a shaking hand. But it's just the usual thick strands. I look back down at the water. A thin, red headband bobs away, not too far from us, and next to it is a white and red swimming cap.

A lump settles in my throat. Cheyenne almost died ... and so did I. The thought is too horrible, too wrong, and I swallow again, trying to push saliva past the growing lump. I need to think about something else. My mind shifts back to the shield of hair that saved us. But it doesn't make any sense.

It couldn't have happened ... *could it?*

CHAPTER THREE

The taxi moves off down the road and I stare at my house. In the fading light, it looks exactly as it always does – small and sad, with a dirty, wooden gate surrounding it.

'You all right?'

Mrs Campbell's voice snaps me out of my daze and I turn to find her clutching a trolley and staring at me. She lives three doors down from us, and her faded brown eyes twinkle with curiosity beneath bright white hair that's always perfectly curled.

I open my mouth to reply, but something in her face stops me. I must look proper odd, standing in the middle of the street, my hair hanging in heavy, wet ropes. I try again, but she cuts me off.

'Heard 'bout your mouthy likkle friend from my niece who works at the pool,' she says. Mrs C was born in Jamaica, and when she's being extra nosy, you can really hear it. 'Hope she's okay.'

Mrs C's expression says she hopes the opposite, and the sick feeling in my stomach gets worse. Cheyenne's been in Mrs C's bad books ever since Chey called her a nosy old bat and Mrs C overheard her. Then a thought hits me. If Mrs C knows about Cheyenne, there's no way Mum doesn't. I ignore the sweat building in my palms and give Mrs C a tight smile.

'Chey's fine,' I croak, my voice still hoarse from all the water I swallowed. 'She's at the hospital, but her dad texted me to say they'll be releasing her soon.'

'Oh?' Mrs C replies with a frown, which quickly morphs into a sly smile. 'I'll let you finish tinkin' 'bout what you're gonna tell your mama 'bout your hair.' With that, she starts pushing the trolley again, cackling as she shuffles away.

Mrs C fully is a nosy old bat, but she's right. What *am* I going to tell Mum? How do I explain that my hair somehow saved Cheyenne and me from drowning? She'll think I'm bonkers, just like the pool manager did when I told him what happened. I wanted to go with Cheyenne to the hospital but they wouldn't let me, so I took a taxi home. I only agreed because the pool paid for it.

I turn back to my house, the closed curtains and darkness telling me that I beat Mum home, even though it's almost seven. Mum thinks it's unsafe to leave them open when we're out ... as if we have anything worth stealing. She should be back by now though. I check my phone, but there's no message. Instead, there's a notification of a new post from my favourite YouTube account.

I force myself to ignore it. CurlyUnicorn02 has the most amazing hair and it's bound to be a new twist-out or wash-and-go tutorial that I'll never be able to rock. I sigh, my wet hair dripping a sad trail down my back. I have *zero* hope of making my hair look smooth or sleek like her curls, especially now that shrinkage has set in and my coils are a tangled mess.

The hallway is quiet as I enter the house. I flip the switch that lights the long corridor leading to the kitchen and living room. On the floor is a pile of letters and a newspaper. The word 'Nigeria' in the newspaper headline catches my attention and I pick it up. Mum usually doesn't let me read stuff like this.

Nigeria announced today that their decade-long effort to slow down the erosion of farmland in the Northern Provinces is proving successful. Using a variety of re-greening programs, such as water harvesting and tree conservation, they have managed to restore vital pasture lands.

It is good environmental news for the powerful nation after ten years of work cleaning up the trarium contamination of local water supplies across the nation. News of this first leaked in 2010, though no one truly knows how long it had been going on for. As the largest producers of solar energy in the world, the environmental disaster has long been a source of embarrassment for Nigeria's ruling Councils—

I stop reading. I don't understand half of it and I'm running out of time to sort out my hair. If I'm lucky, I might be able to pull it into a messy bun before Mum gets home. All my buns are messy to be honest.

'Mum?' I call out, just to be on the safe side.

My voice echoes down the empty hallway, but there's no answer. As I climb the stairs, my eyes are drawn to the bare, white wall opposite. There aren't any pictures, not like Cheyenne's house where every available space is crammed with one family photo after another. She hates them, but I think they're nice. They're much better than our empty walls.

I often imagine what the wall would be like, filled with pictures of me and Mum. Or even the old, faded one of my father that I'm not supposed to know about. You know how vampires never look in mirrors so no one discovers their reflection is missing? I think Mum is worried if we put up our family photos, someone will see we're missing something too.

I hurry up the remaining stairs and into my bedroom. An unmade single bed rests against another bare wall and next to it is a wooden chest of drawers, a broken lamp and a wide, full-length mirror. My gaze shifts to the dressing table opposite and the plastic tub packed with hair products. I have at least three shampoos, four deep conditioners, a ton of leave-ins, butters, custards, soufflés and even an edge brûlée. I still haven't figured out why or how you brûlée your edges.

Every few months, Mum gives me a new miracle product that promises to tame or fix my hair. I don't think my hair needs fixing. Yeah, it's a lot, but it's the way everyone else reacts to it that really bothers me. The way I see it, the only person winning in Mum's war against my hair is the local hair shop.

My gaze moves to one of the soufflés and I reach for it, just as the bedroom door swings open with a loud BANG.

'Onyekachi Adéyẹmí Adérìnọ́lá!'

I nearly jump out of my skin at the sound of Mum's voice. She used *all* of my names too. I turn to find her in the doorway. Her lace front wig is crooked, the middle parting sitting at a funny angle.

Her frantic, brown eyes glare at me from a face so dark it's like staring into the night sky ... if the night sky looked angry and tired. She marches towards me, hard hands grabbing me roughly by the shoulders.

'Kí ló sẹlẹ̀?' *What happened,* she asks. She shakes me so hard my head snaps back.

'Mum, stop. You're hurting me,' I say in a small voice.

She releases me immediately and takes a step back.

'I knew I shouldn't have let you go.'

I lower my eyes but stay silent. Maybe I can still finesse my way out of this.

'I couldn't believe it when Mrs Campbell called me,' Mum continues. 'I had to leave the salon early and I've been searching everywhere for you.' Mum circles me, inspecting every strand in painful detail. 'Look at your hair. Please, o, tell me you did not traipse through Woolwich looking like a ragamuffin?'

I look up then. I don't even *know* what a ragamuffin is. 'Chey got in trouble in the water,' I say quietly.

She hesitates then, but only to gather enough saliva to kiss her teeth at me.

'Are you a water guard?'

I roll my eyes. 'It's lifeguard, Mum.'

'That's what I said.' She circles me again, inspecting my body this time. 'Are you hurt? Is Cheyenne okay?' Her voice sharpens and I almost smile. When Mum is scared, she sounds angry. Most people can't tell the difference, but I can. It sounds like love to me.

'I'm fine, Mum,' I reply.

A soft sigh escapes her lips. 'How many times do I have to

24

tell you? You're not like everyone else. You have to be careful.'

She pauses, then reaches for me. The warm weight of her hand cradles my face gently, but it's not enough to erase the sting of her words. My hands tighten into hard fists at my sides as it washes over me.

'Yeah, I know,' I reply, suddenly tired.

Between Mum's overprotectiveness and the way people react to my hair, I've got the message loud and clear. You'd think I was made of candyfloss the way Mum is always going on. The thing is, her messages are so mixed up it gives me whiplash. It's like with one hand she'll push me away, then with the other pull me back so hard and so close I can barely breathe.

'Kí ló ṣẹlẹ̀?' she asks again in a soft voice.

A hard knot grows in my belly as I try to find the words to explain something I don't even understand. None come, so I give up.

'Chey needed help,' I finally reply with a shrug. 'So that's what I did.'

'But how?' she presses. 'You can barely swim.'

'My hair ...' I begin, but my voice fades away into a thin whisper.

The hand on my face drops and a gruff sound leaves Mum's lips. 'What about it?'

It's her tone that does it. I've heard it a million times before. Annoyance, sadness and a strange fear all rolled into one horrible sound. I don't know if it's a tone she's always had or if it came after my father left.

'Why do you hate my hair so much?' I ask her bluntly. I don't even try to hide the hurt in my voice.

Mum's eyes widen. 'I ... I don't hate it,' she stutters. 'It just makes it harder for us to fit in here.'

I sniff at her answer. I can't help it. 'Then why don't we just go back to Nigeria?'

'You do not get to ask me that,' Mum snaps back. 'When you're grown and have to make difficult decisions then you might understand.'

This again? She says this every time I question her. 'Forget it,' I snap back, twisting away from her.

Mum freezes at my tone and her eyes narrow. 'What did you just say?'

I take a step back at the disapproval in her voice and almost trip on the edge of the worn rug.

'You never want to talk about Nigeria,' I croak out, my earlier confidence vanishing like smoke. 'Everything is always a secret, even my own father.'

'Do not exaggerate,' she replies in a stern voice. 'I do talk about him.'

'When?' I say, throwing my hands up. 'It's like he doesn't even exist.'

Her face hardens and the knot in my stomach feels like a rock now.

'You're not being fair, ọkọ mi.'

I usually love it when Mum uses that pet name, but this time I flinch at the words. I'm probably overreacting, but I can't stop myself. All the fear and panic I felt in the pool crashes over me, and my head starts pounding. My breath locks in my chest, making it difficult to breathe.

'Is that why he left?' I whisper. 'Because you kept so many secrets from him?'

Mum's eyes close as something flashes across her face. It's gone by the time she opens them again.

'Does it matter why he left? He isn't here now,' she says, running a hand across her tired face. 'I am.'

The knot in my stomach loosens like molten lava, burning through me. It boils inside, searching for a way out. I start to count, but something stops me. A small spark I don't recognize. So I let it out and the words pour from me before I can call them back.

'I wish you weren't.'

A pained expression settles over Mum's face and her shoulders drop.

'This is my own fault, I guess, for letting you build this fantasy around your father,' she says in a weak voice. 'I just wanted you to have something. I know how hard you find it here.' Her hand waves around my room. 'With me.'

Mum's voice cracks then, filling me with shame. Mum can be difficult, but I know she loves me, and at least she's here.

My father *is* a fantasy. I have no idea what he would do if he were here. I have no way of knowing if he could fill the great big hole that sits between Mum and me.

A wave of tiredness hits as all the anger drains out of me like dirty water in a sink. But the loud echo of Mum's sadness remains, bouncing silently around us. It's always there, and I'm not enough to make it disappear. It makes me feel lost and helpless.

My vision blurs and my scalp starts prickling, just like in the pool. The air crackles with power as raw energy shoots through my body like an electric current. I am literally buzzing with it.

'Onyeka, are you okay?'

Mum's voice is a distant sound beneath the roaring in my ears. The prickle in my scalp turns into a burn, and as the pain intensifies, so does the power. It's awful – like a million little needles stabbing into my head, over and over again. I bite my cheek, desperately trying to hold back the scream bubbling in my throat. The pain spreads, filling every part of me, clawing for a way out. I realize I'm going to black out as dark spots gather behind my eyes.

Then, suddenly, like someone flipped a switch, the pain stops.

My hair explodes around me in a blue-black cloud, cloaking me like a thick shield. Individual strands drift and dance in mid-air, curling on themselves like playful children.

A strange energy fills the room, and the shield of hair stands to attention, as if it's waiting for me to do something.

'Dear Lord,' Mum breathes, her eyes wide with wonder.

I guess I don't have to explain what happened in the pool after all.

'Mum?' I call out hesitantly.

She doesn't reply, merely points a shaking finger towards my head. I turn to the full-length mirror opposite and my mouth drops as I see my reflection. Coils of hair the colour of blue lightning curl out around me. I reach up to touch them and flinch at the tingle of static electricity that shoots through my hand. My fingers move through the unfamiliar texture. Soft, yet strong, like strands of coarse silk.

I look like a proper badass. But can it move?

Before the thought has even finished, a thick shaft of hair whips out clear across the room, knocking over the bedside lamp.

Mum's gasp is sharp and my gaze swings back to her. She isn't nearly as impressed with the way I look. The terror on her face makes me feel sick and I take a step back.

'This can't be happening,' she whispers, and I freeze. 'I'm not ready.'

CHAPTER
FOUR

There's always been something off about the way Mum avoids talking about my father. The bits and pieces I've managed to discover have either been by accident or when she's in a nostalgic mood, which is when she gets chatty.

That's how I found out about the necklace. I was about nine and Mum was on an early morning shift. She'd left me breakfast and strict instructions not to open the door to anyone but her. As if I would.

She had no choice back then. Where we lived, good babysitters were hard to find; a bit like the money to pay for them.

I'd got bored of the TV and decided my tattered Barbie doll needed a makeover. She only had one arm and no hair, but I knew some of Mum's red lipstick would make her look amazing again. So I did the other thing I was absolutely not supposed to do. I sneaked into Mum's room.

This was before we moved into our current house. Back then, we lived in a damp, little flat that always seemed to smell of pee, no matter how much Mum scrubbed. We moved so often in those days, I used to think Mum was a spy or something cool, like an international criminal mastermind. Then I realized the chances of Mum being a criminal anything were pretty much zero. She can't even bring herself to take the free sample food in the supermarket.

Mum's room wasn't much to look at, with plain walls and an even plainer wardrobe. Her dressing table was something else though. She'd found it in a charity shop, the rich dark wood and delicate curves so beautiful, she'd been unable to walk past it. On top rested various bottles and tubes, and as I reached for the lipstick, something even better caught my eye.

Mum's jewellery box!

Inside she kept all her pretty coloured beads and sparkly bracelets. Exactly what my doll needed. I opened it slowly, holding my breath as Mum's hidden treasures came into view. But it wasn't the bright necklaces or earrings that called to me. Instead, my gaze landed on a bright white shell attached to a simple loop of leather. I picked it up, so lost in the strange beauty of it that I didn't even notice Mum had returned until a heavy hand clamped onto my shoulder.

'What are you doing?' Mum said, a warning in her voice.

I couldn't decide whether to cry or beg for forgiveness, so I did both.

'I'm sorry, Mum,' I howled, as tears streamed down my face. 'I won't do it again, I promise.'

Mum eyed me up and down, then her gaze dropped to the object in my hand and her eyes widened. 'Where did you get that?'

The sadness in her voice surprised me so much, I forgot to be scared. 'In your jewellery box,' I replied.

A faraway look entered Mum's eyes. It was like watching someone close in on themselves, as if she was lost in memories I couldn't see. I called her name, and there was a long pause before Mum slowly came back to me. She bent to look at me, almost surprised to find me there. But whatever she saw in my expression made her drop down to one knee so our faces were level.

'Do you know what this is?' she asked me in a gentle voice.

I shook my head, holding my breath in anticipation.

'It's a cowrie shell and it belonged to your father,' she continued. 'He believed it gave protection to its wearer.'

I knew I should just be quiet and let her talk. She rarely spoke about him. But curiosity won and I opened my mouth, full of a million questions.

She stopped me by placing her finger against my lips. 'He wanted you to have it. Now seems like a good time.'

'Really?' I whispered around her finger. I remember my joy in that moment.

Mum's hand left my lips, moving up to my hair. It was long and thick even then.

'You remind me so much of him.'

My lips parted, ready to reply, but a look passed over Mum's face. Then she stood up and shooed me out of her room.

I still remember that look. It's the same one on Mum's face as she stares at my hair now.

'You need to calm down. Right now!' Mum barks, pointing to my head. 'Use your numbers.'

I almost jump at the urgency in her voice, but I do as she says. With each new number, my hair recedes bit by tingly bit, and a wave of nausea takes its place. By the time I get to fifty-five, I'm me again. I'm also shaking. Unable to control the tremors rattling through my body, I stumble back. Then Mum's arms are around me.

'What's happening to me?' I push out between trembling lips, as darkness begins to close in.

I wake to find myself on my bed. My body feels strange, like it's not quite mine any more. Mum is slumped in a chair beside me; one hand covers her eyes and her shoulders are shaking.

Is she crying?

Memories of my hair going nuts and Mum's reaction rush back all at once. My stomach heaves and I close my eyes again. Then a particular memory hits me and my eyes fly open.

'What did you mean by "I'm not ready"?' I whisper. Mum

33

jerks upright in the chair, her reddened eyes blinking at me. 'You said, "I'm not ready" when you saw my hair,' I repeat.

She watches me for a long minute before speaking.

'Did I? I don't remember.'

I wasn't sure that she was hiding something before, but now I'm certain of it.

'Mum?' I plead.

Her face drops and she takes a deep breath. 'You . . . you're not like the people here.'

'You always say that,' I burst out. 'What does it even mean?' Mum looks away, her mouth thinning. 'Please,' I whisper. 'I need to know.'

Her eyes return to mine, a terrible sadness in them. 'You are not entirely human.'

I stare at her lips, confused by the words coming out of them. For a minute, I thought she said I wasn't human. Which can't be right . . . *can it*?

'Onyeka, did you hear me?'

I didn't imagine it. My hands begin to shake as I try to piece together what her words mean. It's too hard and I can't get them to make sense. I give up, staring at her.

'What am I then?' I rush out.

Mum shrugs. 'Different.'

My jaw tightens. 'Come on, Mum,' I explode. 'That's not good enough.' I'm so sick of her giving me answers that don't really mean anything.

Mum jumps out of the chair, almost knocking it over. 'I'm doing this all wrong. You weren't supposed to find out like this.'

'I'm sorry,' I snap back. 'How *was* I supposed to find out?'

She stops and fixes a narrowed-eyed stare on me. 'Don't you use that tone of voice with me, young lady,' she replies. 'You may have superpowers, but I'm still your mother.'

Superpowers? What the . . . ?

My brain stutters to a stop, totally unprepared for that bit of information. I open my mouth to ask, but Mum's glare is still on full beam and my chin drops.

'Sorry,' I say in a small voice, shrinking down in my bed.

Her face softens a bit, and my mouth starts moving before I can stop myself, desperate to know more.

'Do you mean superpowers as in heroes and comics?'

She sniffs. 'More like mutants, but, yes, something like that.'

Mutants? This just keeps getting weirder. 'How?' I ask.

Mum pauses, as if she's trying to find the right words. Or maybe just any words.

'You are Solari,' she finally says.

'A w . . . what?'

Her lips tighten. 'Solari,' she repeats. 'You inherited it from your father.'

I jerk at the mention of my father, my eyes narrowing. *What does he have to do with any of this?*

'I wish you wouldn't look at me like that,' Mum mutters, and I swing out of bed in a clumsy rush that makes my stomach roll.

'Are you messing with me?' I screech. 'There is no way any of this is real.'

'I assure you; it's all very real. How else do you explain that?' I follow the direction of her pointed finger to find the ends of my hair swirling around in mid-air.

I hadn't even noticed.

Mum's whole body droops, as if she's struggling to hold herself upright. 'You really need to calm down,' she pleads, a wobble in her voice. 'It isn't safe for you to use your powers.'

'I'm not doing it on purpose,' I protest.

'It's your emotions,' says Mum. 'Until you learn to control them, your powers will keep flaring up.'

I take a deep breath, close my eyes and think of my numbers. It doesn't take long for it to work, and my scalp settles. I open my eyes to find Mum looking at me expectantly. I don't know what to say though; my brain feels too full.

If what she's saying is true, then my whole life is one great big stinking lie. What else hasn't she told me? Is my name even . . .

'Onyeka!'

Mum's sharp voice halts my thoughts, forcing me to focus again.

'What?' I snap back, and the air crackles with power. Mum recoils and I take a deep breath, ready to apologize again.

'You need to rest,' she says, and I stare at her. Does she seriously think I'm going to go to sleep? She just destroyed my world.

I start to ask a question, but she throws me another one of her looks, and my lips snap shut. Mum is a bit like the dodgy tap in our bathroom. Once she's had enough, you can't get anything more out of her.

'It's been a very long day,' she says. 'We can talk more in the morning.'

I really want to argue, but I know better. I give her my own stubborn look. 'Promise?'

She sighs. 'I promise.'

CHAPTER
FIVE

I wake up with a scream and lean over the side of the bed instinctively, throwing up on the wooden floor. Everything hurts. My head is pounding like a batá drum, and I can't think past the grogginess clouding my mind.

Mum comes rushing in then. I'm sick and she doesn't know why. I've never seen her so panicked. Each time I throw up, she cleans me up and forces a sugary drink down my throat. I can't keep any food down and Mum keeps muttering about me needing energy.

When the nightmares wake me, she holds my sweating body, whispering that everything will be okay. When Cheyenne rings, Mum makes excuses for why I can't answer. This goes on for two more mornings, until I wake up without screaming or vomiting.

I slump back against the pillows, squinting in the bright

light of the room. I lift my hand to my head and even my scalp is sore. What's worse, my hair is a matted tangle of knots. I groan silently at the thought of detangling it.

My hair!

An avalanche of questions race through my mind as I remember what Mum told me. I frown as I try to recall the word Mum used ... celery ... salary?

Solari!

But where *is* Mum? A small gasp comes from the doorway, and I turn my stiff neck to find her there. Her lace front wig is missing, the fuzzy cornrows she wears underneath visible. There's a strange, grey tinge to her skin and all her make-up is gone.

Her eyes frantically lock on mine. They are so big, they almost leap from her face, and I worry that she's sick too. Mum stumbles towards my bed and her trembling hands reach for me.

'Thank you, Jesus,' she whispers, as she drops to her knees.

I just stare at her because I don't know this woman. The hard shell that usually surrounds Mum is gone, leaving behind something so naked, it almost hurts to look at her.

'Mum?'

My frightened croak breaks through and her clutching fingers soften as she pulls me into her warm body.

'Oh God, I thought I was losing you.'

A giant sob shakes her body, and my throat gets tight as her trembling fingers run through my hair, catching on my curls. I don't know how to stop her tears, so I stay still as her trembling lips trace frantic kisses across my face. Until it becomes a cycle.

Sob ... stroke ... kiss. On repeat. At last she stops and looks at me with a watery smile.

'Are you feeling better?'

I nod back, my throat still raw.

'Hungry?' she asks, a hopeful look on her face.

I'm not, but I nod again. Eating is very important to Mum, especially since we haven't always had food on the table. I feel her reluctance as she lets me go.

It doesn't take long before she returns with some toast and a glass of milk on a tray. Setting it down in my lap, she pulls the chair closer and takes a seat, watching me silently as I grab a browned slice. She doesn't relax until I take a bite, then another, until it's all gone.

'What happened to me?' I finally ask, breaking the silence. 'Why was I so sick?'

Mum's eyes slide away from mine. 'I don't know.'

I don't believe her, not any more.

'It's the Solari thing, isn't it?' I say in a quiet voice. Her startled eyes fly back to my face. 'You said it wasn't safe for me to use my powers, which means there must be something wrong with them.'

Her head turns away again and she sighs. 'Your powers are an amazing thing ...'

I say nothing, waiting for the catch.

'But they're also dangerous,' Mum finally adds. 'Your father always believed that using them could hurt you.'

A heavy feeling settles in my belly at the mention of my father. For years I've known nothing and now he's all Mum can talk about. My head suddenly feels too big for my neck, and it takes all my strength not to sink back down to my bed. An odd noise escapes from my throat.

'Ọkọ mi.' Mum's hand moves towards me, hovering mere centimetres from my face. 'I am so sorry o.'

It's those words and the pain in her eyes that finally breaks me, and I rear back from her hand. 'How could you keep all this from me?' I say with a strangled cry.

Mum's hand wavers for a second, before returning to her side, gripping the other one so tightly her knuckles shine.

'Easily,' she whispers. 'I'm scared all the damn time.' Mum stops as a small tremor wracks her body.

I blink at her. Mum *never* swears and she also never admits she's afraid. Even when it's totally obvious she is. I take her hand and squeeze. She squeezes mine right back before continuing.

'I've spent years hoping and praying that your father would come back. Fearing the day your powers would finally show up. That kind of fear, once you let it in, takes up all the room, until there is no space for anything else. I didn't want you living like that too.'

That shuts me up. All this time I thought she acted the way she did because of me. I thought I was the problem. I tell her as much and Mum's eyes get really big.

'Never think that,' she gasps, pulling me close. 'None of this is your fault, okay?'

A lump forms in my throat and I nod back. But a question hangs between us. One I have always been too afraid to ask. I take a deep breath.

'Where is he?'

She looks at me then, her eyes swimming with unshed tears and a truth I can't ignore. 'I don't know.'

I breathe out slowly, unsure if I'm relieved that she hasn't been hiding him, or angry that she's never bothered to find out.

'Why don't you know?' I finally ask.

Mum grimaces. 'Your father just disappeared one day. Then, soon after, I received a note warning me that if I wanted to keep us alive, I needed to get out of Nigeria. It said powerful people were behind his disappearance.' She points to my neck. 'That necklace was also with the note. It said I should give it to you before your powers activated. I knew then it was serious.'

The heavy weight that permanently lives in my stomach eases a little at her words. For years I've wondered why my father left and why he didn't love us enough to stay.

'Is that why you keep his picture hidden?' I ask.

'How do you—?'

'I wasn't snooping,' I say quickly.

I really wasn't. About a year ago, I'd been looking for a tub of hair grease in Mum's wardrobe when a plastic folder fell from a bundle of clothes. Inside were some old photos, but one in particular caught my attention. It was of a smiling, young man with hair so long, it looked like extensions. It was braided on top of his head in a complicated pattern, like a crown. On the back, written in Mum's scrawl, was the name Benjamin.

That was the day I discovered who my father was and where I got my hair and smile from. It was the day he fully became real to me.

'It doesn't matter now, I guess,' says Mum with a sigh.

Easy for her to say. She doesn't lie awake at night wondering what he sounds like, what his favourite song is or if he likes the doughy sweet taste of puff puff too.

'What were his powers?' I finally ask, the need to know more about him urging me on.

Mum shrugs. 'I don't know,' she repeats for the second time. 'He refused to use them. It was almost as if he was afraid of them.'

'I don't get any of this,' I burst out. 'What was he doing for powerful people to come after him?'

Mum sighs. 'He was working on some big genetics project for the Councils.' Mum shrugs. 'Very secretive and hush-hush.'

Something from history class tickles my memory. 'The Councils of Unity,' I gasp.

'Yes,' says Mum with a small frown. 'They run Nigeria.'

'He didn't say anything else?' I ask.

'He should never even have told me about the Solari. The Councils are desperate to keep their existence a secret and he took a big risk trusting me with that information. When he disappeared and I received that note –' Mum shivers as if she's remembering something awful – 'I assumed someone found out and wanted us out of the way, so they could keep their precious secret. It's why I've been so careful and kept us moving. It's why nowhere truly feels safe.'

So that's why Mum is always moving so mad and why everything feels so complicated all the time. Her favourite warning takes on a whole new meaning now. I'm really *not* like everyone else.

'Am I going to get sick again?' I whisper. Mum is silent for so long, I start to wonder if she heard me.

Mum runs a hand over her cornrows. 'I don't know. Your father spoke about Solari getting sick when they used too much power. I think it's what he was working on – a way to fix it.' Her voice is low and flat.

I close my eyes. 'So I'm stuck feeling like this?' I murmur to myself.

'No!' says Mum, a quiet determination in her voice. 'I'm not watching you go through that again. I'm going to get some answers . . . and that means finding your father.'

My eyes fly open. These are the words I've dreamed of hearing my whole life, but all I manage to say is, 'Huh?'

'There's no other option. We can't hide here any longer.' Mum reaches for me, the look on her face intense. 'The day after your father made a huge discovery was the day he went missing. It can't be a coincidence.' She pauses and pulls me close. 'We're going back.'

'Where?' I ask, my voice muffled by the fabric of her T-shirt.

'Nigeria.'

'B-but . . .' I stutter, pulling away. 'Why?'

'It's where the answers are,' she replies simply. 'I've always regretted not staying and searching for your father. That note scared me and I decided I had to put your safety first.' Her eyes bore into mine and something in her gaze hardens. 'It's different now. Your safety is tied to finding him, and I refuse to sit by and do nothing.'

Hearing her say it again makes it feel real. We're going back to Nigeria and we're going to find my father. The secret thing that has always lived silently inside my head is finally going to happen. A slow smile splits my face. I can't help it.

Mum's eyes narrow. 'You must do exactly as I say. No arguments. Lagos is nothing like London.'

My smile drops at the seriousness of her tone.

'I know it's got loads of tech—'

'It's more than tech. Everything is different there,' Mum interrupts. 'Especially the people and culture. Nigeria has come a long way since independence. It's no longer a bundle of tribes cobbled together by the British. Your Western manners will not serve you well there, so you must remember how I raised you.'

I want to roll my eyes, but then I'd be showing the disrespect she's so worried about. Mum moves to my wardrobe with a determined stride and starts pulling things out randomly.

'We're leaving right now?' I gasp.

She stops and spins back to me, an urgent look on her face. 'No, but within the next few days. You must not tell anyone about your powers. Do you understand?'

I nod. Besides, who would I tell other than Cheyenne?

'Chey!' I whisper.

Mum's eyes soften, as if she's been waiting for me to catch up. 'Not even her.'

I swallow hard. The thought of keeping such a big secret from Cheyenne feels totally wrong. I open my mouth to argue when an even worse thought occurs to me. To find my father, I'm going to have to leave my best friend. I slump back against the pillows as my chest tightens.

I don't know if I can do it.

CHAPTER SIX

The brass knocker on Cheyenne's door is shaped like a lion and it's grinning at me in a cheesy way. I'm supposed to be at home resting, while Mum arranges for us to leave. I don't know the details, and as usual she won't tell me anything. For all I know, we could be travelling by supersonic jet, comic-book style.

So I waited all day until Mum finally left to go to the bank, then I legged it out of the house. Mum's going to kill me when she finds out, but if she gets to do things on the sly, then so can I. Besides, she's having a laugh if she thinks I'm leaving without talking to Cheyenne.

The bus journey was super awkward and tiring. I'm still feeling weak, and I was petrified that my hair would freak out again. I was poking it so much I reckon the old lady next to me thought I had head lice or something.

I grab the knocker and give three hard knocks, rocking back on my heels as I wait for an answer. The door swings open and behind it stands Cheyenne's dad in a pair of jeans and a white T-shirt with an anime character on it. Cheyenne gets her love of anime from him.

Uncle Dàpọ̀ is the coolest dad ever and it's not even because he's a famous TV presenter. He just has natural bants. He's not my actual uncle, but Mum says I'm not allowed to call him by his first name.

'Hey, Onyeka,' he says, giving me a high five. He's always super nice and chirpy . . . in a way that isn't entirely normal for a parent.

'Hi, Uncle Dàpọ̀,' I reply in a squeaky voice, suddenly nervous I'm going to get found out by Mum. I swallow hard to clear my throat, and he takes a small step back, his arm spread out in invitation. I shuffle through the door and take off my shoes out of habit. Cheyenne's mum isn't fond of dirt, but she is super fond of her cream-coloured carpet.

'How's your mum?' Uncle Dàpọ̀ asks me as he leads me along the narrow hallway.

She's a liar, liar pants on fire.

'Fine,' I reply out loud.

'And how's the hair doing today?'

This is our little joke. Uncle Dàpọ̀ reckons my hair has a mind of its own and he likes to check in on it. He has no idea how right he is, so I just smile back.

48

Uncle Dàpọ̀ comes to a stop by the wide, wooden staircase and his face turns serious. 'I just wanted to say thank you.'

I frown, slightly lost by his words.

'For helping Cheyenne,' he says.

He's talking about what happened at the pool.

'Erm, nah, it was nothing,' I reply.

'Hardly that.' He bends down and gives me a quick hug. 'You saved our baby girl's life and we're truly grateful. I can't work out how you did it though. You got some secret superpowers?'

My breath stops until he laughs, and then I breathe out a sigh of relief.

'Adrenaline?' I say with a small smile.

He laughs again. 'Well . . . Chey's in the playroom.'

I don't hang about.

'Thank you,' I call as I head down the stairs to the basement.

Almost the full width of the whole house, the playroom is divided exactly in half by a pair of glass bifold doors. One side houses a sauna and gym, while the other contains a massive pool table, fighting for space with a fifty-inch flat-screen plasma TV. I only know it's fifty inches because Cheyenne's mum is always complaining that Uncle Dàpọ̀ spends more time with it than her. But even though they're rich, Cheyenne and her parents aren't snooty about it.

I find Cheyenne in her usual spot, sprawled on the brown

leather recliner sofa, watching TV. She's dressed in a fluffy, pink onesie with her fox ears on. She hasn't spotted me yet and I hesitate. *How am I going to get her to believe me?*

'Hey,' I call out brightly.

Cheyenne jumps at the sound of my voice, her head swivelling round so fast I think it might fall off. The startled look on her face melts away as a wide smile replaces it.

'Onyeka!' She scrambles off the sofa, coming to a stop in front of me. 'I've been calling for ages. Where have you been?'

'Erm, I had a tummy bug,' I lie. 'I must have swallowed too much water.'

Cheyenne nods. 'As long as you're okay.' Then her grin gets even wider. 'I'm gonna start calling you Super Yeka like in the comic I made you. Everyone says you rescued me from the pool.'

I tense at her words, so eerily close to the truth, except she's just joking. Was it really only days ago we were laughing and playing at the pool? It feels longer. So much has changed since then.

'You don't remember?' I ask her.

'Not really. I remember going after your swimming cap and then getting a stitch, but after that ...' She shrugs. 'Mum says I shouldn't have gone in the deep end in the first place.' Cheyenne's face creases into a frown. 'Hold up ... does *your* mum know you're here?' she asks.

'I sneaked out,' I blurt out before I can think it through.

Cheyenne's eyes widen and she throws me an impressed look. Then puzzlement quickly replaces it. 'Why?'

I try to think of what to say next, but my mind goes blank. 'You know how my mum's always saying I'm different?' I finally say in a rush.

Cheyenne's eyebrows squish together. 'What are you on about?'

I blow out a frustrated breath. There really is no easy way to tell her.

'I know this sounds a bit wild,' I try again. 'But ... I've got superpowers.'

Cheyenne stares at me, then presses the back of her palm to my forehead. 'Did you bang your head trying to save me?'

The sound I make is part laugh, part groan. 'I'm proper serious. I didn't save you in the pool. At least, not by myself. It was my hair.' Cheyenne looks as if she's going to call her dad any moment and I rush on. 'Think about it – how could I have pulled us out? I can't even swim that well.'

Cheyenne shrugs. 'I did wonder about that, but adrenaline can make people do all sorts of things.'

'I'm telling you, my hair saved us. It can move all by itself.'

She crosses her arms. 'Show me.'

'I don't know how. I can't control it,' I continue quickly.

Cheyenne's narrowed eyes size me up as she tries to decide if I'm being serious or not. I can practically hear the cogs in her brain turning. Then she leans in close as if inspecting me.

'I'm getting Dad,' she mutters. 'You did bang your head and now you're chatting rubbish.'

Panic fills me. 'Wait!' I cry.

Cheyenne rolls her eyes and steps around me, heading towards the door. Immediately my heart begins to pound. Uncle Dàpò will call Mum and then I'll really be in trouble. My head starts to pound too and a familiar prickle spreads across my scalp. I look around the playroom in panic.

Please God, don't let me break Uncle Dàpò's TV.

A sharp pain is the only warning I get before my hair erupts like a halo around me.

'Chey!' I call out in a shaky voice, and she swivels around sharply.

Her eyes widen into big, round saucers. 'Woah,' she breathes, backing away from me. Her eyes are glued to my hair in a weird mix of fear and curiosity. 'Wh ... what is that?'

I don't know how to answer her, and I'm petrified my hair is going to do something stupid.

'Super Yeka?' I finally reply.

'When did ... ?' Cheyenne pauses and swallows hard. 'How is this ... ?' She stops again, struggling to find words. I almost feel sorry for her. 'I don't believe this,' she finally pushes out.

'It's still me,' I say softly.

Cheyenne narrows her eyes at me as if I said something silly, but she can't see the expression on her face. She looks proper scared. So I just wait, wondering how she's about to react, but totally convinced she's going to freak out.

As if she's determined to prove me wrong, Cheyenne takes a step closer, then another, and before I can stop it, a strand of hair curls towards her. She freezes as my hair stops just centimetres from her face. Then Cheyenne's hand lifts slowly. It's all the invitation my hair needs, and it wraps around her hand eagerly. Cheyenne stiffens for a second, then her whole body relaxes.

'No freaking way!' Cheyenne squeals as she runs her fingers through my hair.

'Yes way,' I whisper, relieved that she's not running away screaming.

My hair releases her, returning to normal. Almost as if her acceptance was what my hair was after all along. But the familiar wave of nausea soon follows and I swallow it down quickly. Cheyenne is really excited now, and I don't want to spoil it. She's practically hopping on the spot.

'I always knew your hair was amazing. Tell me everything.'

So I do. Her mouth drops as I fill her in on all that's happened since the pool. Mum is going to be so angry, but I'm not as good with secrets as she is.

'Erm, there is one last thing,' I add as I reach the hardest part of my story.

Cheyenne frowns at me. 'What could top this?'

I gulp. 'My powers are making me sick and Mum says it's

really dangerous.' Cheyenne's face falls, and I rush to reassure her. 'But she reckons my father might be able to help.' Her expression lifts, so I continue. 'Which is why we have to go back to Nigeria to find him.'

Cheyenne freezes and I hold my breath, waiting for her reaction.

'You're kidding, right?' she practically shouts, and I throw a worried glance at the door. 'How are you just gonna up and leave like that? What about your mum's job, or school . . . or me?'

Her voice ends on a loud screech, and I wince.

'It's not for ever and I don't *really* want to go,' I mutter. 'I wish I could stay.'

Cheyenne rolls her eyes. 'Stop lying. You fully hate it here.'

What I really hate is that she knows me so well and she's right.

'Okay, fine, but it doesn't mean I'm happy about leaving you behind.'

Cheyenne frowns. 'The way I see it, you don't have much choice. I mean, you've got superpowers, fam. You can't stay here.'

'But—'

'Yeka, you'll finally get to meet your dad!' Cheyenne cuts in, her voice a hushed whisper. 'You'll be a family again, just like you've always wanted.'

Trust Cheyenne to clock right on to the thing I've been

avoiding – the thing I've not let myself think about. Because if I do, it will actually be real and it might be taken away from me. Cheyenne is the only person who truly gets how much finding my father means to me.

Cheyenne and her dad are total mates and she tells him everything. He takes her to all the comic exhibitions, and he even dresses up with her. It's why I like spending time at their house so much. Seeing Cheyenne and her parents together makes me feel good.

Uncle Dàpò always tries to include me too, and for a little while I get to pretend I'm part of a happy family ... that I have a father who loves me. Once, he took us to Comic Con in central London. We'd been queuing for ages to meet the star of Cheyenne's favourite TV show. Finally, it was our turn, and after we got her autograph and picture, she turned to Uncle Dàpò with a smile and told him his girls were adorable.

'Yes,' Uncle Dàpò replied, 'they are.'

The warm feeling that entered my belly lasted a whole week.

I stare at Cheyenne, standing in the middle of her playroom, watching me expectantly.

'I know,' I finally reply.

She grins. 'Scared?'

'Petrified.' I look down at my hands. 'What if he doesn't like me?' My voice rises to a squeak. 'What if I don't like him?'

Cheyenne takes my left hand and squeezes. 'He has to like you, and you're gonna think he's awesome.'

I look up. 'What if he doesn't want to be found?' I whisper.

'Then you come home, innit?'

I don't feel myself move, but the next thing I know, I've closed the distance between us and my arms are wrapped round her. 'I'm gonna miss your big mouth and your crazy fox ears,' I whisper as tears fill my eyes. 'I'm even gonna miss the way you always smell of coconut oil.'

Cheyenne sucks in some air. Her arms hang loosely at her side for a moment, as if she's unsure what to do. She's never been much of a hugger. Then they wrap round me too.

'Don't forget my amazing playroom,' she says.

I flick her on the arm. 'I'm being serious. I'm really gonna miss you.'

'Please, you'll be too busy living the Naija life,' she replies with a small snort. 'Besides, we can chat on the phone and I'll try not to be too jealous.'

I pull away and we stare at each other. There aren't enough words. At least, not the right ones.

Suddenly, the playroom door bursts open and we spring apart.

'Onyeka, why didn't you tell me?' Uncle Dàpọ̀ demands as he walks in. But it's the woman behind him that makes my chest tighten.

Mum!

CHAPTER SEVEN

I risk a quick look at Mum's face. The expression on it is thunderous, and if her eyes were laser beams, I'd totally be dead.

Uncle Dàpọ̀ wraps an arm round Cheyenne's shoulders. 'You okay, baby girl?' he asks. 'The news about Onyeka leaving must have been a shock.'

Cheyenne and I exchange a quick look. *How does Uncle Dàpọ̀ know?*

Mum steps forward then. 'I know this must be difficult, Cheyenne, but the job in Nigeria is a fantastic opportunity. We have to leave urgently or I'll lose it.' Mum makes an awkward sound. 'We've still got a ton of packing to do, but I know how important it is for Onyeka to say goodbye.'

'Well, congratulations again,' Uncle Dàpọ̀ says before Cheyenne can reply. 'We've been thinking about moving back to Nigeria too.'

Mum nods, then gives me a meaningful look. 'Thank you, Dàpọ̀. We really must go now,' she says. My eyes meet hers in a silent plea. *I'm not ready to leave Cheyenne.* She glares at me even harder, shooting me a clear warning.

'Goodbye, Chey,' I say obediently.

As Mum pulls me away gently, I turn to look at Cheyenne one final time. She lifts her hand to her ear, as if she's holding an invisible phone, and I nod back. My eyelids feel hot and my legs don't want to move.

A secret worry niggles at the back of mind. *What if I never see Cheyenne again?*

'Are you happy with yourself?' Mum huffs as the car speeds along an unfamiliar road. We've been driving since she all but dragged me out of Cheyenne's house.

'I just wanted to say goodbye,' I reply. She's been ignoring me most of the journey and I'm beginning to miss the silence.

Mum gives me a sharp glare. 'Well, I hope it was worth it.'

It was, but I don't tell her that.

'You can't do things like that any more,' she adds, her eyes returning to the road. 'Now you've come into your powers, you have to be more careful. You can't control them yet and you could expose us.'

I know she's right, but I'm not admitting that either.

'Where are we going anyway?' I ask, hoping to distract her.

'The airfield,' she replies after a pause. 'We're staying with a man called Dr Dòyìnbó at his school. He was your father's old mentor and he's got enough power and influence to keep us safe . . . I hope.'

I suck in a sharp breath of shock. *We're leaving tonight to go to some school in Nigeria?*

Before I can ask any more questions, the car begins to slow down and we pass a sign for Enfield Airfield. I almost smile. Someone was definitely having a laugh when they came up with that one. The car turns past a metal gate and onto a small dirt road. Soon the light strip of a runway comes into view and it finally hits me that we're really leaving.

The car stops and Mum gets out. I follow reluctantly, when suddenly a huge, black jet materializes in the sky out of nowhere.

'You got us a private jet?' I squeak, but my words are lost beneath the roar of the powerful engine and a gust of wind that nearly knocks me off my feet.

Woah! I wasn't actually serious about the whole supersonic jet thing.

Swooping low, it hovers in mid-air, its four rotor blades spinning furiously. Twin beams of blue light home in on us, like eyes in the dark, and I'm reminded of a bird of prey. Then it starts to descend, settling its great hulk on the ground in a soft perch. An emblem I don't recognize is etched onto the side. It looks like the Nigerian flag of green and white, but in the centre of it is a blazing, yellow sun.

My jaw drops and my neck tips back as I try to take it all in. The jet is beyond cool, and I wish Cheyenne were here to see it. She'd totally freak out. I look at Mum. *How did she swing this?*

A circular doorway opens in the side of the jet, light beaming out of it. In it stands a tall boy wearing a pair of patterned shorts and a yellow short-sleeved shirt. He reaches out a hand and blue mist emerges from it. The minute the mist hits the air, it solidifies into a glass step in front of his feet.

No, not glass . . . ice!

I gasp as the step grows bigger, bending and twisting into a whole staircase that stretches from the plane to the ground. I want to call Chey to squeal in excitement, and I also want to run and hide all at the same time. *It's too much!*

The ice boy climbs down and walks towards us quickly, his body stiff and dead straight like a toy soldier. Across his nose sits a pair of glasses, the lenses reflecting a strange, luminescent glow. He reminds me of a drawing of a noble warrior I once saw in a library book. Except he's still a kid, like me.

'Ms Adérìnọ́lá?' he says to Mum in a thick Nigerian accent. His voice is sharp and clear, like the ice that leaped from his hand. 'My name is Niyì Olúbọ̀dé. Dr Dòyìnbó sent me to bring you home.'

Home … The word sounds strange. I've never thought of Nigeria as home before. He turns to me then with a small smile.

'You must be Onyeka,' he says. Then he nods towards my head. 'Nice hair.'

'Hi,' I reply, eyeing him suspiciously. *Is he making fun of me?*

He stretches out a hand and I stare at it. The dude shoots ice from his hands; does he seriously expect me to shake it?

As I stand there trying to decide what to do, Mum leans towards me, a tightness in her voice. 'Niyì is Solari.'

Really, Mum? I hadn't guessed.

I take a breath and shake Niyì's hand, surprised at the warmth of it.

'It's always great to meet a new Solari,' he says. It takes me a minute to realize he's talking about me and a shiver of excitement races down my spine.

I'm Solari now and everything is about to change.

CHAPTER EIGHT

The inside of the jet, or Gyrfalcon as Niyì calls it, looks like something out of a movie. Six seats resting in two columns fill the large space. In front, a giant viewscreen stretches from one edge to the other, but it's been blacked out since we arrived. On either side of me are more screens and buttons than a video arcade, each one a glowing invitation to touch.

I don't dare. Besides, I'm too busy pretending to be asleep. I have been since we left England. Meeting another Solari feels so strange, and I don't know how I'm supposed to behave. Neither Mum nor Niyì seem to care anyway.

I peek at them through half open lids. In the seat in front of me, Niyì fiddles with some controls and an Afrobeat song I don't recognize pours out of a very impressive speaker system. Sat next to him, Mum nods along in time to the heavy rhythm. My body is still and my breathing even, yet inside a million questions are fighting to burst free.

Where exactly are we going?

Just how many others like me are there?

Why am I only finding out now that Mum likes Afrobeat?

They swirl inside my head, but fear keeps them locked there. Instead, I try to focus on Mum's and Niyì's voices as they talk.

'How much does she know about us?' says Niyì.

'Not much. I thought it best to explain when we arrived.'

'Does she really have follicular psychokinesis?' Niyì says, excitement creeping into his voice. 'I've never encountered that combination before.'

Great! So even as a mutant, I'm weird. I don't catch what Mum says next, but I feel a shift in the air as one of them gets up. Forcing my body to relax, I quickly close my eyes.

'Are you really planning to pretend-sleep the whole way?' Niyì's voice startles me. *If he's here, who's flying the jet?* Still, I manage not to move. I even throw in a snore for bonus points.

'I know you're awake,' he presses, but I don't even twitch, determined to stick to the plan.

'I'll answer any question you have,' he finally offers.

He's so obvious, but I'm too hungry for information to ignore him any longer.

I crack open one eye. 'Anything?' Niyì nods and I sit up. 'How did you do that?' At his confused look I point to his hands. 'With the ice stairs, I mean.'

Niyì smiles. 'Ike and several years of training at AOS.'

Two new words I know nothing about, but the way Niyì says them tells me they're important.

'AOS?' I repeat.

'Yeah, that's where we're going.' Niyì eyes me strangely. 'You really don't have a clue about any of this, do you? I thought your mum was exaggerating.'

'Mum doesn't exaggerate,' I tell him.

'Then I guess I'd better back up a bit,' Niyì replies. 'AOS is an elite school called the Academy of the Sun. Its actual name is the Academy of Surùlérè, but no one calls it that.' Then he grins at me. 'Dr Dòyìnbó, our head teacher, founded it almost twenty-five years ago. Solari have been coming to it ever since, to learn how to use their powers.

'For most of us, getting our powers was a scary and strange experience. Our Ike is unpredictable and left unchecked can cause some major damage.' Niyì's awed gaze runs over my hair. 'I bet your Ike is spectacular.'

Ike? So that's what it's called. Spectacular isn't exactly how I'd describe it, but I don't bother to correct him. I'm more concerned about the *unpredictable* and *major damage* bits.

Does Mum know any of this? She must know. I look over at her, but her head is still bopping along to the song. It doesn't even seem like she's listening, which is proper strange as Mum doesn't believe in minding her own business.

64

I turn back to Niyì. 'So kids just leave their families to go to some strange superhero school?'

Niyì stiffens, as if my words have offended him or something. 'It's an honour to be Solari and to serve our country. We get to use our Ike to keep Nigeria safe, and even though we can't keep in contact with our families, they understand it's important. The government makes them swear to secrecy anyway.'

AOS sounds more like a training camp than a school to me, but the look on Niyì's face warns me to keep the thought to myself.

Niyì's chest lifts with pride. 'I'm on track to graduate PP in two years.'

'What's PP?' I ask.

'Sorry, I keep forgetting how new you are to all of this. PP is the Protector Programme.' Still confused, I raise one eyebrow, and Niyì coughs. 'Right ... Protectors are elite government operatives who help the navy, army, air force and the new space programme. They're covert so the public don't even know they exist, never mind that they're Solari.'

Woah! Secret spies, a space programme? It's like I've stepped into a comic book. One where the kids get to act like the grown-ups. Then a new thought occurs to me.

'Did my father go to AOS?' I ask excitedly.

From the corner of my eye, I see Mum flinch. She *has* been listening.

I knew it!

Niyì frowns. 'I don't know—' he begins.

'Your father was a student, but he preferred test tubes to fighting,' Mum cuts in, though she makes no move to join us.

'Well, that explains it then,' says Niyì. 'He probably works in a government research lab.'

As Niyì talks, frustration wells up in me. How come I don't know even the most basic things about the country I was born in? If I'm honest, I'm a little jealous too. It doesn't seem fair that Niyì has all this knowledge, while I'm wading through what feels like a dense fog.

'He's missing actually,' I snap back.

Suddenly, Mum is there, glaring at me as if I've lost my mind. Maybe I have. I feel as if I'm losing *something*.

'I'm sorry,' Niyì says. The excitement on his face dims and guilt slithers across my skin. 'I didn't know ... I'm just so happy to meet you. We've never collected a new Solari your age or from another country before.'

What does he mean *my* age?

Before I can ask, Mum places a gentle hand on Niyì's shoulder. 'It might be best to leave the rest of the explanations until tomorrow. It's been a long day.'

I don't argue. Firstly, because I won't win, and secondly, because I don't think I can take any more.

An uneasy look settles over Niyì's face, but before he

can reply, a deep, metallic voice says, '*In approximately ten minutes, we will arrive at AOS. Descent protocols activated.*'

I look around for the source, but there's no one else. Which must mean . . .

'Thanks for the update, DAMI,' Niyì replies, as if it's totally normal to chat with a jet.

I suddenly have so many more questions.

'*Not a problem, Niyì. Though you may want to buckle up, given what happened last time.*'

Niyì looks embarrassed.

'I thought I wiped your memory processors.'

'*You know how Adanna likes her backups,*' the voice replies. '*She asked me to remind you not to touch my processors again or she'll be very displeased.*'

Niyì's short bark of laughter is loud. 'Abeg o. I know she did not say that!'

'*I believe her precise words were: "If he touches you again, I'll break his head for him."*'

Niyì laughs once more. *Who is Adanna?* She sounds proper scary. Though I guess I'll find out soon enough. My stomach clenches at the thought, and before I can stop myself, I move closer to the huge glass window stretching across the front of the jet.

Niyì steps up beside me. 'Do you want to see?'

I nod, unable to trust my voice to work.

'DAMI, viewscreen please,' says Niyì.

The darkened glass in front of me blinks awake and my jaw drops as I get my first view of Nigeria's capital city.

Even though I've seen it a few times on TV, the reality is something else. In the darkness of the night sky, the mainland and smaller islands that make up Lagos shine like a bright beacon. The Gyrfalcon heads towards the mainland and I see a strange network of bridges and tunnels crisscrossing over it, like a giant spiderweb with trains and cars crawling across them. Then there are the lights.

Millions of them shimmer off the water of the lagoon surrounding the city. Buildings rise for miles, stretching into the sky like giant points of a never-ending concrete and metal crown. Some are so thin and tall, I can't understand how they're even standing. But it's not all metal and glass.

There's green too, so much green. Lush spaces filled with plant life are scattered amongst all the concrete. Some even burst from the buildings themselves. When I ask, Niyì tells me they're called vertical farms. He says it allows people to grow their own food.

Weaving between the buildings is a strange system of clear tubes, and through them zoom small, silver pods. I squint harder . . . there are people inside them.

'The Hyperloop,' I whisper. I've seen the high-speed, floating pods in magazines, but up close they look even cooler.

Mum joins us, and I look into her troubled face.

'I can imagine how exciting it must be to see Nigeria

for the first time, but remember, we're here to find your father,' she says, gesturing to the city below. 'AOS is just a temporary stop.'

My eyes return to the window. The Gyrfalcon lowers as we approach a sprawling campus of buildings. At the heart of it is a circular one, surrounded by trees and a small strip of water. It looks like a strange doughnut. The light of the jet bounces off a staggered roof made of solar panels that slope across different levels and sections of the building. The hole in the middle yawns at us like a dark, gaping mouth, and as the Gyrfalcon lines up over it, I realize it's about to swallow us.

'You ready?' says Mum in a quiet voice.

'No,' I whisper back.

Instead I'm falling – falling into something I don't understand. Mum takes hold of my hand and I grasp it tightly as the jet lowers into the darkness. I'm glad she's here with me and I don't have to do this alone.

CHAPTER
NINE

From the ground, the Academy of the Sun is even more amazing than it looked in the air. The school is huge. Transparent, circular walls of glass and metal surround us. At its centre is a jet-black landing pad – the doughnut hole I saw from the air. Several brightly lit pathways shoot off it like arteries towards the main structure of the school.

I bet my eyes must be huge as I try to take it all in, but I can't help it. I've never seen anything like this up close before. It's so shiny and perfect-looking.

'We grow our own food on campus and recycle water by harvesting rainwater, especially during the wet season,' says Niyì proudly.

'The dry season is called Harmattan, right?' I ask.

Niyì nods. 'We also have an Olympic-size athletics field, swimming pool and a Premier-League-quality football field,' he adds as he leads Mum and me down one of the pathways.

The air is warm and spicy like Mum's pepper soup, and sweat is already trickling down my back. We pass a flagpole holding a flag with the same emblem I noticed on the Gyrfalcon.

'Where is Dr Dòyìnbó?' Mum asks, a note of impatience in her voice. 'I'd like to speak to him about my husband.'

A tight feeling settles in my chest and I gawp at Mum.

'You were married?'

Mum looks at me and sighs. 'I changed our surname back to my maiden name when we left Nigeria. I hoped it would make us harder to find.'

'So I'm not an Adérìnọ́lá?' I squeak.

What else is Mum hiding? She reaches towards me and I flinch back. Mum hesitates for a moment, then her hand lowers again.

'Your last name is really Uduike.'

Uduike. I repeat it, trying to get my tongue around the strange sound, but it means nothing to me. My own name feels like it belongs to somebody else. Niyì's eyes dart about as if he doesn't know where to look, then he clears his throat.

'Dr Dòyìnbó is busy this evening, but he's asked me to get you both settled and he'll see you tomorrow.'

'Where is everyone?' I ask, trying to distract myself.

'At this time?' Niyì shrugs. 'In their dorms or the common rooms.'

71

'Do all Solari live on campus?' Mum asks.

'Dr D likes to keep us close,' Niyì replies. A passing student calls out to Niyì and he pauses to return the greeting before continuing. 'This is the main building,' says Niyì, coming to a stop in front of a set of glass double doors. 'There are four other buildings on campus, including the dorms. But this is where all the classes and major school events take place.'

The doors part and he leads us into a brightly lit atrium that's proper grand. It's like something out of one of the interior design magazines in Mum's salon. Above me, a massive network of black and grey pipes hangs from the ceiling and a web of lights weaves between them. Their bright glow reflects off the white marble floor and a huge baobab tree grows in the centre of the space. Arching away from it like an upside down U are two wide, metal staircases, leading up to the second floor and the corridors beyond.

It's big and beautiful and scary. Nothing like my worn-down school at home. My stomach tightens. I already know I won't fit in, and I don't even have Cheyenne to make things easier. The reality of my new surroundings begins to creep in and all I want to do is run and hide.

A massive digital screen with a list of colour-coded names hangs from the balcony. Not just names, but also *rankings*. In first place is a name I recognize ... Adanna Okeke. I see Niyì's too, but otherwise the names are unfamiliar and I stop reading.

Just how many Solari are there?

'About a hundred and sixty,' says Niyì, when I ask. 'We go from primary school, right through to junior secondary school. The school is split into four houses based on Ike. There are the Enhancers. Their Ike tends to amplify an already existing ability, like super speed or strength. Then you have Emitters, like me. Our Ike allows us to create different types of energy external to our body.'

I think back to his icy staircase and it suddenly makes sense.

'You'd better watch out for the Transformers,' Niyì adds. 'They can change their physical form and they're a tricky lot.'

'What about me? Which house would I be in?'

'Psionic,' Niyì says with a grin. 'Their Ike uses the psychic power of the mind to move or manipulate things.'

I blink at him. There's so much new information coming at me, I can't help but feel like the kid in the park who still has a tricycle, while everyone else has already moved on to two wheels.

'You're going to need this.' Niyì holds out his hand to Mum and me. Resting in his palm are two pairs of glasses, just like the ones on his face. 'So you don't get lost while you're here,' he finishes. Mum grabs one, then hands me the other.

The minute I place the glasses across my eyes, the lenses flash to life and a 3D map pops up across my vision, like something from a game console. I blink in surprise. *Is this what Niyì sees all the time?* In the bottom corner of the display is a digital version of the rankings list.

'What am I looking at?' I ask, my voice a breathless rush.

'We call it Second Sight,' Niyì replies. 'It's a device that adds extra digital information to the real world, through a connection to your brain. It lets you access and view data about the academy that's embedded across the campus. It also activates DAMI.' He smiles at my look of confusion. 'You met on the Gyrfalcon. He's an artificial intelligence system and he pretty much controls everything here.'

'So I just speak to it?'

Niyì puts a finger to his lips in a shushing motion. 'Him, if you don't mind. He can get a bit funny about that.'

'DAMI, where is Dr Dòyìnbó?' Mum barks out loud, and I jump.

Niyì's laughter is sudden and loud. I stiffen, waiting for Mum to finish him.

'Sorry, Ma, I should have been clearer,' says Niyì with a final chuckle. 'You need to *think* your commands. We only speak directly to DAMI on the Gyrfalcon and the Beast.'

Mum nods and my mouth drops. I'm torn between awe that she let him get away with laughing at her, and curiosity at whatever the Beast might be.

'Come on, let's get you settled in the visitors' wing,' Niyì continues, and I remember that I'm not actually going to be a student here.

We follow in silence as he leads us through the atrium. By the time we get to our room, we've gone through what feels like a million corridors and I'm totally lost.

'Here we go,' says Niyì, coming to a stop in front of a doorway. 'Your Second Sight will give you access.'

'Thank you, Niyì,' Mum replies in a subdued voice, before stepping forward. The door slides open with a soft *whoosh*. I move to join her when Niyì's voice stops me.

'Dr D thought Onyeka might like to bunk with one of us.'

My heart speeds up, then just as quickly drops. I look at Mum, waiting for her to squash the idea. There's no way she's letting me out of her sight.

'That won't be necessary,' Mum says. The tight smile on her face is the only sign of her displeasure.

Niyì smiles back, totally oblivious. 'It's no trouble, Ma. Her room-mate is expecting her.'

My stomach tightens. *Who am I sharing with?*

'Do you want to go?' says Mum, turning to me. 'You don't have to.'

I swallow. I don't want to upset Mum, but I'm also really curious. I have so much to discover and I won't be able to if I let her hide me away like she usually does.

'Yes,' I reply quietly. 'If that's okay.'

I hold my breath and wait, but Mum doesn't say a word.

She nods at me, then turns, the door of her room shutting behind her.

'You're in the upper dorm,' Niyì tells me as we hurry down the halls of another dormitory. Kids slip in and out of rooms, some dressed in a uniform like Niyì's. 'Our junior secondary school has three year groups and you're in JSS1 with me,' he continues. But I'm barely listening.

The sound of easy chatter and laughter lowers as we pass through. It feels like the time in Year Six assembly, when I had to go up to collect a music award. Everyone went quiet then too, until the giggling and pointing started. I hold my breath, waiting for it to begin now.

'Who be the new girl?' a boy wearing a baseball cap calls out.

'Face your business, Chidi,' Niyì replies with a grin, and laughter breaks out.

'And you should mind your elders,' Chidi grumbles back, but there's a smile on his face.

Slowly the attention moves away from me, and I even get a wave or two. Then a girl bursts from the wall to my right and barges across the hallway, almost knocking Chidi over. She doesn't stop and instead jumps straight through the opposite wall.

'For solar's sake, Balu. Do you have to phase out like

that? Can't you just use a door like everybody else?' Chidi grumbles before storming off.

I don't realize I'm staring until Niyì pokes me. This is not normal. Like at all. My head swivels in every direction, trying to make sense of what I'm seeing. So many kids, but no grown-ups!

'What are you looking for?' Niyì asks me.

'Oh, nothing,' I mutter, feeling silly.

'Come on. You can tell me.'

My mouth suddenly feels dry and I swallow. 'I ... I guess I thought there'd be adults around or something.' I shrug self-consciously.

Niyì grins. 'You mean teachers?' His grin widens when I nod back. 'We're pretty self-sufficient up this side. I mean the littles have a dorm mummy, but they have a habit of blowing things up.'

'Littles?' I ask.

'Most Solari get their Ike between age four and eight,' Niyì replies.

So that's what he meant on the Gyrfalcon about my age. I'm way too old to be a little.

'They're in the primary wing on the east side.' Niyì throws me a wink. 'Away from the explosives.'

'You have explosives?' I gasp.

Niyì lifts his hands in mock surrender. 'I'm just joking. Though, to be honest, with the firepower some of us have, we don't need them.'

His reply isn't reassuring at all, and I move closer to him, just to be on the safe side. Some of my hair has escaped my bun and I tuck a loose bit behind my ear, twisting it around my finger as I do.

Niyì stops in front of a door and knocks once. 'I'm sure you and Adanna are going to get on great.'

Adanna? *I'm rooming with the girl who wants to break his head?* I twist the strand even harder. There's no answer, and Niyì tries again, more loudly this time.

'Come on, Ada. I haven't got all night.'

The door springs open. A girl about my height leans against the doorway and that's where our similarities end. Suspicious eyes stare at me from behind a pair of bright pink frames. Her tiny micro locs hang down her back and I can tell she has dimples. They probably make her look cute when she smiles. She's not smiling now though. In fact, the look on her face is anything but welcoming.

Maybe the rankings list is for unfriendliness.

I don't know what to say, so I just stand there staring, an uncomfortable silence hanging between us. Cheyenne would probably say something rude to break the ice. My chest tightens at the thought of Cheyenne and a wave of sadness rolls over me.

Adanna's face creases into a grimace, as if she's tasted something sour.

'Cherries,' Adanna mutters. 'I hate cherries.'

'Come on, Adanna. You know how it is with the new ones,' Niyì replies. 'You're not exactly helping.'

'Fine, whatever,' she says, before spinning around and disappearing back into the room.

I turn and give Niyì a *don't make me go in there* look.

He laughs. 'She's harmless, trust me. Just don't touch her books.'

I don't believe him, not for a second. The hair wrapped around my finger tightens even more.

'Cherries?' I ask.

He gives a small shrug. 'I'll let Adanna tell you about that.' I frown as he gently takes my hand and releases the hair wrapped around it. 'I'll see you tomorrow.' Then he turns and walks away.

'Are you coming in or what?' Adanna calls from somewhere inside.

We're here to find my father, I remind myself before taking a deep breath and stepping into the room.

CHAPTER TEN

The room is empty when I wake, and I stretch with a wide yawn. I turn to face the bright light streaming through the open window blinds, getting my first proper look at my temporary home. Adanna wasn't very talkative last night. She turned the lights out the minute I entered the room and I had to feel my way to my bed.

My big toe is still throbbing.

A neatly made single bed rests against the wall opposite, and next to it is a bedside table, wardrobe and desk. The same as my side of the room. On top of Adanna's desk sits a clear glass screen, surrounded by devices I don't recognize. The desk looks as if someone took a ruler and carefully measured and positioned each item.

Then there are the books, stacked from floor to ceiling

and stuffed into every space imaginable. There's even one on genetics where Adanna's pillow should be.

I grab my phone from my bedside table and turn it on. The network speed is incredible. I'm scrolling through CurlyUnicorn02's feed when a new text message from Cheyenne pops up.

> **What's going on? Where are u? Have u arrived? Seen a Hyperloop yet? Met any other Solari? Come on, I'm dying here!**

I stare at the message with a smile, my thumb quickly moving over the keypad as I type a reply.

> **We flew on a super jet that talks. I met a boy who makes ice cubes with his hands and we're staying at a special boarding school. My room-mate is proper grumpy though xx**

With a grin, I throw my phone on the bed and get up to find the bathroom. Cheyenne's going to freak out when she reads it.

The atomised shower is weird, like a cloud of steam surrounding me, and it leaves my hair a mess. It probably didn't help that I slept without my satin bonnet. I pull the tangled strands into a thick braid that takes three hairbands to secure. Then a rumble in my stomach reminds me I haven't eaten in hours. I could go and find Mum or I could get some breakfast. *Okay, food first.* I deal better with Mum on a full stomach. I just need to find out where to go.

Placing my Second Sight on my face, I grimace, unsure how to activate it.

DAMI? I think, feeling really silly until words flash across my vision.

Yes, Onyeka. How may I help you this morning?

Erm, where do I get food around here?

Meals are served in the canteen. Would you like me to direct you?

The rumbling in my belly turns into butterflies at the thought of walking into a room full of kids on my own. I don't really have a choice though.

Yes, please, I finally reply.

I follow DAMI's directions through what feels like a maze of corridors, until at last I reach the double doors of the canteen. The doors slide apart like magic and a loud hum of kids talking hits me. That changes the minute I step through as a hushed quiet settles over the space. Uniformed students stop all activity just to take me in. Some even get out of their seats so they can gawp at me more easily.

Do not be alarmed. The words flash up and I blink in surprise. *They do not bite and I believe most have eaten already.*

I smile at DAMI's attempt at humour, but I keep my head down as I weave my way through the tables and whispering bodies. A few kids wave at me and I nod back shyly. Finally,

I reach the serving station and breathe a sigh of relief. It turns to awe when I see the set up and spread of food. It's proper amazing.

Plates of fried egg, yam, bacon and plantain chug along on a conveyor belt, like a souped-up sushi restaurant. It's the akara that grabs my attention though. Mum doesn't like beans, so I rarely get to eat the golden-brown fritters. I load a tray with as many plates as I can fit, grab some agege bread to mop the food up and head to the nearest empty table.

It all tastes so good and I'm halfway through it when a pretty girl in a violet shirt drops down into the chair next to me. Dark hair peeks through her violet headtie.

'Hi,' she says with a smile. 'You're Onyeka, right?'

'Yeah,' I reply around a mouthful of akara. Just my luck that she wants to talk when I'm eating.

'I'm Ẹniayọ̀, but you can call me Ẹni,' she replies, her smile growing wider. She places a tall glass of dark red liquid on the table. 'I thought you might like some zobo,' she says. Then she points to a table to the right of us and a group of kids wave back. 'You should come over to our table. Everyone's *so* excited to meet you.'

Why? I want to ask, but that's probably not the best way to make friends. The thing is, I've learned the hard way not to trust overly confident people. There's always a catch. Whether it's the joke I'm about to become the butt of, or some creepy Afro fascination that'll see me dodging wandering hands.

'I'm still a bit tired from the journey,' I blurt out.

'Don't be silly,' says Ẹni, calling me out on my rubbish excuse. 'England's not that far away.'

'Erm . . .' I begin, unsure if I'm even allowed to talk about yesterday.

'I love your hair by the way.'

Ẹni's voice is like honey now, and I know I need to get out of here sharpish. *No one* loves my hair.

Just as I search for the words that'll help me escape, a familiar voice says, 'Let's go.' I turn to find Adanna behind me. 'Dr Dòyìnbó asked me to show you around, and I'm already missing chemistry to do it.'

I can tell from her face she's not very happy about it.

'Sure, let me just finish eating,' I reply, forgetting that a moment ago I was desperate to escape Ẹni. To be honest, I'm desperate to avoid Mum too after ditching her last night, and the sooner I finish breakfast, the sooner I'll have to go and look for her.

Adanna's expression doesn't change. 'We'll start with the classrooms. I might still be able to make biology if you don't slow us down.'

'I can take her,' says Ẹni with a sugary smile.

Adanna turns narrowed eyes on her and I almost shiver from the chill of her glare. 'Did you receive instructions from Dr Dòyìnbó this morning to take Onyeka?'

Ẹni's face tightens. 'No.'

'I thought not,' Adanna replies in a matter-of-fact tone. 'Come on, Onyeka. Professor Sàlàkọ́ doesn't like being interrupted once he's started class.'

Adanna spins away and a heavy silence hangs over the table. I get up with a small shrug to Ẹni and grab a slice of agege bread before hurrying after her. I stuff it in my mouth.

Is it too late to change room-mates?

CHAPTER
ELEVEN

Professor Sàlàkọ́'s classroom is full when we reach it and a tall man stands in the centre, his long face animated as he talks to the students in the room. The professor's dark eyes sparkle with interest when he catches sight of us.

'Class,' he calls out. 'It seems we have a new student.' Every head in the room swivels towards me and I don't know where to look. 'Please introduce yourself and then take a seat next to Chigozie,' he finishes, pointing at a small girl with a friendly smile.

My eyes widen and I turn to Adanna for help. *I thought we were only doing a tour?* She stares at me, a curious emptiness in her eyes. It's like I'm being studied by a robot.

My hands begin to shake, and I'm thrown back to all the times at school I had to give a presentation and the giggling would begin before I even opened my mouth. Once, my hairband snapped while I was talking, and I had to finish with my hair surrounding me like a thick blanket. For the rest of the day, everyone called me Onyeti.

Silence stretches across the room like a strange stand-off. I reach up to tug on a stray strand of hair and my elbow connects with something solid. I turn my head, but there's no one there. I look back up and Professor Sàlàkọ́'s face has gone from interested to concerned.

'This is Onyeka,' Adanna finally says. 'She's a guest of Dr Dòyìnbó and he asked me to show her around.'

'I see,' says Professor Sàlàkọ́. Suddenly he stills, his eyes swivelling to a point in the opposite corner of the room. I follow his gaze, but there's nothing there.

'Will you be staying, Mr Adamu?' Professor Sàlàkọ́ calls out in a bored voice. 'Or are you also just visiting?'

A mumbled, 'Chai!' comes from the empty corner and I jump.

Giggles fill the room.

'Joker,' Adanna mutters as, piece by flickering piece, a boy materializes before us.

His skin is so dark, it gleams blue like my hair, except for a small, light brown patch surrounding his right eye. Even stranger is the way he continues to flicker in and out of view, like a dodgy light bulb. A piece of gum dances about in his mouth, and I frown when he gives me a wink. Then he blows the gum until it bursts with a loud pop.

Professor Sàlàkọ́ grimaces. 'If you want to sneak into my class successfully, Hassan, perhaps you should chew your gum a little more quietly next time.'

'Make you no vex, prof,' the boy says in Pidgin English, before taking a seat. A grin splits his face, flashing brilliant white teeth.

I recognize the language immediately. Uncle Dàpọ̀ uses Pidgin when he's talking to his friends. It's nice hearing the familiar sound. It makes Cheyenne feel just a bit closer.

'Hassan—' the professor begins in a warning tone.

'Sorry, sir,' says Hassan, tucking his smile away. 'I dey pray.'

The professor's eyes narrow. 'Well, I've told you before I don't appreciate lateness. Do try and finish your prayers on time.'

Adanna retreats from the room. 'We'll be going now.'

I turn to follow her, and Hassan calls out in a dramatic whisper.

'Bye, Onyeka.'

'Hassan!' barks Professor Sàlàkọ́.

'Nonsense boy,' Adanna mutters as she starts walking down the hallway.

I don't even bother trying to hide the smile that breaks out across my face. Hassan's antics are almost enough to make me forget how silly I must have looked to everyone.

'I don't know why you're so pleased,' Adanna calls out in a bored voice. 'He's like that with everyone.'

The smile drops from my face pretty sharpish and my scalp prickles with annoyance. *What is up with this girl?* I open my mouth to give her a Cheyenne-worthy clapback when I remember I'm on her turf.

'How long have you been at AOS?' I ask instead, pushing my irritation down. I rush to catch up with her.

'Six years,' Adanna replies without stopping.

Rah, I think, feeling a bit sorry for her. That's a long time to be away from your family.

'I don't want to hear your pity,' she continues, as if I'd spoken my thoughts out loud. 'So keep it to yourself.'

I frown. *What is her deal?* I hope she's not a mind reader, although I guess that would explain her crankiness. If I had everyone's thoughts invading my mind, I'd probably be a bit cranky too.

'I'm sure you've made lots of friends,' I try again, determined to make an effort.

Adanna stops and turns so suddenly I almost bump into her. Her face is tight, like one of Mum's perm rods just before it snaps.

'What do you mean by that?' she hisses at me.

I lift my hands quickly in surrender. 'Nothing. I . . . I was just being friendly, that's all.'

Adanna looks me up and down like I'm some sort of slug. 'You've been talking to Ẹni, haven't you?'

'Adanna!' a sharp voice commands. It's so deep and

powerful, Adanna freezes in place, and we both realize someone's been listening to us.

A big man walks up behind her and my gaze locks onto a pair of stern, brown eyes beneath the bushiest brows I've ever seen. Laughter lines crinkle at the corners, feathering up into his hairline.

Adanna turns to him and her whole body seems to shrink. 'I . . . I'm so sorry, Dr Dòyìnbó.'

'Thank you, Adanna, I'll take over from here,' he says in a gentler voice. 'You can return to class now.'

'But I've only just started the tour,' she mumbles.

Dr Dòyìnbó's expression doesn't change and, with a resigned nod, Adanna shuffles away.

'Hello, Onyeka,' says Dr Dòyìnbó, turning to me with a wide smile. 'It's a pleasure to finally meet you.'

So this is the man everyone's been talking about. He's much older than I imagined and I wasn't expecting the fully grey Afro that sticks up in fuzzy tufts above his forehead. Nor the pink bow tie that clashes with the orange shirt beneath it. Now the sternness has left his eyes, he looks like someone's lost grandpa.

'If you'll follow me?' he says, leading me into a large office with a glass-top desk and tons of framed pictures lining the walls. 'Please excuse Adanna,' he continues. 'She's dealing with a lot at the moment.'

Somehow, I doubt that's why Adanna's decided she hates

me. She could have at least given me a chance to earn it. You'd think I'd be used to it by now. Back home, my hair always spoke for me, long before I even opened my mouth.

'It's so good to have you here,' Dr Dòyìnbó continues. 'Your father was one of my best students.'

I lean forward, wanting to hear more, but before I can ask, Mum walks into the room. I can't help but stare at her. Her wig is gone and her hair is fully out. *She never leaves it out!* She looks totally different, as if she's put away her armour. I guess she's glad to be back in Nigeria. Maybe when we find my father, she'll be completely happy.

Mum approaches me slowly . . . too slowly.

'Good morning, ọkọ́ mi. Did you sleep well?'

I nod. There's no point complaining about my new room-mate. We're not going to be here long enough for it to matter. Mum comes to a stop in front of me and our eyes meet. Something feels off though, and I frown at her.

What is it now?

Mum tries a smile, but it looks too tight to be real. 'Did you eat yet?'

I nod again in reply. 'The canteen is so cool. I had some akara.'

'The academy is great, isn't it?' Mum's tone is off too, and I eye her suspiciously. 'Do you think you might be okay with staying here a little bit longer?'

My hands clench beside me. 'Why? You said we were coming here to find my father?'

91

'I think I already have,' Mum replies, and I blink at her. 'Uncle Ṣèyí ... I mean Dr Dòyìnbó, has been doing some digging into your father's disappearance on our behalf. He's found something that he thinks will lead me to him.'

Don't say it ... please don't say it.

'That's why I need you to stay here, where it's safe,' Mum finishes.

My scalp prickles and a heavy lump forms somewhere deep in my belly. Dr Dòyìnbó clears his throat once, then fiddles with his wonky bow tie. Everything in me stills and a strange ringing begins in my ears. *She's leaving me here.*

Sweat breaks out on my upper lip. 'How can you—' I begin, but my voice catches. I swallow and try again. 'We came all the way to Nigeria and you're just going to dump me on the first day?'

Mum steps back. 'I am not *dumping* you. It's too dangerous for you to come with me and your safety is my number one priority.'

But what about us sticking together? Isn't that a priority too?

Pain blooms across my entire head and I close my eyes and turn away, trying to push the power bubbling in me back down. But it won't go. My heart begins to race as panic rises in my chest, threatening to take over. Mum stares at me as if frozen in place. Her face is a mask of worry, but it's the fear in her eyes that finally breaks me.

Hairbands snap as my hair shoots out like super-fine

arrows, tearing through everything in its path. The top of Dr Dòyìnbó's desk shatters and shards of glass fly around me in a shimmering rainstorm. I barely feel it.

'Onyeka, control yourself,' Mum shouts.

It's too late. My emotions are taking over and I'm not sure I want to stop them.

CHAPTER TWELVE

Zero is a rich purple with the sweetness of toffee.

One I give a fiery red with the sharp tang of lime.

The next *one* is a bright blue and salty like the ocean.

Two is a deep black, bitter like burned toast.

A hot anger claws up my throat, but I don't stop counting ... I can't. If I do, I'll remember that Mum is leaving me here like a sack of potatoes and I might start breaking stuff again.

Three looks like the green of freshly sprouted leaves, with the soothing flavour of mint.

'Onyeka, are you okay?' Dr Dòyìnbó's voice breaks into my thoughts. It comes at me as if from a distance and I try to ignore it. But he won't let me. 'Your mother says you like to count. Are you doing it now?'

I laugh – I can't help it. He makes my numbers sound so

simple, even though they're not. Then the strangest thing happens. With each giggle, the anger I thought was about to eat me whole weakens. Like a toothless tiger, it scuttles back into its box in my mind. With it goes the power and my hair drops like a heavy curtain.

'I'm fine,' I finally say with a small hiccup.

I try not to think about how much I really want to throw up or the way everything hurts. I rock back on my heels as I take in the mess I've made of Dr Dòyìnbó's office. The pictures on the wall are all wonky and there's glass everywhere. The metal legs where the glass desk once was have buckled outwards as if something tried to punch its way through.

'Hmm,' says Dr Dòyìnbó. 'That's quite an impressive trick to use the Fibonacci sequence to regulate your emotions. I knew Benjamin used it when he was young, but I've never seen it in action before.'

Slowly, my eyes move to Mum and Dr Dòyìnbó, ready for the major trouble I must be in. My mouth drops when I see the scratches dotting his face and Mum's hair looks like it's been attacked by a leaf blower. Yet somehow, Dr Dòyìnbó is grinning.

Is he for real? I just destroyed his office and he's looking at me as if I gave him a really cool present.

'Onyeka.' Mum's voice is high and tight. 'Apologize this second.'

Dr Dòyìnbó waves her words way. 'It's fine, Tópé.' He turns to me again. 'While I'm sorry you find your mother's news so distressing, I'm quite glad I got to witness that little display in person. Is your Ike always so explosive?'

Shame crawls up my belly and my head drops. Mum is right to be horrified by my *little display*. A finger beneath my chin startles me and I look up to find Dr Dòyìnbó staring at me in a way that makes me feel even worse.

'It's all right, Onyeka. There's no permanent damage done yet.' I frown, confused by his words. His office is trashed. Dr Dòyìnbó's smile returns, then he steps away and Mum takes his place.

'I know you're scared and that's my fault.' Her hand is warm as it closes around mine. 'We had to hide in London, but you're safe here, I promise. Your father trusted Dr Dòyìnbó and so do I.' She squeezes my hand. 'Besides, I'll be back before you can even miss me.'

I bite my lower lip and look down. It's not just about Mum being away. I wanted to be there when we found my father, not stuck in some strange school.

'Thank you,' says Mum, turning back to Dr Dòyìnbó. 'I feel much better knowing Onyeka will be looked after here.'

'Think nothing of it. We'll keep her monitored while she's at AOS,' Dr Dòyìnbó replies.

I look up then. 'Why?'

'It's just a precaution,' he assures me. 'Ike usually shows

at a much younger age, and we need to ensure your body is handling the transition well.'

Mum nods. 'You'll keep me informed?'

'Of course.'

'I guess I'd better get going then,' says Mum, suddenly looking lost. 'I don't want to miss my Hyperloop.'

I swallow hard. I'm not ready for this. Even though she probably won't be gone long, it somehow feels as if I'm losing her as well. I can still remember the look in Cheyenne's eyes when we said goodbye.

Mum cradles my face in her hands. 'I'll make sure I call you and you can message me whenever you need to, okay?'

I nod. 'You'll be back soon?'

Her smile feels forced and I pretend not to notice. 'As soon as I find your father.' She pulls me in for a hug, and then with a quick kiss to my forehead, she turns and walks briskly out of the room.

I stare after her and the panic begins to rise in my chest again. What if she doesn't come back? What if she doesn't find him?

What if she does and he doesn't want anything to do with me? a dangerous voice whispers inside my head. My shoulders droop and my breath hitches.

'Your father used to look at your mother that way too,' says Dr Dòyìnbó softly, and my startled gaze swings back to him. 'As if she were his world.'

My stomach jolts and the queasy feeling intensifies. Mum *is* my world.

'Are you feeling nauseous by any chance?'

I look at Dr Dòyìnbó in surprise. *How did he know?*

He smiles at me gently. 'It's quite normal. Using Ike takes a toll on the body. You can expect to feel some discomfort until you gain better control of your emotions.'

I press a hand to my stomach, relieved. *So that's why I've been feeling so sick.*

'I certainly wouldn't advise overusing Ike,' Dr Dòyìnbó continues with a small wince, almost as if he knows how it feels. 'I hear it can be quite unpleasant.'

My curiosity stirs. 'So you're not Solari too?'

'Heavens no,' Dr Dòyìnbó's splutters, his face twisting. 'That kind of power? I wouldn't know what to do with it.'

I stare at him, confused. *Then why set up a whole school just for us?* I'm about to ask this, but Dr Dòyìnbó shuffles past me towards his mangled desk. A new wave of embarrassment washes over me and my eyes drop to a large piece of glass on the ground.

'What am I supposed to do now?' I ask instead.

'Your mother insists that you continue your schooling,' says Dr Dòyìnbó, and I grimace.

'But I'm on summer holidays!'

Dr Dòyìnbó shrugs in sympathy. 'I thought you might enjoy a different kind of learning,' he says with a meaningful look at my head.

'Huh?' I squeak.

He bends to pick up some papers from the floor. 'You need to improve your connection to your Ike. Unless you plan to spend the rest of your life counting?'

If I could blush, I'd probably be a million shades of red, and I'm thankful for my dark skin.

'What else can I do?' I fire back, crossing my arms over my chest. 'You saw what my hair is like.'

Dr Dòyìnbó frowns. 'Ike is as much a part of you as the nose on your face. You don't have to think about letting air in and out when you breathe, it just happens. It's up to you to choose how you use your Ike, though I hope it will be for good.'

I'd never thought of my power that way before. To be honest, I haven't let myself think about it much beyond the complete mess it's made of my life. The idea that it could be something good or useful feels strange.

Then I remember how it saved me and Cheyenne and how excited Niyì is about being a Protector. *Maybe it's not so bad.* Then a new thought occurs me. Something both scary and exciting.

'Are you saying that if I learn how to use my powers, I can be a Protector?'

Dr Dòyìnbó laughs. 'Let's start with: so you don't destroy my office the next time you get some unexpected news.' I hesitate, and his caterpillar brows lift. 'Do you have something more important to do?'

He's right, I don't.

But I could. I could have control of my Ike by the time Mum returns, then maybe she won't be so worried. The tight feeling that's been sitting in my chest since Mum left loosens and I shake my head in answer to Dr Dòyìnbó's question.

'Good,' he replies. 'We start tomorrow bright and early.'

'Where?' I reply with a frown.

Dr Dòyìnbó's face lights up. 'HOME.'

CHAPTER
THIRTEEN

HOME turns out to be a building on the east side of campus, near the littles' dorm. With DAMI's help, I make my way over after breakfast the next day.

Dr Dòyìnbó suggested I finish my tour yesterday, but I wasn't in the mood, so I spent the rest of the day in my room texting Cheyenne and watching CurlyUnicorn02 videos. Cheyenne couldn't believe it when I told her Mum had left. Adanna didn't turn up until after I'd gone to bed and it's beginning to feel like she's avoiding me. Good thing I had DAMI to show me how to get to HOME.

Inside the building, I follow a long, grey hallway to a set of metal doors. It's so quiet I can hear myself breathing. The double doors slide apart suddenly and I squint as bright light hits me. My vision clears and I gasp.

No freaking way!

A sea of yellow grass stretches out as far as I can see. It

gleams underneath a yellow sun that shouldn't be there, shining out of a blue sky that doesn't exist. Proud looking trees are scattered everywhere and a herd of gazelle shimmer in the distance, like some sort of hazy mirage. All of it sits in the shadow of a steep, rocky mountain.

I blink, shaking my head. There's no way any of it can be real. Then I see Dr Dòyìnbó, striding through the golden grass towards me.

'Come in, come in,' he hollers.

I step inside the room uncertainly and the doors close with a *swish* behind me. It's hot and I pull my T-shirt away from my neck. The sound of whispers catches my attention. A group of three students are huddled around a tall tree in the distance. I recognize Niyì immediately, but it takes me a moment to place Hassan, the flickering boy with the gum. I freeze when I clock the girl with them.

Adanna!

Hassan waves at me. 'Sannu,' he calls out with a smile.

I recognise the Hausa greeting from the Naija films Cheyenne's mum likes to watch. Before I can even respond, Adanna yanks his arm down and glares at me.

Seriously, what is her problem? And what are they even doing here? They look super cosy too. I look away quickly and focus on Dr Dòyìnbó as he reaches me.

'Good, you found your way,' he says with a cheerful grin. 'Let's begin.'

He leads me through the grass, towards another tree that's off to one side.

'Welcome to HOME – the Holographic Offensive Multi-sensory Environment,' says Dr Dòyìnbó in a firm voice. 'It's a state-of-the-art holosuite that allows students to train in a realistic but safe virtual environment.'

I nod, still too shocked to say anything. I'm standing in the middle of a savannah, inside a freaking building!

Dr Dòyìnbó gives me a reassuring pat. 'It's just fancy lights, a bit of smoke and lots of mirrors, but it's where you'll learn to use your Ike.' His voice turns serious again. 'Ike means "power" in Igbo. For the safety of everyone in Nigeria, it's vital that all Solari learn to master it and keep it a secret. Do you understand?'

I do, but his warning is a bit late. The trio have stopped talking, their attention now focused on me. I shift from one foot to the other and force myself to look away.

'Erm . . . I might have told someone already,' I reply in a quiet voice.

Dr Dòyìnbó's eyebrows come crashing down. 'Who?'

I swallow hard. 'My best friend back home. She promised not to say anything,' I rush on. A low whistle comes from Hassan. 'Chey's not in trouble, is she?' I add anxiously.

Dr Dòyìnbó pauses for a moment, a thoughtful look on his face. 'I'm sure it will be fine,' he finally replies. 'You didn't know, and I doubt anyone would believe your friend, should she decide to talk.' Then his expression sharpens. 'But there must be complete secrecy from this moment on, understood?'

I nod quickly.

'Good,' he says, and his voice softens. 'A Solari's powers are a gift, but they must only be used to serve and benefit this country.' He pauses to adjust his lilac bow tie. 'Now the first thing you need to understand is that Ike is the energy source that fuels your psychokinesis. All fuel requires a spark to ignite it and the same is true of Ike. Can you guess what it is?'

I open my mouth to say no when a memory stops me. I remember the fear I felt in the pool, the first time my powers showed up. Then pain with Mum, and just yesterday, blinding rage.

'My emotions?' I whisper.

'Precisely,' says Dr Dòyìnbó with an approving smile. 'Thus far you've been suppressing them with your Fibonacci technique. Now you need to learn how to harness and release them.'

Release them? Is he actually kidding?

I look over at the group again. Adanna is pretending to ignore me, but Niyì and Hassan are watching with zero shame. I turn back to Dr Dòyìnbó with a frown. Has he forgotten what I did to his office?

'I don't think that's a good idea.'

'Of course it is,' he replies in a cheerful voice. 'You can't do any damage in here. You just need to find your anchor then you—'

'Wait!' I interrupt. 'What's an anchor?'

'An anchor stabilizes your emotions,' Dr Dòyìnbó replies. 'It can be anything really – a belief, a memory or even a person. The key thing is faith. If you believe in it completely, without a shadow of doubt, it will help you connect with your Ike. Otherwise, your emotions will continue to overwhelm you.'

A lump forms in my throat and I swallow it down with difficulty. I don't think Dr Dòyìnbó realizes what he's asking me to do. I wish Mum were here. She understands why I can't just let my emotions go.

'I can't,' I tell him, trying to make him see sense. 'It ... it will take over, like it did yesterday.'

'Only if you let it,' he says calmly. 'If you don't learn to master your powers, they will master you.'

I think back to each time my power came through. I was totally not in control, my emotions taking over as I reacted to the things happening to me. Dr Dòyìnbó is right and I shift from one foot to the other, disturbed by the discovery.

'What do I need to do?' I mutter.

Satisfaction spreads across Dr Dòyìnbó's face and he steps towards me.

'Let's start with an easy emotion – fear. You must be feeling some right now. I want you to try to capture it in your mind. The shape and the colour. You'll know once you have it.' He stares at me, an expectant expression on his face, and I bite my bottom lip.

I'm proper baffled now. I have no idea what he's talking about. How am I supposed to *capture* a feeling?

'I don't understand.'

'It's just like your Fibonacci sequence,' says Dr Dòyìnbó. 'But instead of focusing on the numbers, focus on the emotion.'

I blink at him. I hadn't thought of it that way. But still, I've spent way too long running away from my feelings and the thought of running *towards* them . . .

'I'm scared,' I push out through gritted teeth.

'There's nothing wrong with being scared, Onyeka, but you must embrace the feeling,' Dr Dòyìnbó insists. 'Then trust your anchor to contain the power.'

I don't even have an anchor!

Before I can say as much, a new voice beats me to it.

'Sir, if I may . . .'

Dr Dòyìnbó swivels round in surprise. But I already know the owner.

'That's not going to work with her. She's not a little,' Adanna continues.

Our eyes lock. She steps forward as Dr Dòyìnbó moves aside, then places a hand on my chest.

'Your Ike isn't separate from you.' Her words push at something buried deep inside me, and I clench my teeth against it. 'It's part of you ... here.' She presses down hard against my heart, before moving to my head. 'And here.' I stumble back, the grass brushing against my legs. 'Stop hiding from it.'

Her eyes bore into me, willing me to understand. Sweat breaks out on my forehead as I try to focus on her words.

'Close your eyes,' Adanna commands, and I do it instinctively. 'You need to push deeper. What do you fear most?'

I hear Dr Dòyìnbó gasp.

'Adanna, that's much too dangerous. She's not ready—' But the rest of his sentence is lost as Adanna's words act like a key, opening something inside my mind.

I stiffen as the ground beneath my feet shifts and my eyes fly open in time to see the sunny savannah disappear. Bright blue beams spring up around us like a cage of light, and the air shimmers for a moment before the cage solidifies into faded white walls that are all too familiar. As are the wooden chest of drawers and the broken lamp.

I'm in my bedroom again.

I look around wildly. How is this even possible?

'This is a holographic room,' Adanna reminds me. 'DAMI is tracking the synaptic activity in your brain and HOME manifests it.'

As if on cue, Mum materializes in front of me. I stare, my mouth hanging open.

'Mum?' I finally whisper.

'I'm so sorry, Onyeka, I couldn't find him,' she says. 'I couldn't find your father.'

My face wrinkles. Mum only left yesterday morning. I reach out to touch her arm and my fingers move right through her, as if she's a ghost. Then Mum's face glitches – she's not a ghost, she's a holographic projection.

'Not that I blame him,' the hologram continues. 'Why would he want to come back to us?' The voice deepens suddenly and Mum's face morphs into my father's.

'I don't want you in my life,' it says. 'I don't even love you.'

'No,' I gasp.

Even though it's obvious this thing isn't my father, that it isn't even real, the horrible words coming from its mouth drill through me like a blunt screwdriver.

As if sensing my pain, the thing pretending to be my father steps closer. 'Did you enjoy pretending you were part of Cheyenne's family?' it hisses at me. Another glitch and the features change again. I flinch as Cheyenne's face stares back at me.

'I'm having a blast with *my* family and all my new friends now that you're not butting in all the time.'

'Stop it,' I scream. But it's no use.

'You're better off alone, you know,' Cheyenne goes on. 'You'll never fit in anywhere. Even here.'

I jerk as terror like I've never felt before floods me, until

I'm almost shaking with it. I reach for the Fibonacci numbers desperately.

Zero is turquoise with the fiery taste of scotch bonnet peppers. Just like the burning fear that I try to shove back down.

'Don't fight the emotion,' Adanna reminds me. 'Find your anchor and use it.'

Don't fight the emotion, I repeat to myself. With a deep breath, I close my eyes and push the next number away. It's time to stop running.

Then something strange happens. A memory flickers inside me. It opens slowly, a small thing really, but the brilliance of it glows brightly as it overpowers my fear like a floodlight.

Cheyenne standing up for me in after-school club when Joshua Effiang said my hair looked like a dirty mop.

The memory begins to glow bronze and the taste of chocolate floods my mouth.

Cheyenne sharing her food with me whenever I didn't have any dinner money.

A silver shine coats the memory, this time ham-flavoured like Cheyenne's sandwiches.

The image shifts again and now it's Cheyenne going after my swimming cap, because she didn't want anyone to laugh at me. Even though she could barely swim. Even though it nearly killed her. The memory burns a blazing gold, with a metallic edge . . . like blood.

This final memory is so strong, it wraps around the fear like a net, harnessing it. It grows stronger and stronger until I'm pulsing with power.

With Ike!

A ripple of energy sparks across my scalp, and I feel a stirring as everything else fades away. My eyes snap open again, just in time to see my hair converge into a solid mass of wiry strands. It whistles through the air, punching through the hologram of Cheyenne. The projection of my room shatters into tiny fragments of light before fading away, leaving behind a dark grey room, lit by blue beams criss-crossing the walls.

'I did it!' I whisper into the shocked silence.

Niyì gives me an amused smile and Hassan raises his thumbs. I'm so giddy with excitement that nothing can ruin this moment, not even Adanna's smirk as she steps away from me.

'Unorthodox and rather dangerous,' says Dr Dòyìnbó to Adanna. 'But also effective,' he adds with an approving smile, and I beam right back. 'Now let's do it again.'

A churning begins in my stomach and my triumph melts away like ice cream left out on a sunny day. A sharp pain fills my head and half-digested akara shoots out of my mouth and onto the hard floor.

I was wrong ... there *is* something that can ruin this moment.

CHAPTER FOURTEEN

A few hours later, and I'm staring down at the uniform on my bed. It looks weird sitting on top of the white bedsheet. It's a pair of patterned ankara shorts in a loud mix of colours and a bright blue polo shirt that does nothing to calm it down. But the embroidered AOS crest on the breast pocket looks really cool and I reach for it, studying the intricate design.

Red and orange threads spiral out from a yellow circle – a flaming sun. According to Dr Dòyìnbó, it represents the power of the Solari. A power I still don't fully understand.

Like how to use it without throwing up.

I push the embarrassing memory aside. Dr Dòyìnbó assured me that the sickness would ease up. I pull the uniform on quickly, just as there's a knock at the door. I open it to find Niyì, dressed in matching shorts and a yellow shirt.

'How far?' he says with a big grin, and I frown, unsure

what he means. 'You look better, so you must be feeling better,' he adds, studying my new uniform.

My eyes narrow, waiting for the gag. My hair isn't as dry and tangled as it was this morning. I'm not sure if it has something to do with learning how to access my Ike. Still, it took for ever to pull it into a simple braid that's frizzing up already. But Niyì's face doesn't change.

'I look like a box of crayons,' I finally reply. 'What's with the rainbow uniform?'

'House colours,' Niyì replies. 'Emitters burn yellow, you guys are blue, House Enhancer is green and House Transformer is violet.'

I frown as I remember something. 'Why only four houses?'

Niyì laughs. 'They're the only Ike we know about, and believe me, it's more than enough. The way your house and House Transformer are always bickering.' Then he puffs his chest out. 'It's a good thing House Emitter is here to keep the peace. Speaking of bickering, where's Adanna?'

I shrug. I woke up to an empty room again and I'm beginning to wonder if Adanna thinks I stink or something.

'I don't know. She keeps disappearing on me.'

Niyì's grin turns rueful. 'Ada's okay once you get to know her.'

'How am I supposed to do that if she's never around?'

'You'll figure it out,' Niyì replies. 'Ready for a proper tour before your first class?'

My brows lift. 'I thought Adanna was doing it?'

Niyì suddenly looks uncomfortable. 'Dr D thought you might prefer me.' Then his grin returns. 'Besides, you haven't *fully* experienced AOS until I take you around.' He inspects me again. 'Good, you've got your Second Sight on. You'll need it for all your classes. You can call up your schedule on it too. Dr D is starting you slow and easy, so you only have history today.'

He looks at me like he thinks I'm lucky, but I don't *feel* very lucky. I have to deal with a whole bunch of new people, and I can't be sure I won't throw up on them.

Out in the hallway, students scurry past. A small boy zooms by, almost knocking me over as his wheelchair hovers away.

'Watch it, Muhammad,' Niyì yells after him, before turning back to me. 'Sorry about that. He's been banned from teleporting after he went missing for a whole day, so now he insists on speeding around instead.'

We pass a group of students dressed in green shirts and Niyì calls out a greeting. They ignore him.

'JSS3,' Niyì says with a shrug. 'They think they run the place because they're graduating soon. As if we're not all going to be Protectors one day ...'

Well, I'm not going to be a Protector, I think. I swallow hard, trying to memorize their faces so I can avoid them.

'I can't wait for Ìdánwò,' Niyì says with a wide grin. 'I'm going to smash the record for house points and show them.'

I just stare at him and Niyì smacks his head.

'Oops, sorry! Ìdánwò is part of our annual house tournament. It's a competition between the houses that decides the final placement of every student on the List.'

The List. So that's what the rankings are about.

'Two houses go up against each other to complete a set of trials,' Niyì adds.

Wow, and I thought school at home was tough. The last time I checked the List, Adanna was still first. Niyì and Hassan were in eighth and tenth places.

'You get points for academic achievement and points for completing Ìdánwò,' Niyì continues. 'The person in each year with the most points in total gets ranked first on the List, as well as winning full bragging rights. Then they tally everyone's points and the house with the most points overall wins for that year group.'

Before I can ask any more questions, we arrive at the canteen. I grab some fried plantain called dodo with suya for lunch, while Niyì goes for the pepper soup. Afterwards, Niyì takes me to the shared JSS common room. The open-plan space is split into colour-coded zones, one for each house. Though no one seems to care much as kids mix together in their polo shirts like a bag of M&M's.

Some lounge around chatting on the comfy-looking sofas, while a big group gathers around a game of tabletop football. I guess football is big here. Niyì introduces me to two of the six JSS prefects on campus – a boy and a girl with straight backs and arrogant smiles. Niyì tells me that's just how prefects are, and that he can't wait to be one, so he can do a better job of it.

Afterwards, we head to the library. A bright white space where the walls themselves are shelves, crammed with books rising right up to the ceiling. Mum would love it here. The floor is a lush carpet of green so vivid, it almost seems like real grass. Pink and orange tinted light streams through colourful panels in the roof that look like stained glass windows.

'It's solar glass,' Niyì says, seeing my confusion. 'It generates solar energy and also allows light to pass through like a window.'

Students lounge in little alcoves, noses deep in the pages of their books. A large picture of Dr Dòyìnbó catches my eye, but something about it looks strange. I move closer to get a better look. *Dr Dòyìnbó is moving!* Every few seconds his expression shifts, morphing into a smile. It's an augmented photograph.

'Rah,' I breathe.

A girl in violet standing nearby gives me a strange look. But I barely notice because underneath the picture is a plaque that reads: 'In honour of Dr Şèyí Dòyìnbó, Father of Solar'.

I frown, and before I can stop myself, I'm already speaking. 'What does it mean by "Father of Solar"?'

Niyì comes up behind me. 'Dr D discovered a new element

called trarium in 1979. He was only twenty,' he replies in an awed voice. 'He used it to create a solar cell that's five times more efficient than what the rest of the world uses. It powers our tech and without it –' he waves at the room – 'all this wouldn't exist.'

'So he's a scientist?'

Niyì nods. 'He used to be on the Council.'

'Which one?' I ask, remembering that there are two.

Niyì smiles at me approvingly. 'The Upper one. The Lower Council is made up of locally elected members from over three hundred tribes. They run the provinces. The Upper Council is like the big boss. You have to come from one of the seven largest tribes to be a member.'

'Why isn't he on the Upper Council any more?' I ask.

The girl beside us sniggers. 'He got demoted.'

Niyì scowls at her and his jaw stiffens, then he moves away. 'Come on, Onyeka. We've still got loads to see before Professor Sàlàkọ́'s history class.'

I follow, startled by his response. 'What did that girl mean when she said Dr Dòyìnbó was demoted?'

Niyì gives me a tight smile. 'Don't mind her, she's just a loudmouth Transformer.'

The hallway is full of rushing kids and the sound of chatter and laughter fills the air. Colourful posters and banners hang from the walls, reminding us that we serve Nigeria, as well as pictures of former students. I look for one of my father, but I don't find him.

My hair draws a bit of attention as we continue walking ... even here where people hover above the ground and walk through walls as if it's the most natural thing in the world. I reckon what happened in HOME must have got around. But for once the stares feel harmless and I let myself relax a bit.

Outside, we follow one of the criss-crossing gravel paths across the grassy quad and towards the sports fields. A uniformed guard waves at Niyì and he waves back.

'They guard the campus,' he says, seeing my curious stare. 'Though I can't decide if they're here to protect us or the rest of Nigeria.'

We continue on, and as we pass the football pitch, a coach yells orders at a group of players sprinting across the field. Suddenly, one player sprints away so fast, she looks like a blur. Then a whistle blows.

'For solar's sake, Pèlúmi, what have I told you about being offside?' the coach barks after her.

Rah, she's fast! I look around, but no one else seems bothered by her easy show of power, as if it's totally normal ... expected even. Will I ever be able to use my Ike like that?

Niyì points out the indoor gym and basketball court, before continuing along a path that takes us further away from the main building, the trees growing denser and thicker the more we walk on. I'm still getting used to the constant heat and sweat begins to gather on my back.

As we near the lake that borders the campus, the busy sounds of the quad fade away, replaced by the chirping of strange birds and small animals scuttling off to places I'd rather not know about.

Maybe that's why it's such a surprise when I hear the sound of little children playing. Then a playground appears, bordered by a thick fence. Dressed in academy colours, they shout and run around the wooden playground. It must be the littles Niyì was talking about before. They look so happy and confident, but they also look really small. Too small to be in a boarding school.

I ask Niyì about it and he frowns.

'It's better this way. The younger we find Solari, the easier it is for them to learn how to use Ike safely.'

I shake my head. 'Don't they miss their families?'

Niyì shrugs. 'Probably, but there's no other option. It's too dangerous otherwise.'

My gaze drops back to the children. 'How? They're so tiny.'

He snorts. *Am I missing something?*

'They're Solari.' Niyì's voice is gruff, and he turns away from the playground, walking quickly. I follow him, even more confused. *What did I say?* Then a thought occurs to me. Maybe he used to be one of them.

'How old were you when you came here?' I ask him.

Niyì grinds to a halt, like a toy soldier whose batteries have died.

'Six.'

'It must have been hard for your parents to let you go,' I say uncertainly.

A sound leaves Niyì's throat, and he kicks a small rock with his foot.

'They couldn't wait to get rid of me after what I did ...' His voice trails off as a shudder runs through his body. 'It wasn't hard either. The Councils do a really good job of keeping our existence a secret. Even if it means having to bribe or threaten people. There are always rumours about us, but no one's been able to prove anything yet.'

My mouth goes dry. I probably shouldn't ask, but I can't help myself.

'What did you do?'

He doesn't answer immediately, just stares at me, as if he's trying to figure something out.

'You don't have to tell me,' I whisper, suddenly nervous.

Niyì's expression shifts then, as if he's made a decision.

'It's fine.' He runs a hand across his head. 'I was playing with my best friend, Débọ̀. We were arguing about something. I can't even remember what it was, but I lost my temper. I could feel something growing inside me, but I couldn't stop it. Then there was ice everywhere, covering everything. The ground, the trees ... Débò.' Niyì rubs his eyes. 'My ice isn't like the normal kind. He's still stuck in a coma and no one knows if he'll ever wake up.'

'I'm so sorry,' I whisper. I reach out a hand towards him, but he steps back before I make contact. A tight feeling spreads across my chest and my hand drops back down to my side.

'Dr Dòyìnbó personally came to get me,' he continues in a flat voice. 'He's so famous my parents didn't even hesitate. Plus, I'm sure the money the Councils pay them helps my parents to forget about me. Dr D is always looking out for strange news reports or sightings of paranormal activity, just in case it's a Solari. He promised that if I went with him, nothing like that would ever happen again – that he would protect me and all other Solari.' An urgency burns in Niyì's eyes now. 'It's why the academy is so important. It exists so bad things don't happen when Ike is left unchecked.'

'But it wasn't your fault,' I reply. 'You were only little.'

Niyì blinks, as if seeing me properly after a long while.

'So are they.' He nods towards the playground full of young children. 'It doesn't make our powers any less dangerous.'

CHAPTER
FIFTEEN

Niyì is quiet as we approach Professor Sàlàkọ́'s class. Neither of us has spoken since we walked back from the littles' playground. A flash of violet fabric catches my attention. It's Ẹni from the canteen. She's so busy talking to another student that she doesn't see us immediately.

'See you later,' says Ẹni to the girl, then she turns away, finally spotting me and Niyì.

'Oh, hi, Onyeka.'

She narrows her eyes at Niyì, then with a small wave at me, she strolls into the classroom. I look at Niyì, my brow raised. He just shrugs and waves me forward. I hesitate for a second, then take a deep breath.

Please, God. Just let me get through this without messing something up!

We step through the automated doors and into a large,

white room with tiled walls. The staggered seats are arranged in a circular pattern, two rows spiralling outwards like a maze.

Most of the seats are already filled and I spot Hassan on the opposite side of the room, Adanna next to him. I look away, feeling awkward. I'm not fully sure why. She's made it clear she doesn't want to be friends and I'm totally fine with that. But why then did she help me in HOME this morning? The girl has even seen me throw up.

In the middle of the circle of seats is a large, flat, metal disc embedded into the floor. Floating above it is a set of bright blue numbers – a 3D timer . . . and there's less than a minute left. Curious, I lift my Second Sight away from my face and the numbers disappear. I do it a few more times, my face splitting into a grin.

Niyì nudges me. 'Having fun?' I nod, and he grins back. 'Come on, Professor Sàlàkọ́'s about to start.'

Sure enough, the professor is glaring at us with narrowed eyes. We move quickly, grabbing two empty seats as the clock hits zero. The classroom doors swish closed and the lights dim.

Professor Sàlàkọ́ coughs to get everyone's attention, then he turns in my direction. 'I see you've joined us properly, Ms Uduike.'

It's strange hearing my real surname used for the first time. Then I realize why the room is laid out the way it is. I can see everyone in the classroom. But what's worse, they can see me too. Too many eyes zero in on me and I struggle not to fidget in my seat.

'Do you think you could introduce yourself now?' the professor asks.

My voice is frozen, as if Niyì used his Ike on it, and I shake my head. A few students gasp and even Niyì sucks in a breath next to me.

Professor Sàlàkọ́ stares at me for a long moment and I hold my breath too.

'We're discussing the history of Nigeria's Unity Councils,' he finally begins, and I release my breath on a sigh. 'I'm assuming you already know how Nigeria got its independence back in 1960?'

I nod eagerly. We covered it in Year Six.

'Good to know you're learning about something other than Vikings and murderous Tudor kings,' Professor Sàlàkọ́ responds, and I cringe. I actually quite liked learning about Henry VIII. 'This is probably a good opportunity to revise and recap our learning. Can anyone tell me the most important thing the government did after independence?'

'Do we have to go over all of this again?' says Adanna in a bored voice. 'I don't want to get behind. If she needs to catch up, why can't she use her free study period?'

The room goes real quiet and Professor Sàlàkọ́ glares at Adanna. I want to curl up like an embarrassed caterpillar.

Everyone knows we're room-mates, but the way Adanna's acting, they probably think I'm a nightmare to live with.

'I don't mind recapping, Professor Sàlàkọ́,' a voice says. It's Ẹni and she's grinning at me. 'I can imagine how difficult it must be for Onyeka. We should all do what we can to make her feel welcome.'

Adanna rolls her eyes and Ẹni's grin grows wider. It looks a bit smug, but I'm too relieved to care. I give her a grateful smile back.

'But maybe Adanna should start since she's ranked first,' Ẹni adds in a sarcastic voice.

I cringe as Adanna goes as still as a rock. I'm suddenly really glad my name isn't up on the List. Adanna's eyes narrow, as if she's heard my thoughts, then she begins to speak in a flat voice.

'Almost twenty years after independence, the government decided to focus exclusively on solar power as a source of energy. Dr Dòyìnbó's trarium solar cells, together with the superconducting alloys he also invented, means that Nigeria is now the largest and most efficient producer and transporter of solar energy in the world.'

'Excellent, Adanna,' says Professor Sàlàkọ́. 'Please continue.'

Adanna's expression doesn't change. 'Our leaders also realized they needed to make the country better for everyone.'

'How?' Professor Sàlàkọ́ asks.

'Health care,' a deep voice booms across the room, and I clamp my hands over my ears. A bald boy in a green shirt, an Enhancer, smiles sheepishly.

'Thank you for whispering this time, Amandi,' the professor replies as he lowers his hands from his ears.

My eyes widen. *That was a whisper?*

'What else?' Professor Sàlàkọ́ continues.

A boy in a blue shirt with a huge hi-top fade raises his hand and the professor nods. 'Education and technology.' The boy's pupils are so big and dark, I can't see the whites of his eyes at all. He catches me staring and winks. I look away quickly.

'That's correct, Ọ̀rẹ́bíyì,' Professor Sàlàkọ́ says, before moving to the metal disc in the centre of the room.

A 3D map of Nigeria pops up on my Second Sight, showing three regions – northern, western and eastern. Now I understand why Niyì said I'd need the glasses.

'Our leaders also realized no one knew what it truly meant to be Nigerian,' Professor Sàlàkọ́ goes on. 'We only had the fragile systems that the British left us with after independence.' The regions on the 3D map break apart into nineteen new provinces as he speaks. 'But they understood that for new Nigeria to survive, it would need to be truly united.'

'That's when the Unity Councils were created,' Ẹni cuts in quickly. 'Members are called Elders, though they can be any age really. The Laamu-EzeOba is the leader of both the

Councils and Nigeria and is elected from the Upper Council every ten years. The tribal origin of the Laamu-EzeOba is rotated at each election.'

Professor Sàlàkọ́'s face is fully alight with excitement now. 'Why do they do this?'

'It's supposed to ensure that only those who have earned the respect of other Elders are chosen to lead the country,' Adanna cuts in before Ẹni can reply. 'That no one tribe is ranked above any other.'

Her voice is biting and there's a mocking twist to her mouth. I'm getting proper fed up with her attitude.

'You don't sound like you think it works,' I say in a sharp voice, surprising myself.

Adanna shrugs. 'It doesn't. No one from the smaller tribes has a chance of joining the Upper Council, so they'll never get a shot at being Laamu-EzeOba.'

'Ignore her,' Ẹni says to me. 'She thinks she knows everything.' Then she turns to Adanna. 'Just because you have more than one Ike doesn't make you smarter than the rest of us.'

I stare at Adanna, surprised. I didn't even know Solari could have multiple powers.

Adanna straightens in her chair, ignoring Ẹni. 'Sure, the Councils are better than what a lot of other countries have, but they're not perfect. Look at us . . . we're only here because a big mistake was made.'

'It's being fixed!' Niyì snaps, and Adanna flinches. 'The Councils have shut down all the dodgy trarium factories and cleaned up the contaminated areas. We haven't even had a new little for a while.' Niyì takes a breath, then continues. 'Dr Dòyìnbó left the Upper Council and created AOS to keep us safe and he's kept his promise.'

My head shifts between them as I try to keep up. What does trarium have to do with Solari? Then I remember the article I read in the newspaper the day my powers showed up.

Before I know it, Professor Sàlàkọ́ is in front of me.

'Apologies, Onyeka. I should probably explain.'

'Explain what?' I reply, suddenly nervous.

The professor nods and the map in the centre of the room disappears, replaced by a hologram of a silver lump of metal. The shimmering ridges look so real I could reach out and touch it.

'On its own, trarium is a fairly harmless metal,' says Professor Sàlàkọ́. 'But Dr Dòyìnbó's mining process made it capable of mutating humans and no one realized at the time. For at least twenty years, local groundwater supplies across the country were being contaminated by the runoff water used to process trarium ore. By the time this was discovered, many women had already been exposed to the contaminated water. At first, it seemed the mutation only affected babies still in the womb.' Professor Sàlàkọ́ pauses, as if he's choosing his words carefully. 'But we now know the mutation can be passed on genetically to the next generation. Dr Dòyìnbó took full responsibility for the contamination, but the damage had already been done ... Solari started cropping up everywhere.'

I blink at him in surprise. *Like me. He's talking about me.*

'How ...?' I begin, but my voice fades away as I struggle to process Professor Sàlàkó's words.

We're an accident, and not even a happy one from the sounds of it. My powers aren't supposed to exist, and the only reason they do is because someone messed up big time. I stare around the room. *How come everyone seems to be cool with it?*

CHAPTER
SIXTEEN

The classroom grows quiet again as everyone watches me, waiting for my reaction.

'Does that mean other countries that use solar power have Solari?' I ask.

'Not at all,' says Professor Sàlàkọ́ quickly. 'Solari seem to be specific to Nigeria. Dr Dòyìnbó couldn't have anticipated it, of course, but as the technology is his, Dr Dòyìnbó is doing his best to help Solari here at AOS.'

I remember then what Niyì said about Dr Dòyìnbó protecting us. *He must feel really guilty.*

Adanna rolls her eyes. 'What about the Rogue Solari who aren't here any more? Is anyone helping them?'

'Maybe they shouldn't have left the academy then,' Ẹni replies with a sneer. 'Why should we care about them when they keep attacking us and risking our safety? You're such a traitor, always defending them.'

I wince at the venom in Ẹni's voice, but Adanna seems totally unbothered. She pulls her Second Sight off and gives the lenses a wipe, then looks straight at Ẹni.

'And you're such a lizard.'

Ẹni gasps and the class erupts with laughter. Professor Sàlàkọ́ throws both of them a warning glare.

'Differing opinions are fine, but I will not tolerate disrespect in my class. Is that understood?'

Ẹni nods, her face an angry mask. A warm flush settles under Adanna's golden brown skin and she stares down at her feet. I almost feel sorry for her. Her eyes shift to me immediately, rejection blazing back at me. I swallow hard and look away.

The rest of the lesson goes quickly and quietly after that. When the bell rings, I head back to my room as Niyì and the other students go to their next lesson. Except it doesn't really feel like my room. I sit on my bed, trying to get my head around everything I've just learned.

This place is so strange. My mind keeps going back to how Solari were created. It all seems so wrong somehow. And who are these Rogues Adanna mentioned? Why would they attack AOS?

My thoughts shift to Mum then, and I can't help but worry if she's okay. *Has she found my father yet?* Just then, my

Second Sight flashes up an incoming message. Niyì helped me move my text messages onto it before we left Professor Sàlàkọ́'s class.

How's ice-cube boy?

I smile at Cheyenne's text.

Niyì's cool. I met some more Solari today

I sit back, knowing she's going to be so excited.

OMG! It's not fair. And u get to eat akara every day too

I laugh at that. Cheyenne loves akara even more than I do. I wait as she continues typing. It's taking for ever though, as if she keeps changing her mind. Finally, the rest of the message pops up.

How's ur mum?

So that's why she took so long. Trust Cheyenne to get straight to the point, even when she knows I might not want to talk about it. It's like she has a sixth sense.

She's still gone

Any luck with finding ur dad??!!

Not yet but I'm learning loads. They've got some amazing tech here

Can't u use some of it to find him? 🙂

Just as I'm about to reply, a new call alert flashes up, and I almost topple over as Mum's number springs up across my vision.

Gotta go, TTYL x

NP. See ya xx

'Ọkọ́ mi,' Mum says with a smile when I accept the call. 'How are you?'

'Mum!' I squeal with delight. It's as if the universe heard my conversation with Cheyenne.

'Have you been eating?' she asks me. I nod back and her smile widens. 'Are you paying attention in class? You're being good?'

What she's really asking is if I've damaged any more offices.

'Yes, Mum. Everything is fine,' I reply. 'Are you coming back soon?' I add hopefully.

'Not yet. I may have found someone with more information, but she's proving tricky to pin down.'

Mum found someone who might actually know where my

father is? Excitement builds in me at this bit of news and I forget myself for a minute.

'Maybe I could help,' I begin eagerly. 'If you just let me come—'

'No!'

Mum's voice scrapes harshly through me, and I shrink a little inside. Then she takes a deep breath.

'I told you already, it's not safe.' Her voice softens a bit. 'I can't do what I need to if I'm worried about you.'

'Yes, Mum,' I whisper, my voice shaky.

Her sigh is tired, and I feel even worse.

'I have to go. I just wanted to check how your first full day went. Be good. I love you.' Then, before I can reply, she disappears as the call disconnects.

I yank my Second Sight off, tossing it onto the bed. *Why won't she let me help?* I'm learning to use my powers now – I could protect us. Then something Cheyenne said hits me.

Nigerian tech *is* pretty powerful. I mean, I can surf the net with just my mind. Cheyenne was only joking, but she could be on to something. Maybe I *can* use some of it to help Mum with the search.

I put my Second Sight back on and start by searching for Benjamin Uduike on AOSnet, the school's closed intranet. I get a hit almost immediately. I tried googling him back at home, but I could never find anything. *Probably because I was searching for the wrong surname.*

I select the first link and suddenly my whole world shifts as the same face in Mum's faded picture stares back at me. Except this one is so full of colour, he looks almost real. I reach out before I can stop myself and my stomach clenches as my fingers come away empty. I grab the shell around my neck, needing something solid to hold on to.

Quickly, I move to the next image, whizzing through picture after picture. I can't get enough of his face. I keep searching until I hit one that's different from the others. It looks as if it came from a magazine or newspaper clipping. My father is in some sort of lab and he's holding up a model of DNA with a proud smile on his face. But he's not alone.

Behind him, in the background, is a woman, but she's too blurry for me to make out. I quickly search for any clues as to who she might be and find a short description: 'Dr Benjamin celebrates with partner, Dr Naomi.'

My heart races. I might have just stumbled upon something useful. Maybe she's the woman Mum is trying to find. I enter Dr Naomi into the search bar, but it turns up over a thousand results. That's way too many for me to look through, especially without a surname.

Whether I like it or not, it looks as if I'm going to need some help . . .

CHAPTER SEVENTEEN

The next day I'm eager to get to my first class, physical training. Not because I like PE, but because it's my first chance to ask Niyì for help. I couldn't find him at dinner, so I had to eat alone. I would have asked Adanna, but she was missing too, and then this morning she ignored me when I tried to speak to her and took off without a word.

As soon as I enter the gym, it's obvious I'm in trouble. It's huge, with a high ceiling and bare concrete walls. Treadmills and bikes line the room, and in the dim lighting, they glow and wink at me like evil vending machines.

In the middle of the room, the floor slopes downwards like a pit. A large mat with the AOS emblem on it rests in the centre, and on one wall is the List none of us can escape. A dozen or so robotic drones float around, and every so often one sends out a blue beam as if scanning us.

I'm early and there are only a few other students here. Ẹni waves at me from across the room. I nod back, distracted. She isn't the person I'm looking for and I find him talking to Hassan and a really tall boy, whose legs are almost as long as my whole body.

'Niyì!' I call out.

His head turns and his face breaks into a smile. He bounds over to me.

'How far?' he says. It turns out that means 'hi' here. His eyes move up to my hair. 'Did you do something different to your hair?'

I reach up with a tentative hand. I didn't think anyone would notice. The jumbo braid is still there, but the strands now have a strange sheen to them. They also feel different, like they're more flexible. But the strangest thing is that it took me way less time than usual to braid my hair this morning.

I shake my head, unsure how to reply, and instead dive straight in.

'Are you any good with AOSnet?' I ask in a hushed voice. 'I'm trying to find something.'

He looks at me curiously. 'Have you tried using the turbo search engine?'

'Yeah, but I got too many results and there's no way I can search through them all on my own.'

'Then you're going to need Ada.'

I groan. 'Why? She won't even talk to me, never mind help me.'

Niyì shrugs. 'She's a technopath and the smartest person I know.'

I stare at him. 'She's a what?'

'She can control technology with her Ike,' Niyì says, grinning at me. 'Hardware, software, even nano technology. It's why she's so good at the science stuff.' His grin widens and he nods towards the door. 'Why don't you ask her now?'

I turn in time to see Adanna step through the entrance. Her face is blank as usual. It tightens into a scowl when she spots me with Niyì.

'Maybe later,' I reply, and Niyì laughs again.

His laughter stops as a tall woman wearing a pair of black leggings, a matching T-shirt and a turban stalks in behind Adanna. Her skin gleams like the glazed pot Cheyenne uses to hold hair accessories at home, and her deep-set eyes dart around the room, taking everything in. She looks dangerous.

'Is that our teacher?' I mutter.

'Yeah,' Niyì whispers in a breathless voice. 'Aminatu Bello, but we call her Ms Bello. She's a five-time Dambe boxing champion and has a black belt in taekwondo and Krav Maga.'

I'm impressed, and also a little scared. Why would anyone need a black belt to run a PE class?

Ms Bello walks down to the middle of the mat. 'Mu taru!' *Gather!* she commands.

The sound booms across the room and everyone scrambles into a tight circle around her. Everyone except me. Ms Bello's head turns to me and a finely arched eyebrow lifts. I scurry forward.

The soft mat gives beneath my feet as I move into place, close to Ẹni. Ms Bello inspects us, her hooded eyes bright and sharp. A thrum of anticipation spreads along the circle, like a charge of electricity.

'Who are you?' she demands suddenly in a loud voice, and I jump, thinking she's talking to me.

'We are Solari,' the circle bellows back in one voice. The hair on my arms tingles at the sound of it.

Ms Bello nods, satisfied. 'Who do you serve?'

'We serve Nigeria!' comes the united reply.

Power hums in the air like a solid, living thing. It weaves between each Solari, connecting them in an invisible chain. I want to reach out and touch it . . . become a part of it.

'Yayi kyau,' *Good*, Ms Bello says in a softer tone, and the chain is broken. 'You can start on the treadmills.'

The circle dissolves as the class moves to the machines. Ms Bello makes us run for thirty minutes and I'm wheezing by the time we finish, the muscles in my legs twitching.

Ms Bello stares at us without sympathy. 'Now you're all warmed up, we can begin.'

I gape at her. *That was a warm-up?* Sweat slides down my back, as if I just came out of Cheyenne's sauna. My nose wrinkles. Someone forgot to wear deodorant. I look around to see if it's just me who's noticed and spot Adanna, Niyì and Hassan clustered together whispering. Just like in HOME. Adanna looks proper unhappy, then she glances up at me and frowns.

I look away. *What are those three up to?*

'Mu taru!' Ms Bello commands again. This time I fall in line with the others immediately. 'Shooting ice from your hands, walking through walls and even messing with people's heads is all very good,' says Ms Bello as she scans the room with narrowed eyes. 'But you can't always rely on Ike. You must learn to defend yourselves without your powers.'

'Especially if they're rubbish,' a quiet voice whispers to my right. It's Eni and she's looking straight at Adanna.

Adanna stiffens as nervous giggles travel around the circle and Hassan places a warning hand on her arm. I cringe. I know what it feels like to be the butt of a joke. Adanna doesn't move, but her face tightens.

'Silence,' Ms Bello roars, and a deadly hush settles over the room again. 'Since you're all so excitable today, we'll run sparring drills.' There's a chorus of groans, before Ms Bello's thunderous face shuts them up. 'Partner up and don't forget — no powers! Òré, try not to float away this time, please.'

Bodies scurry around me, pairing up, until there's only one other person left without a partner ... Adanna.

Great!

I look over at Niyì. He's totally buddied up with Hassan and he throws me a sympathetic smile.

'Come on then,' says Adanna. 'Let's get it over with.'

We take our positions along with everyone else. Adanna drops into a crouch and I look at her helplessly. She must know I have no clue what to do.

'That run was tough, right?' I try in a friendly voice, hoping she'll take it easy on me.

'Can you at least pretend to focus?' Adanna replies. 'This isn't a game, and I don't want to get behind in class because of you.'

So much for being friendly. I shut up and try to mimic her stance. We circle around each other, neither of us willing to get too close. Tired of the dancing, I look for Niyì and Hassan, hoping we can swap partners.

But I can only spot Niyì, standing at the edge of the sparring mat. The space next to him flickers once. *It's Hassan!* I blink in surprise as his flickering form moves stealthily towards the exit. *What is he up to?*

Then, suddenly, from the corner of my eye I see Adanna rushing towards me. I swivel around quickly, but it's too late. Her arm whips out and I stumble back, gasping as it hits me right in the face. With it comes a blinding pain and my Ike rises like an avenging phoenix. Power surges through me before I can anchor it back.

'Gbaghara m,' *I'm sorry*, Adanna pleads in Igbo. 'I thought you were going to block—'

Adanna doesn't finish her sentence as my thick braid whips around in the air, slamming straight into her. She flies backwards, hitting the ground with a hard crack.

Solari rush to Adanna's side, gathering around her. Niyì is there too, and I watch as Ms Bello pulls her up. No one comes to me.

I cradle my nose as blood drips from it, my Second Sight sitting at a wonky angle. Every eye in the room turns to me then and a shocked silence settles. I can feel them judging me and guilt pools in my belly.

Ẹni is the only person who isn't horrified. She looks pleased that Adanna is hurt and I feel sick. With a small cry, I put a hand over my mouth and rush out of the gym, my braid flying behind me.

The taste of my half-digested breakfast is sour and I stare as lumps of agege bread mix with the green lawn of the quad. A stray strand of hair flutters past my cheek and I push it away angrily.

The pounding in my head and churning in my stomach finally fades long enough for me to think clearly. I didn't even check if Adanna was okay. Shame wraps around me like a vicious snake. I really messed up this time and everyone is going to think I did it on purpose! I'm not even sure myself. I don't think I did, but all I can remember is the pain I felt and how I couldn't stop my Ike from reacting.

I reach for my necklace, tucked inside my shirt. The hard shell digs into the palm of my hand as I clutch it tightly. I thought I had finally started to understand my Ike. I take a deep breath and the smell of newly cut grass mixed with vomit fills my nose.

I've got this. I'm fine.

As I straighten up to wipe my mouth, someone bumps into me, and I turn quickly. Chigozie, the small girl from history class, blinks at me. Her body jerks for a second before going really still.

'Don't worry,' she says in a whisper, then hands me a tissue. 'This place gets easier.' She dashes away before I can ask her what she means.

I press the tissue to my still-bleeding nose and frown after her, but I don't have time to worry about it. I need to talk to Cheyenne ... now! With a thought, my text messages pop up and I begin to type.

I want to come home

The words float across my vision as I wait for Cheyenne to reply. Nothing comes, not even the three little dots to tell me she's typing. Tears fill my eyes and I sweep them away angrily. *It's fine. I'm fine.* The message disappears and the path towards the gym lights up in warning – a reminder from DAMI that I should be in class. But I can't go back in there.

Instead, I follow the path towards the lake that Niyì showed me a few days ago. A familiar fence comes into view, but there are no sounds of playing children this time. As I get closer, it becomes clear the playground isn't completely empty either.

Near the swings I see Hassan kneeling on a small woven mat. *So this is where he sneaked off to.* A white cloth hat covers his head and his eyes are closed, but his lips are moving silently. I stop, ducking behind a tree. My nose presses close to the trunk and the earthy smell of moss hits me as I peek around to watch him . . . *pray?*

I stay where I am, waiting for Hassan to finish. There's no way I'm going to be able to explain why I'm behind this tree.

Suddenly, Hassan's eyes fly open.

'You can come out now, Onyeka,' he says in a loud voice, and I freeze.

CHAPTER EIGHTEEN

I slink out from behind my hiding spot and walk over to Hassan on legs made slow with embarrassment.

'How did you know I was there?'

'You should leave being invisible to me,' he replies with a smirk and pulls the hat from his head.

The collar of my shirt suddenly feels really tight, and I tug at it.

'I'm sorry.'

'It's fine,' he says as he stands and folds up the mat.

Hold up ... Hassan hasn't been speaking in Pidgin English.

'What happened to your ...' My voice trails off, unsure how to ask without offending him.

'You mean the Pidgin?' Hassan says with a smile. 'Do you even understand it?'

I shake my head and look away. 'Sorry, no.'

'Why are you sorry?' he replies with a shrug. 'My father taught it to me and my brothers. Using it helps me feel close to home.' Then a thoughtful look comes over his face. 'Tell you what. I dey speak English, but you dey try learn Pidgin.'

His mouth lifts in an encouraging smile and, after a moment, I return it with a nod. He seems really cool and I can see why he and Niyì get on so well. Adanna, not so much. Thinking about her reminds me of Ms Bello's class and Hassan's disappearance.

'Why did you sneak out of PE?' I ask carefully.

He watches me for a long moment, as if he's searching for something. I stay still and hold his gaze, hoping he'll answer, but knowing he probably won't. Finally, he nods.

'I try to perform salat five times each day, but praying doesn't always fit with my class schedule. Besides, I don't like fighting.' He looks away suddenly and rubs the back of his neck like he's embarrassed. 'What about you? Ms Bello's class isn't finished yet.'

My eyes drop away. What if he looks at me the way the others did?

'You can trust me,' says Hassan in a gentle voice and I meet his gaze again. His face is so friendly and something inside me really wants to open up to him. Besides, he's going to find out anyway. I take a deep breath.

'I hit Adanna during the sparring drill.'

Hassan frowns. 'So? You're supposed to do that.'

I blow out my breath in frustration. 'No, you don't understand.' Then I explain what happened.

'Chai,' Hassan whispers. 'Ada *can* be a bit uptight sometimes, but—'

'I didn't do it on purpose,' I cut in. 'I just lost it and . . .' My voice trails off helplessly.

'Is that why your nose looks so big?'

Hassan leans in to inspect my face and I rear back, covering my swollen nose. Pain shoots across my face and I wince. I'm totally going to have a bruise tomorrow.

'Everyone was staring at me,' I tell Hassan. 'It was awful.'

Hassan grins. 'Niyì threw an icicle at Dr Dòyìnbó once if it makes you feel any better.'

My eyes widen; I can't imagine it.

'We're all here to learn, so it's only natural that we're going to mess up,' Hassan continues. 'Just don't do it with Ms Bello.'

Hassan moves to the wooden swing and climbs on, pushing off with his feet. I join him, perching on the other swing.

'Why *is* Adanna so uptight?' I finally ask as he swings back towards me.

Hassan stops and looks at me. 'How much do you know about the Rogues?'

'Not much,' I reply.

He takes a deep breath. 'About fifteen years ago a student

named Gbénga led some sort of revolt on campus. No one knows why, but it ended with him and a few other Solari leaving the academy. Since then, they've been attacking us and trying to break back in.'

'Why?' I ask, shocked.

Hassan shrugs. 'Maybe they miss the food.' We both laugh, then Hassan's face turns serious again. 'Ada and Ẹni used to be friends.'

I straighten up abruptly, nearly tipping out of the swing. 'What?'

'Ada won't tell us what happened, but a couple of years ago they just stopped talking. Then the rumour started about Ada being a Rogue spy. Gbénga is the only other Solari we know of that has more than one Ike and some people think it's proof that Ada can't be trusted. With the Rogues attacking the academy, everyone is paranoid.'

'That's so wrong,' I breathe.

Hassan sighs. 'Then there's the List. Ada is always first. For most of the year she tops it. No one can beat her when it comes to academic stuff and it doesn't exactly help her make friends, you know?'

I nod. 'If she wins every year, I can understand why everyone else gets annoyed.' *Especially with her snarky attitude.*

Hassan shakes his head. 'She doesn't.'

'You just said—' I begin, but Hassan cuts me off.

'I said she's first for *most* of the year. Ìdánwò changes everything because it's about using Ike.'

'How?'

Hassan's face lights up. 'Each Solari must complete three trials that test Ike, physical strength and teamwork. The more trials you complete, the more points you get.'

'So why does Adanna lose? She's got two Ike.'

'Teamwork,' Hasan says simply. 'No one trusts her, so they won't work with her.'

Before I can ask more, a loud *crack* comes from the path. I look up to find Dr Dòyìnbó striding through the trees towards us, a serious look on his face. The sick feeling in my stomach returns. I smooth down my shorts with shaking hands as he stops in front of me and Hassan.

'You know about Adanna,' I say in a strained voice. It's not a question; I can already see the answer in his worried eyes.

Dr Dòyìnbó nods, his bushy eyebrows crinkling. 'We need to talk.'

CHAPTER NINETEEN

The *talk* consisted of me apologizing and Dr Dòyìnbó trying to make me feel better. Then he suggested that I work with Adanna to improve my connection to my Ike. Apparently, it was Adanna's idea. I only agreed because I hoped it would be a chance to fix the problem between us.

Boy, was I wrong! It's a total nightmare ... Adanna is a nightmare.

I spend the next few weeks either training with her, Ms Bello or studying. My hand-to-hand combat is getting better and Ms Bello even taught me a few of her signature moves. But with Adanna, nothing I do is ever good enough.

I'm either not trying hard enough or trying too hard. At least I'm doing okay in all my other lessons. We don't have many teachers as DAMI runs most of the lessons through

Second Sight. History and PE are the only exceptions. Dr Dòyìnbó says it ensures Solari remain a secret.

Mum still hasn't returned. It's been a full week since we last spoke and before that we had been talking every few days. She says she doesn't understand why it's taking so long to find my father. I don't either, but there's no point offering to help. My birthday is in a month and I don't even know if she'll be back for it. The last few times I tried to call her to ask, her phone just rang out.

The only thing that's kept me going is Cheyenne. She's impressed that I've managed to get my detangling time down to three hours, but she isn't so impressed with all the classes I have to take. She also thinks Niyì sounds cute. I must have described him wrong.

Despite spending so much time with Adanna, I haven't been able to ask her for help with the whole Dr Naomi mystery. We've never talked about what happened in the gym. In fact, she only speaks to me when she's kicking my butt during our training sessions.

Just like right now!

It's our free period before lunch and the gym is full of Solari. Hassan and Niyì decided to tag along as usual. The three of them do everything together, including disappearing at the same time. I'm always looking for them.

My worry about Mum is making it difficult to keep control of my Ike and I'm proper distracted. I'm supposed to be working on my aim by trying to hit some drones with my hair. After I miss the target a third time, Adanna sends it flying at me and I dive to the ground just in time.

'Oi!' I shout, the hairs on the back of my neck prickling. 'What was that for?'

Adanna crosses her arms. 'Do you think this is a joke?'

'Uh oh,' whispers Hassan, flickering until he completely disappears.

'What is your problem already?' I snap back, sick and tired of Adanna's attitude. One minute she's helping me, the next she's trying to kill me.

'You're wasting my time. I have a million other things I could be doing instead of babysitting some lazy Solari.'

My eyes narrow at her. *Lazy? Is she for real?* It's not like I even asked for her help.

'Look, this was your idea—'

'Trust me, I regret it already,' Adanna interrupts. 'If you're not going to put in the work, just go back to wherever you came from.'

I lose it then and my Ike flares out of control. My hair whips around me in a frenzied cloud. 'You think I don't want to? You think I'd be here if I had a choice?'

The robotic drones gather defensively behind Adanna. I forgot she's a technopath.

'Chai!' she exclaims, stepping closer to me. 'AOS isn't some fun summer camp. Some of us actually want to be here.'

Niyì moves between us. 'Come on, Ada, that's not fair. We don't know the full story.'

Adanna blinks, noticing for the first time the attention we're drawing from the other kids.

'Whatever,' she says, throwing her hands in the air. 'I already have a permanent headache from using my Ike so much. I don't need to listen to your nonsense feelings as well.' The drones drop to the ground with a loud crash as she turns and leaves.

'That could have been worse,' says Niyì, picking one up.

I gape at him. *Seriously?*

'Why is she always moving mad?' I ask.

'Moving mad?' says Hassan, reappearing next to me. 'Oya, you dey teach me more cockney.'

'You're such a chicken,' I reply with a smirk. He always disappears when Adanna and I get into it. 'And I already told you, I no dey speak cockney.'

Hassan gives me an impressed look. He's fascinated by my accent, the same way I am with Pidgin. He's been teaching me and I can mostly understand him now.

'You know I no like wahala,' he says, grinning.

I roll my eyes and bend to pick up a drone. 'Does anyone like trouble?' I reply. 'Seriously, though, why is she always so angry?'

'It's not personal,' says Niyì, and I give him a look. 'Okay, fine, but you need to speak to her.'

I straighten up with a frown. 'Why? She's the one being funny with me.'

Niyì sighs. 'This thing between you two is getting annoying. You need to sort it out.'

The canteen is packed when I finally arrive for lunch, but I barely notice as I struggle to get Niyì's words out of my mind. *Why do I have to be the one to sort things out?*

There's a crowd near the food and the atmosphere is buzzing. I reckon there's something about the smoky taste of jollof rice or the spicy kick of efo riro that gets Solari super excited. I never know what strangeness I'm going to find in here.

Yesterday, some students decided to have a dance battle in the middle of the canteen. As the heavy rhythm of Afrobeat filled the room, one of the boys created a copy of himself. He straight up became his own dance troupe and his moves were fire.

Next was Pèlúmi, the girl with super-fast speed. I've never seen anyone do the shoku shoku dance that quickly. It looked like she was about to take off.

But the best by far was Ẹni's group. The six girls were perfectly in sync, and when it was Ẹni's turn to do a solo, she did the weirdest thing with her body. A member of the group grabbed her legs and another her arms, then they pulled. I swear I nearly fell over as Ẹni's body started stretching. They kept pulling until she was impossibly thin, before turning her like a skipping rope. When the other members of the group jumped in, in time to the beat, the canteen went nuts.

They won, of course.

By the time I get my pounded yam and efo, there aren't too many empty tables left. As I pass the recycling station, I scan the room looking for a free seat.

'Onyeka! Over here.'

I turn to find Ẹni waving me towards her table. I hesitate, thinking of Adanna. But then I stop myself. I'm done with letting her affect what I do. Besides, I need to at least try to make new friends and Ẹni has been nothing but nice to me. If Cheyenne were here, she'd tell me to get my butt over there. So I do.

'Hi,' I say, putting my tray down.

'Hey,' Ẹni replies. 'Love your hair today.'

I tense and stare down at the table, waiting, out of habit, for the insult that must be coming. But my hair has actually been looking all right lately. Styling it is getting easier too, and I mostly wear it in a thick braid now, though it still tries to escape.

'It's such a cool Ike,' says a girl wearing yellow, a pair of matching earrings dangling from her lobes. 'I'm Oluchi, by the way.'

154

I nod back, feeling slightly dizzy from all the attention.

'That's Fa'idah,' Oluchi adds, pointing to a girl wearing a hijab that matches her patterned leggings. 'I think you know Amandi already.' The boy with the supersonic voice gives me a wave. 'Welcome to the cool table,' Oluchi finishes, arms spread wide.

The table erupts in laughter, like she said something funny.

'So you've been training with Adanna,' says Ẹni, a slow smile spreading across her face. 'Bet that's fun.'

'Ugh, she's so annoying,' Amandi whispers, though he still sounds incredibly loud. 'She's always sucking up to Dr Dòyìnbó and she thinks she's so brilliant.'

My fists clench in my lap and the hairs on my arms tingle. I'm always complaining to Niyì and Hassan about Adanna, but it feels wrong listening to these kids do it.

'Erm, yeah, it's been okay,' I reply.

'I heard she lost it in the gym today,' says Oluchi with a laugh. 'I mean, we all know she hit you first, that time with Ms Bello.'

Ẹni's smile shifts. 'She's dangerous and totally a Rogue spy. I don't know why Dr Dòyìnbó lets her stay at the academy.'

Their laughter flows like acid, burning a hole in my stomach. The sound is very familiar. I've heard it too many times before. But usually, I'm on the other end of it. I totally shouldn't have come to Ẹni's table.

'I know, right?' says Fa'idah as she pushes a piece of moin

moin around her plate. 'I can't wait for Ìdánwò. Then we can put her back in her place.'

I'm not sure what she means by that, but it doesn't sound good for Adanna.

'What are you going to do?' I ask with a frown.

The whole table goes quiet.

'Make things fair,' Ẹni says with a smirk. 'Adanna had better watch her back during the trials. It's not right that she has more than one Ike, even if they're pretty useless.'

A bitter smile twists Ẹni's face ... *she's jealous!* She's probably the one who started the rumour in the first place about Adanna being a Rogue spy. I think of each time Adanna has helped me. First in HOME when she showed me how to connect with my Ike, then later, offering to help me learn to use it properly. Even after I accidentally hurt her. My chair scrapes loudly across the floor as I stand up quickly.

'That's just wrong,' I snap. 'Adanna might be rude, but at least she isn't nasty and jealous like you lot!'

Silence settles over the table and their stunned faces lock on mine. Then every eye shifts to a point over my left shoulder and I just know I'm going to be in a ton of trouble. Knowing my luck, it'll be Dr Dòyìnbó.

But it's not our head teacher. I turn to find Adanna staring at me, holding a tray full of jollof rice.

CHAPTER TWENTY

My face heats, and without a word, I stalk out of the canteen. Hurrying through the hallways, I reach my room and the door opens immediately.

What did I just do? I'm not going to make any new friends at this rate. Though I wouldn't want Ẹni and her lot anyway. I pace across the room, imagining all the things they must be saying about me.

'You didn't have to do that, you know,' says Adanna out of nowhere, and I jump.

I spin around to find her in the doorway, a strange expression on her face.

'It's cool,' I say, shuffling from one foot to the other. 'They weren't being very nice.' I pause as she enters the room. 'Are they always like that?'

'Let me guess . . . they were saying stuff about me being a

Rogue?' I nod and Adanna sighs. 'Ẹni and her friends don't like me. Dr Dòyìnbó says I should ignore them.' Seeing my curious expression she continues. 'Dr Dòyìnbó's been helping me. I have an interest in genetics and he lets me use his personal library.'

Well, that explains all the books. I swear they've doubled since I arrived.

'Yeah, I noticed,' I say with a grin.

Adanna stares at me for a moment, as if she's trying to decide if I'm making fun of her.

'Everyone takes our powers for granted, but I need to know more,' she finally replies. 'Since we're going to be Protectors, shouldn't we understand Ike? Like, why does using it make us feel so bad? It's why I've been researching my genetic profile. I'm trying to understand us better, and maybe even find a permanent cure for the headaches and nausea.'

Adanna moves to her desk. I open my mouth to ask her why I've been feeling worse lately, but I'm distracted by a bigger question that has been burning for weeks.

'Just ask already,' says Adanna, her eyes locked on the glass screen. 'Your curiosity sounds awful.'

Her words startle me and I frown. She's always making strange comments like this.

'Why did you help me with my Ike that first time?' I finally say. 'I mean, I'm proper grateful, but I still don't understand why.'

She swivels away from the screen, turning to face me. 'Dr Dòyìnbó is a great head teacher, but his methods can be a bit traditional. He uses the same technique with all the new students and usually it's fine as they're younger. But with you, something felt off. Your fear was as loud as a batá drum.'

I blink in confusion. That's the second time she's mentioned *hearing* my emotions. 'What are you talking about?'

Adanna looks at me strangely. 'You must know what my Ike is by now?'

I nod. 'I know one of them. You're a technopath.'

'I'm also a synaesthetic empath,' she replies. 'I can smell and hear people's emotions, and yours are especially strong.'

'I knew it,' I gasp. 'I knew you could read minds.' Then a horrible thought occurs to me. Is she reading mine right now?

'I don't read minds, Onyeka.' Adanna's voice is dry. 'I sense feelings. When you're curious, it sounds like a drum roll, and when you're freaking out, you smell like bananas, like you do right now.'

'Cherries!' I cry suddenly, remembering her odd comment from my first night at AOS.

Adanna pushes her Second Sight up higher on her nose. 'Yeah, that's sadness. New students always smell like cherries. I hate it almost as much as bananas.'

'Rah, that's got to suck,' I say.

'It can be difficult to filter out everyone's emotions, especially as we use them to power our Ike. It's one of the reasons why I keep to myself. Although Dr Dòyìnbó insisted that I try to socialize more.'

'What do you mean?' I ask.

'I'm sorry I've been *moving mad*, but I haven't had a room-mate since Ẹni and I stopped being friends.' My face heats and I make a mental note to kick Hassan the next time I see him.

I get a flash of dimples as Adanna gives me her first true smile. But it quickly fades. 'When Dr Dòyìnbó said I was going to get another room-mate, I got scared and shut you out. Then I saw you talking to Ẹni that first morning and it looked as if you'd decided to become friends with her. I didn't want to get hurt again.'

'Why would you think I'd want to hurt you?' I ask, bewildered.

Adanna's fingers move restlessly across her desk. 'I only got my technopath abilities a few years ago. At first it was great and everyone was fascinated by them. But the more attention I got, especially from Dr Dòyìnbó, the more jealous Ẹni became. She tried to hide it, but I could smell it all over her.' She takes her Second Sight off and wipes the lenses, as if she's trying to buy herself more time. I wait silently, knowing it must be hard for her to tell me all of this.

'When I confronted Ẹni, she denied it and accused me of thinking I was better than her,' Adanna continues, putting her Second Sight back on. 'After that, she moved to another room, and then the rumour about me being a Rogue spy began. I'm pretty sure Ẹni started it.'

I knew it! I remember then what Ẹni said in the cafeteria.

'You need to be careful,' I warn her urgently. 'Ẹni's got something planned for you during Ìdánwò.'

Adanna rubs her forehead, looking totally unsurprised. 'I work really hard all year for first place, hoping it will show everyone that I don't care what they think – that despite what they say about me, I'm going to succeed here. But every year I have to watch it slip away from me because of that stupid tournament.'

She looks so defeated, I move closer. I used to pretend that it didn't matter when all the kids at home laughed at my hair. Cheyenne always saw through me though. She helped me to try to ignore them, even if it didn't always work.

'Maybe you'll make it this year,' I say with an encouraging smile.

Adanna slumps in her chair. 'That's not likely.'

'If it makes you feel better, I'm stuck here because my mum dumped me. Plus, I still can't get my stupid powers to work properly.'

Adanna looks at me strangely again.

'You don't like your Ike very much, do you?' she asks in a quiet voice.

I flinch, startled by her observation. Then I look away, unable to deny it.

'I just . . . I don't know what I'm supposed to do with it,' I finally say. 'I've always been the odd one out, even here.'

'I get it. I don't fit in here either, but it's not always a bad thing,' she replies with a grin. 'Besides, it's not as if you can change who you are, so you might as well own it.'

I stare at her. That's the kind of thing Cheyenne would say.

'Where is your mum, by the way?' Adanna asks, her eyes going back to the glass screen. 'I heard she arrived with you, but no one's seen her.'

I bite the inside of my cheek. How do I explain? Am I even allowed to?

'You're hiding something,' Adanna mutters in a distracted voice, her eyes flickering as they pass over the screen. 'I can hear you buzzing like a bee with it.'

My mouth falls open as I jerk back. It's just my luck to get an empath as a room-mate.

I shrug. 'Mum and I came to Nigeria to find my father. She left a few weeks ago after getting some information that she hopes will lead her to him.'

Adanna turns to me, her face fully confused. I have her total attention now.

'Huh?'

'My father's a geneticist and he used to be a student here. Maybe you've heard of him? He disappeared about ten years ago.'

Adanna studies me and I can almost feel the invisible

touch of her Ike as it tests my words. Finally, her eyes widen as she realizes I'm serious. Then the shock changes to something else.

'Chai!' she exclaims loudly, and my heart starts to pound. 'You're *that* Uduike!'

Now it's my turn to be confused. 'What?'

Adanna pulls a book from the huge pile on her desk and hands it to me. 'Is that your dad?'

I nod as the same picture I found online appears in front of me.

'I can't believe Benjamin Uduike is your dad,' she says in a hushed voice. 'I've been reading his research papers on AOSnet for years.' Adanna brings up a series of web pages on the glass screen.

'This is the one he wrote about clinical research findings in pycnodysostosis and gene mutations of cathepsin K.'

The words mean nothing to me, but I lean forward for a better view. Rows of text and funny-looking diagrams fill the screen. I can't make sense of any of it, but it almost doesn't matter. This is my father's work.

These are his words. The necklace around my neck suddenly feels heavy.

'Would you like to see another one?' Adanna asks.

I nod, feeling overwhelmed. I don't trust my voice not to shake or make me look stupid.

Adanna loads up a new tab and I catch a glimpse of the

latest CurlyUnicorn02 video as she switches over. I'm so shocked, I forget about my father's research for a second.

'You follow CurlyUnicorn02?' I squeak.

Adanna turns to me. 'You too?'

'I swear she's a hair magician,' I reply with a grin.

A snort of laughter bursts from Adanna and she quickly opens the video.

'Her hair is so cool,' says Adanna when the clip finally ends. 'I think that style would look good on you too.'

I don't like the way she's looking at my hair and I back away, tucking a stray strand behind my ear.

'Erm, nah,' I reply. 'I can never get her styles to work on me.'

Adanna stares at me for a moment. 'I can.'

CHAPTER TWENTY-ONE

There is so much confidence in Adanna's voice that I just stare at her. I hate wash days, and I always avoid doing my hair until the tangles have tangles.

Before I can answer her, Adanna gets up and pushes me down into the chair. She presses a button and I gasp as the glass screen turns into a mirror. I stare at our reflections, fascinated by the differences between us. We're like night and day.

Adanna reaches for my hair and I pull away sharply.

'Aren't you going to detangle it first?' I ask.

She rolls her eyes at me. 'Of course.'

I tense. I really hate this part.

'Where's the comb?' I ask, getting ready to face the instrument of torture head on.

Adanna lifts her hands and wiggles her small fingers. My eyebrows lift, but I say nothing.

'I need to soften your hair first.' A black sphere rises from her desk and floats towards us. I jerk and a gentle hand on my shoulder stops me. 'Relax, you're channelling bananas again,' says Adanna. 'It's my personal grooming device.'

It pauses a couple of centimetres away from my head as Adanna controls it with her Ike. A red light in the middle flashes at me, then a small window opens and a nozzle appears, followed by a fine liquid mist that fills the air around my head.

The smell of roses hits me first, then other spicier scents I don't recognize.

'It's rose water with nano conditioners,' says Adanna. 'One of my own formulas.'

She grabs some oil, and gentle hands slide into my hair as Adanna takes a dampened section and smooths it in, from root to tip. She begins working through the section with her fingers. Stretching and separating until she's satisfied that it's knot-free. My eyes are wide with amazement. It never occurred to me that I could use my hands or that it could be so easy.

The personal groomer follows her hands, pushing out rose water like my very own sprinkler system. Once she's finished detangling and moisturizing my hair, Adanna grabs something I finally recognize. Mum calls it ilarun, but it's really just a wooden cutting comb with three prongs. Then Adanna is parting and braiding with a speed that should hurt like hell.

But it doesn't.

There's no rough yanking of my head or heavy sighs as she works through the thick strands. For the first time in my life, I'm not hating having my hair done. A happy satisfaction fills me, like when you slot the final piece of a complicated puzzle into place.

Does this mean we're friends now? It's kind of hard to stay angry at someone once they've done your hair.

'How are you doing that so easily?' I ask quietly.

'What?' Adanna replies, her fingers flying along my scalp.

'My hair.' Our eyes meet in the mirror and I look away quickly.

Adanna drops the braid from her hand. 'It's not magic, you know. Your hair is a bit dry, but if you moisturize it more regularly it will be fairly easy to style.'

My eyes swing back and I gape at her. 'But I can never get it to look like everyone else's.'

Adanna rolls her eyes as if I'm still missing something obvious. 'Why would you want to?'

I blink in surprise. *Then how do I fit in?*

She picks up the braid again. 'It's a part of you, just like your Ike,' she reminds me. 'Yet you keep fighting both of them.'

She's right. No wonder my hair has always felt like a battle Mum and I could never win. Maybe that's why it's been easier to style lately . . . because I'm not fighting it as much. I wish again that Mum were here so I could share this moment with her. I wish I could share it with both my parents.

Then I remember my father's mystery lab partner and my quest to find her.

Adanna's hands go still. 'Just ask o,' she says with a sigh. 'You sound like a marching band.'

Our eyes meet in the mirror again and I take a deep breath.

'I need to find information about someone.'

Adanna eyes me curiously. 'Who?'

'I only have her first name,' I reply. 'She's a scientist and I know she was working with my father.'

'Sure, let me just finish this last braid.' Adanna releases my hair. 'Can you pass me the hair cuff?' I reach out towards it. 'No, with your hair,' she says, and I rear back in shock.

I shake my head quickly. 'I can't.' The shiny metal cuff is so tiny, and my connection with my Ike is still shaky.

'Yes, you can,' Adanna insists. 'Find the joy you were feeling just a minute ago and use it.'

The look on Adanna's face reminds me of the way Cheyenne used to look at me and a small part of me starts to believe that I can actually do it. A spark of happiness ignites, and with it comes a memory. It's faint at first. The image of a hand-drawn comic. The main character has long, thick hair like mine and her name is Super Yeka. Cheyenne made it for me and it took her weeks.

As the memory grows more vivid, the joy from the past

collides with this newer, tentative one. It bursts like a bubble that got too big, spreading through me, and suddenly my hair springs to life. The braided strands dance in the air like the finest of ropes. I concentrate hard on the hair cuff resting on the table, just beyond my reach. Nothing happens at first as my hair continues its rhythm, wrapping round Adanna's hand instead.

'Try again,' Adanna says.

I shake my head as I focus harder on the memory, picturing each page in the comic. A braid brushes my cheek, the shiny strands intricately wrapped around each other, and seeing it sparks another wave of joy. My connection solidifies. The braid snakes out across the table and hooks around the cuff, before drawing it back to me. I grin as I wave it at Adanna triumphantly.

She grins back. 'Told you.'

Adanna takes the cuff from me and grabs the braid, her hands moving once again in my hair. After a moment, her hands drop, and my eyes grow wide as I properly see what she's done with my hair.

I've never had Bantu knots before. Each braid has been wrapped on itself into tightly coiled stacks all over my head. They look like mini pyramids, the gold cuffs glinting like tiny points of light from each knot.

Adanna smiles at me. 'You should find it easier to use your Ike with this style and it should reduce the tangling.'

Then Adanna returns to the screen and activates it again. I ask her to search for Dr Naomi and she goes to work. Her gaze flies so fast across the screen I almost feel dizzy watching her. She whizzes through page after page of data. Then she stops suddenly and looks at me with a worried frown.

'Her name is Naomi Uduike. See?' Adanna's eyes move back to the screen. 'I had to use a Boolean search with some truncation and a bit of Ike.'

I barely hear the strange words coming from Adanna, I'm too busy staring at the screen. *How is her name Uduike too?*

'Are you sure?' My voice is breathless with confusion and excitement as my gaze locks onto Adanna.

'Of course,' Adanna replies, looking insulted. 'Is she related to your dad or something?'

I turn back to the screen and shake my head, trying to clear it.

'I don't know. But I know who might.'

'Who is Dr Naomi Uduike?'

My voice bounces loudly across Dr Dòyìnbó's office, and he stares at me, a bemused expression on his face.

'Good evening to you too, Onyeka.' He puts the book in his hand down. 'Shall we try that again?'

My face feels hot as I shuffle closer to his desk. I'd spent the rest of the day bursting with questions and I'd rushed straight to Dr Dòyìnbó's office after lessons ended. I was so desperate for answers I didn't even knock before barging in.

'Sorry, sir. Good evening,' I say in a quieter voice. 'Please can you tell me who Naomi Uduike is?'

'Where did you hear that name?' he replies slowly, and I blow out an impatient breath.

'AOSnet.' My eyes narrow when I notice he doesn't seem surprised at all. 'Who is she?'

Dr Dòyìnbó coughs once, then adjusts his bow tie. It's blue with orange fish today.

'She's your aunt.'

I recoil, my denial instinctive. 'I don't have an aunt. Mum would have told me.'

Dr Dòyìnbó looks at me and I realize how silly I sound, especially since Mum's been keeping my superpowers a big, fat secret my entire life. I look away from the pity in his expression, my eyes suddenly itchy.

'It's okay, Onyeka.' His voice is so gentle it's almost painful and something inside me cracks a little. 'This information must be something of a shock.'

I start to pace around his office. My anger at Mum quickly builds as I think about all the lies she's told and how she's left me here to deal with everything alone. I lean into the emotion and my scalp prickles.

'Use your anchor, Onyeka,' Dr Dòyìnbó warns sharply. 'Master the emotion before it overwhelms you.'

I don't need his warning though. I quickly wrap a memory of Cheyenne around the anger until it simmers down. When I'm sure I'm fully in control, I turn to Dr Dòyìnbó.

'Where is my aunt?' I say quietly.

His head tilts slightly. 'I don't know. She disappeared shortly after your father did.'

'Does Mum know about her?'

There's a long pause and I watch as he tries to decide how to answer me.

'Yes,' Dr Dòyìnbó finally replies. 'She's the lead I discovered – the one your mother is currently trying to find.'

I grind my teeth. I'm so sick of Mum keeping things from me. When will she trust me with the truth?

'Your mother felt it best not to tell you about your aunt as you already had so much to contend with,' Dr Dòyìnbó continues. 'I wasn't in a position to argue with her judgement.'

Dr Dòyìnbó gives me a sympathetic look and I blow out a frustrated breath. It isn't fair to expect him to go against Mum's wishes, no matter how wrong I think they are. So I thank him and turn to leave.

'One moment, Onyeka. Now you're here, there is another matter I wish to discuss with you,' Dr Dòyìnbó says, and I spin back around. 'It's been brought to my attention that you should be taking part in Ìdánwò, since you're an enrolled student. It wouldn't be fair to your fellow students otherwise.'

I stare at him. *Me, take part in Ìdánwò?* I just got here, so how is it unfair? Then understanding dawns.

'It was Ẹni, wasn't it?' I mutter. She's the one who had complained about fairness at lunch and I bet she's got it in for me too after what I did.

'I'm not at liberty to say. However, the observation is valid. I didn't expect you to be here this long so I made no provision for your inclusion.'

I suck in a sharp breath. 'Are you saying I have to take part?'

Dr Dòyìnbó spreads his hands wide. 'I'm afraid so.'

'What if I win?' I mutter, only half joking.

He frowns at me. 'That won't be possible. You will remain unranked as you don't have a full academic year of achievement. Your performance during Ìdánwò also won't count either for or against your house.'

Why am I even taking part then? This is all Ẹni's fault. I think of Adanna and how nervous she seemed about the tournament. My stomach sinks. If she's worried about it, then I should probably be petrified.

I open my mouth to argue when something stops me. Ẹni proper has it in for Adanna and it doesn't seem right leaving her to handle Ẹni alone. Cheyenne would be there in a heartbeat if she thought it would help me. I don't know if I can help Adanna, but I'd like to try.

'What's Ìdánwò like?' I ask.

An intense look enters Dr Dòyìnbó's eyes. 'It's a test of determination and loyalty. Protectors are tasked with defending Nigeria and our future. They must be prepared to win at any cost and Ìdánwò is but a taste of that.'

Win at any cost? I frown. It sounds a bit much.

Dr Dòyìnbó must have seen my thoughts mirrored on my face because his jolly smile returns.

'Don't worry, it's only a game, after all,' he says. 'I'm sure you'll have fun.'

CHAPTER TWENTY-TWO

Adanna and I spend the next two weeks training together, and as my connection with my Ike improves, so too does my confidence about my hair. By the time the morning of Ìdánwò arrives, I still don't feel prepared, but at least my hairstyle is looking good.

Adanna, however, is even grumpier than usual. After she snaps at me for the third time, I quickly coil my hair into the Bantu knots she taught me and leave our room. I find Niyì and Hassan in the canteen and join them for breakfast.

'How's Ada doing?' Niyì asks me around a mouthful of yam.

I throw him a look and he bursts out laughing.

'Watch it!' says Hassan, brushing chunks of yam off his arm. He gives Niyì a sharp look before turning to me. 'She see di List?' he asks quietly.

I nod. House Emitter and House Enhancer had their trials first thing this morning and Niyì moved up to first place. Hassan is third, Adanna dropped to second and Ẹni went from second to fourth. Our trial with House Transformer will decide the final rankings and the winning house for our year.

Niyì puts his fork down. 'Abeg! I'm not going to feel guilty because I worked hard and did well. This place is all I've got.'

I stay quiet, feeling torn. I want to be happy for Niyì, but being first means so much to Adanna too. Even though I think the ranking system is weird, I get why it's important to each of them.

'How you dey?' Hassan asks me, changing the subject. 'You ready?'

I shake my head and Niyì jumps in. 'You guys are going up against House Transformer. They're tough to beat.' He nudges Hassan. 'Remember how Fa'idah changed size to battle that robot last year?'

I swallow. 'We're going to battle robots?'

Hassan nudges Niyì back . . . hard.

'Don't worry, it changes every year,' says Niyì with a reassuring smile. 'You won't know what the trial is until it starts.'

I don't feel reassured. Just then Ẹni, Balu and another boy from House Transformer called Rótìmí appear next to our table.

Ẹni grins at me and I tense. 'Are you and your pathetic friend ready to lose?'

Balu giggles, reminding me of a hyena. My scalp prickles and I let my Bantu knots uncurl. The braids sway in the air and Rótìmí steps back. He's never seen them in action before.

'Ignore am,' says Hassan, with a worried look in my direction.

He's right – losing it with Ẹni isn't a good idea. I nod back, letting my Ike retreat. When Ẹni finally clocks that she's not going to get a rise out of me, she throws the three of us a dirty look.

'I'll see you later,' she says with a sniff, before slinking away with her friends.

I stare after them, worry churning in my stomach.

As I step into HOME, a blast of cool air hits me. Yet I barely feel it through my blue leggings and matching T-shirt; I'm too nervous. I look around, but there's not much to see yet. Solari are gathered in their respective houses and I count about thirty of us in total. The holographic projectors haven't even been activated yet, but the air is already so thick with tension, I could choke on it. I look for Adanna, but I don't see her anywhere.

'Welcome to Ìdánwò.'

Dr Dòyìnbó's voice startles me, and I turn, trying to find

177

him. It takes me a moment to realize that he's not actually in HOME and it's just his voice we can hear.

'Who are you?' he commands in a tone I've never heard him use before.

I recognize the question though, and this time I'm ready with an answer.

'We are Solari,' I cry, along with everyone else.

'Who do you serve?' Dr Dòyìnbó demands.

'We serve Nigeria!'

As our united voices die away, flashing blue beams surround us and a strange mist fills the air. Dark grey walls dissolve away, replaced by solid rock, the colour of rusted metal. We're in some sort of huge cavern and the smell of damp is strong. There's a gasp beside me and Balu takes a frantic step back. I look down and realize why.

Stretching out not far from where we're standing is a yawning pit. Jagged rocks line an almost vertical drop into its inky darkness, and even though it's just an illusion, it looks endless, like you'd be falling for ever. It's easily half as wide as a football pitch and my stomach tightens.

Murmurs rise around me as the mist clears, revealing the other side of the pit and the rocky edge waiting for us.

'Are we supposed to cross that?' says Balu in a voice that isn't quite steady.

I'm still staring at the chasm wondering the same thing when small rocks appear like floating islands, bridging the gap.

I guess that's her answer!

'Solari!' Dr Dòyìnbó's voice fills the cavern. 'The first of your three trials is to get across the pit within fifteen minutes. If you fall, you'll be eliminated. If you run out of time, you'll be eliminated. Though it's a simulation, everything you feel is real, even the pain. But rest assured, there will be no lasting damage. You may use your Ike during one trial and one trial only, so choose wisely.'

I blink as a countdown clock appears in the corner of my Second Sight.

'Make me proud . . . make Nigeria proud.'

His words are followed by the short, sharp beating of talking drums. It acts like a starter gun and Solari burst forward, eager to win. Then Fa'idah starts to grow. Her body triples in size in a matter of seconds, until she's towering over the rest of us like a mythical giantess. She steps easily onto the first floating rock, then turns back, a smirk on her face.

'This will be a piece of puff puff,' she crows.

'Typical Transformer,' someone mutters.

Before Fa'idah can move to the next rock, something shifts above us. Every eye turns upwards as an army of orange drones descend from the darkness. One hovers directly above Fa'idah and she stares at it curiously. Then bright red flames burst free, shooting straight at the rocks. Fa'idah screeches as the rock beneath her feet dissolves and she falls away into the dark pit below.

I gasp, my jaw dropping. Even though it's a holographic projection, it looked so real. My feet suddenly feel glued to the ground. *Why am I even here again?*

Then Òrẹ́ and his hi-top fade are in front of me. He uses his power of telekinesis to float past everyone, avoiding the drones and rocks altogether. He's not the only one who chooses to use their Ike. A Transformer called Kelechi suddenly inflates until he looks like a giant ball-shaped boy, bouncing from rock to rock. Then I see Ẹni stretching her way across like a smug elastic band.

'Let's go, Onyeka,' a voice says in my ear, and Adanna streaks past me.

She avoids the gap where Fa'idah's rock was, jumping swiftly onto the next one.

Two minutes gone!

My feet come unstuck then and I dart after Adanna, trying to keep track of the path she takes. The shouts and grunts of falling Solari surround us, but somehow the drones are avoiding her completely.

She's using her Ike to control the drones! I push forward, knowing I need to stay close, and soon we're halfway across.

'Help!'

A sharp shout behind me brings me to a stop ... I recognize the voice. I turn to find Chigozie clinging to a rock. She must have slipped. I freeze, unsure what to do. I only have nine minutes left. Then her frantic eyes meet

180

mine and I sigh. Somehow, I doubt her telepathic powers would work on the drones and I can't leave her to get flame grilled.

I sprint back, landing on her rock with a grunt. I reach for Chigozie and pull her back up.

'Watch out,' Chigozie screams, and I know before I even look up what I'll find. A drone hovers over us, its mouth opening as it prepares to send out a burst of fire. I look at Chigozie helplessly. There's no way we can move to the next rock in time. I close my eyes and brace myself.

But nothing comes.

I peek one eye open. The holographic drone is still there and a blazing streak of fire races from its mouth but it's frozen in mid-air. Then the hologram flickers, as if it's malfunctioning, and I turn to find Adanna grinning at us. She must have stopped it.

'Don't just sit there,' Adanna yells. 'Move!' She turns and sprints back the way she came.

I leap to the next rock, pulling Chigozie with me, and we follow her. The numbers continue to blink at me ... *Two minutes left.*

We dodge the gaps where rocks used to be ... *Sixty seconds left.*

We dive past tumbling Solari and random bursts of flames ... *Twenty seconds left.*

Until at last we reach the other side.

I collapse on the hard ground, gasping as I try to push air back into my tired lungs.

'Thank you!' Chigozie wheezes beside me. She's staring at me as if I'm a unicorn or something.

I shrug shyly. 'It's okay. Besides, it wasn't just me.' I nod towards Adanna. She's bent over, clutching her head as she tries to catch her breath. 'Ada helped too.'

Adanna looks down at us and a wide grin splits her face. I grin right back. Chigozie stares at the two of us like we've lost the plot. I don't think we're supposed to be enjoying this.

Òrẹ́ appears suddenly, still gliding above the ground.

'I saw what you did for Chi,' he says, looking at Chigozie. I almost burst out laughing at the embarrassed look on her face. 'It was cool,' he adds.

I nod back at him, still a bit dazed. It was close, but Adanna and I made it. The look on her face is a mix of excitement and fear. I get it. Neither of us thought we'd even get past the first trial, and now that we're here, it feels too good to be true.

We must have been some of the last to get across the pit because the ground begins to move again and the rocky cavern fades away. In its place is a grassy riverbank hugging a fast-flowing river. The water churns a foamy white as it gushes past. On the other side is a line of green trees, yet they aren't what's grabbed our attention. It's the churning whirlpool we can all see in the distance that has made us freeze.

My hands begin to shake as fear races through me. I squeeze my eyes shut and anchor the feeling so my Ike doesn't take over. I haven't been near this much water since the pool . . . since Cheyenne and I nearly drowned.

The second trial hasn't even begun, and I already don't want to do it.

CHAPTER
TWENTY-THREE

The other side of the river suddenly looks very far away. I'm still knackered from the first trial ... we all are. There are only fifteen Solari now and I recognize Ẹni, Kelechi and Rótìmí. Then I spot Tómi, a Psionic with mind-control Ike. That means with him, Chigozie, Ọ̀rẹ́ and Adanna, there are just five left from my house.

'Look,' Adanna cries.

I let out a huge breath when I see the line of wooden boats on the bank, near the water's edge. At least Dr Dòyìnbó doesn't expect us to swim across. Then, as if my thought conjured him up, his voice booms around us.

'Congratulations on completing your first trial, Solari. Your second trial is to cross the river.'

I look at Adanna, but she shrugs back. There's no time limit for this trial and a tingle of alarm skates down my back.

And it's not just me that's nervous, because when the talking drums beat, no one rushes forward.

Until Kelechi makes a dash for it. He ignores the boats and I frown, wondering what he's doing. When he hits the water's edge, he inflates again, using his arms to paddle through the water. I gasp. *He already used his Ike in the last trial. He must know he's going to be eliminated.*

He doesn't get far before the water beneath him begins to stir. Then a huge wall of liquid rises behind him like an angry monster. It crashes over him, bouncing him downstream towards the whirlpool. Kelechi's scream doesn't stop until he disappears into its depths. Beside me, Adanna is still and Chigozie's hands are shaking. I wipe my damp palms on my leggings and swallow hard.

Nobody wants to go in now.

Eventually, Tómi sprints forward and pushes a boat into the water, before jumping in. He rows fast and soon he's near the centre of the river. Then everything changes. His arms slow down and he looks as if he's struggling to move them.

'It's the water current,' Adanna cries. 'He's not strong enough to make it by himself.'

Tómi must be tired, but he refuses to give up, pulling his oar as if his ranking depends on it. It doesn't matter how hard he pulls, his boat drifts further away from the shore, until at last he too disappears into the mouth of the whirlpool.

Others start to move then. Ẹni and Rótìmí are already

in a boat, but neither of them bothers to row. Then Rótìmí stands up.

'No way,' I whisper as his whole body ripples, before turning into a column of blue-grey water. Rótìmí flows over the side of the boat, slinking underneath it. Then the boat begins to move towards the opposite bank, powered by its Solari engine.

'Come on,' Adanna calls to me and Chigozie as she sprints towards a boat. 'If we work together, we can make it across.'

We dash after her. Each of us grabs a corner of the boat and we push it towards the water. A fourth pair of hands appears next to mine and I look up to find Ọ̀rẹ́'s black eyes staring at me. He raises an eyebrow and I nod back silently.

It doesn't take us long to get the boat in the water. But as soon as we reach the middle of the river, the current Adanna was talking about strikes. I grit my teeth as the oar in my hands grows heavy. It would be difficult even if we hadn't just completed a trial, but now it feels as if we're rowing through peanut butter.

Adanna yells at us to keep moving, until I want to whack her with the oar instead. But I'm kind of glad in a way. If I'm focusing on her, I'm not thinking about the swirling water beneath us. I'm not remembering how it felt to choke on the water in that swimming pool in Woolwich. I can even pretend I'm not picturing the look on Tómi's face as he sank into the whirlpool.

Eventually, we reach the other side, each of us shaking with the effort. I look around to see who else made it and my head jerks. There are just six of us left. Ẹni and Rótìmí are staring at us, but it's the venomous look on Ẹni's face that fills me with worry.

My dread increases as the trees start to flash, signalling the start of the final trial. The boats melt away and the temperature is the first clue of what's coming. A suffocating heat spreads over us and the river disappears, replaced by an ocean of golden sand as far as the eye can see.

The huge dunes roll endlessly, shining strangely in some places. They're broken only by the thick trunks of palm trees dotted across the sand. In the distance is a small cluster of trees. A holographic sun blazes down, glinting off a tiny pool of water nestled between them. Next to the pool, a huge rock stands guard, the AOS emblem engraved into it.

'Congratulations, Solari,' says Dr Dòyìnbó. 'You have made it to the third and final trial. The first to cross the dunes and touch the AOS emblem will win the bonus points.'

Then the talking drums beat their familiar rhythm.

'Come on,' Òrẹ́ urges as he darts forward.

Adanna grabs his arm. 'Look!'

She points to the right of us, where Rótìmí and Ẹni are fighting. Rótìmí ducks as Ẹni aims a kick at his head. He sweeps around, knocking her over with his foot, then he dashes away, heading for the oasis.

Ọrẹ́ wriggles out of Adanna's grasp. 'He's going to get there first.'

'Just wait, for solar's sake,' she snaps.

Rótìmí is halfway across the dunes when something strange happens. His left foot lands on a shiny patch of sand and begins to sink. He wiggles, trying to free himself, but the sand isn't having it.

'Chai!' Chigozie gasps, and I see what she's already noticed.

The rest of Rótìmí is sinking too. The more he struggles, the faster his body disappears into the yellow sand. I turn away as his neck vanishes, followed by the rest of him.

It's just a simulation, I say to myself. *It isn't real!*

When I look back, Ẹni is already standing, and she quickly disappears over a sand dune.

Chigozie wraps her arms around herself. 'I'm not doing this,' she whispers. 'Did you see Rótìmí's face? I'm fine with not being in the top ten.'

Nobody says anything for moment and a part of me really wants to join her. I'm not even ranked, so I doubt anyone would care if I sat this one out.

'This is going to be a race to the finish line,' says Adanna, looking at Ọrẹ́.

I understand then. This is their last chance to win points and get the best position possible on the List. Last I checked, Ọrẹ́ wasn't even in the top twenty.

Ọrẹ́ nods once, then sprints away, Adanna right behind

him. With one last look of concern at Chigozie, I turn and follow.

'I wondered where you were,' Adanna pants as I catch up with her.

'I'm not letting you have all the fun,' I reply, my chest heaving. 'Besides, we have to make sure Ẹni doesn't win.'

Adanna grins at me. 'Fine, but keep up and avoid the shiny patches.'

As we dash across the desert, flying grains of sand sting my eyes and nose, disturbed by the movement of our feet. I can't help but marvel at how real it all feels.

A cry somewhere ahead has us speeding up over a huge dune, but we're too late. We find a shiny patch of sand near two tall palm trees a short distance apart. All that's left of Òrẹ́ is the very tip of his hi-top fade as he sinks into the quicksand.

'We need to keep moving,' Adanna wheezes, pointing towards Ẹni shimmering in the distance. 'She's getting close.'

As we pass the closest palm tree, I look up. The glare from the artificial sun hits me dead in the eye, blinding me for a moment. My foot snags on a rock and I stumble forward, knocking into Adanna.

'Watch out . . .' she yells, but it's too late. Adanna staggers sideways and then freezes. She stares at me, horror stamped on her face as her legs begin to disappear into the shiny sand.

There was another patch of quicksand!

I steady myself and stretch my arms towards Adanna, making sure to avoid the shiny edges of the sand.

'Come on,' I yell, but she shakes her head.

'By the time you get me out, Ẹni will have won.' I try to reach for her again, but she waves me away. 'You need to continue for the bonus points.'

'What?' I cry, wiping a sandy hand across my face.

'I can't win them now, and the only way I can still get first place is to stop Ẹni from getting them,' Adanna replies. 'You're not on the List, so you can't win the points either.'

She's right, but it's my turn to shake my head. Adanna is up to her thighs in sand now and Ẹni is almost at the oasis. Even if I ran super fast, I don't think I'd catch up with Ẹni. I stare at Adanna helplessly as guilt claws at me. She's going to lose because of me.

I can't let that happen.

The thought booms through my mind and anger at the unfairness of it all flares to life. I grab a memory of Cheyenne and then another one joins it . . . Adanna doing my hair. They wrap around each other, like the braids in my hair, anchoring my Ike. My scalp prickles to life as the braids uncoil from their knots with ease, erupting around me.

Adanna was right about the Bantu knots.

'Use your hair as a slingshot,' Adanna says excitedly, staring at the two trees.

I understand immediately. My braids lengthen, wrapping

around themselves until I have a thick rope of hair on either side of me. I take a deep breath as my hair loops around the trunk of each tree, leaving me in the middle. Then I push my body backwards, straining as I try to build up as much kinetic energy as I can.

With a loud cry, I push off the ground, and the momentum sends me flying across the dunes. The air whips around me as I sail over a bug-eyed Ẹni, landing on my butt in the sand with a gentle thud. Right at the base of the rock.

I don't move for a moment, disorientated and unable to believe what I just did. Then I hear the pounding of Ẹni's feet as she speeds up, desperate to reach the rock first. I turn my head, looking for Adanna. She's up to her chest in sand now and Ẹni is almost on me.

'Move!' Adanna screams as she sinks deeper. And then three things happen at once.

Ẹni launches herself forward, arms outstretched; I scramble towards the rock and push my arm out; the sand creeps up to Adanna's neck. Time slows down to an aching drag as my hand inches forward slowly, until at last it touches the AOS emblem, just a breath ahead of Ẹni, her fingers landing after mine.

The sand around us begins to dissolve away as the talking drums blare out. I spin around as Adanna, now free, sprints the rest of the way to the oasis. When she reaches me, she flings her arms round my neck.

'You did it!' Adanna screeches in my ear, and I wince.

'We did it,' I reply with a grin.

Then, like a mirage, the pool and trees shimmer away until there's nothing left but the plain walls of HOME. Ẹni stares at us, a sour expression on her face. It takes every warning Mum has ever given to stop me from sticking my tongue out at her.

Luckily, the doors open and Dr Dòyìnbó strides in, followed by the rest of our year. Everyone is excited and anxious to find out the final results. I ignore Rótìmí's and Kelechi's scowls and focus instead on Niyì, Hassan and Chigozie, who are grinning at us. Even Ọ̀rẹ́ is smiling. I beam right back, unable to believe it. Adanna might just win this.

My hair is still loose and I use my Ike to pull it back into the Bantu knots. As the strands curl around themselves high on my head, nausea boils up the back of my throat. I force it down with gritted teeth. *I can't throw up. Not right now.* Sweat peppers my face from the effort and I catch Adanna giving me a strange look. I work to keep myself together but pain pounds through my head as I try to focus. *I used my Ike properly, so why do I feel even worse than usual?*

Dr Dòyìnbó smiles at us with pride. 'I think I speak for everyone when I say that was an incredible finish. DAMI, will you do the honours?'

The scoreboard flashes up across my vision. My heart sinks when I see that Niyì is still at the top. *It wasn't enough.* But then his name shifts, moving downwards as Adanna's drifts up to the top. I blink, before turning to her.

Adanna lifts a hand to her stunned face and it's clear she can see it too. Everyone is silent for a moment, then a loud cheer goes up from Niyì and Hassan, and soon Solari surround her with congratulations. Adanna turns to me, her lips mouthing something I can't hear above the noise.

Thank you.

My chest lifts as I smile back. For the first time since I found out, I understand what it means to be Solari – to be a part of something so incredible.

To finally belong.

The moment is soon interrupted by the sound of the talking drums. The rhythm is different this time, more urgent. Around me Solari go still, as if recognizing the unspoken message behind the beat.

'All Solari are instructed to return to their dormitories.' The voice belongs to DAMI. 'I repeat, return to your dormitories. This is not a drill.'

There's a startled pause after the announcement ends. Then, as if someone pulled a starter gun, the bodies around me scatter. And with them goes my excitement.

CHAPTER TWENTY-FOUR

A quiet sort of chaos breaks out around me as I search HOME for Adanna. I can't see her anywhere and even Niyì and Hassan have disappeared. Then I spot Chigozie waving frantically at me.

'What's going on?' I ask, totally confused.

'It's the emergency alarm. We have to get back to our dorms,' she says, pulling me along with her.

'What emergency?'

She shrugs. 'It could be anything.'

'I bet it's Rogues again,' Òré mutters, coming up beside us.

Together, we make our way across the quad and back to our dorms. There's a practised sort of order about the way everyone moves that tells me they've done this before. Soon, I'm outside my room, and I wave to Chigozie as she enters hers. I open the door and slide inside quickly.

'Ada, where did you go . . . ?'

My voice trails off. The room is empty. *Where is she?* I was one of the last to leave HOME and I fully thought she'd be back by now. Then a worrying thought flashes through my mind. What if Òrẹ́ was right? What if it *is* another Rogue attack and Adanna is caught up in it? *What if she needs my help?*

I swallow hard, pushing down the panic trying to crawl out of my skin. It's the same one I felt when Cheyenne disappeared under the water. I try to focus, but my worry won't let me.

I should tell someone Adanna is missing . . . Dr Dòyìnbó or even DAMI. I start to activate my Second Sight when something stops me. *What if I'm wrong and Adanna is fine?* I don't want to get her in trouble, but I can't just sit here and do nothing either. I only have one option left. I have to find her myself.

The hallways are deserted as I dash back out of my dorm. Probably because everyone else is where they're supposed to be. I move quickly across the quad, hurrying through a set of double doors and down a long hallway. My legs feel heavy. They know I shouldn't there.

The thought of Adanna in trouble keeps me moving though. As I head for the main atrium, the sound of something hitting the ground sends me spinning towards the hallway to my right. Wiping clammy hands on my leggings, I take a deep breath and follow it. Then I find the source.

Niyì crouches protectively over something, his hands in the air as an icy mist weaves around him. But it's the young girl nearby dressed in black from head to toe who turns my legs to jelly.

A thick braid hangs down her back and golden flames burst from her hands, turning the hallway orange. I must have made a sound because her head shifts my way and bright red eyes burn straight at me.

She's a Rogue! She has to be, because she's definitely not one of us.

Then I see what Niyì is protecting and I freeze. It's Adanna! Her body is still and her eyes shut.

'No,' I scream, and Niyì looks my way too, his face breaking into a horrified expression.

'Run, Onyeka,' he yells, but my feet are like lead.

The Rogue's eyes widen as if she recognises my name.

'You,' she breathes.

Huh?

She takes a step towards me, but before I can reply, Niyì releases a blast of ice. The Rogue dodges it, then sends her own blast of heat in his direction, before barrelling straight towards me.

She doesn't get far as a flickering shape emerges in front of her. The Rogue grunts, then flies backwards, knocked away by an invisible force. My mouth drops as Hassan materializes in front of me.

But another ball of fire is already forming in the Rogue's hands and she hurls it at us. It's like the first trial with the drones all over again. Except this time, Adanna can't save us. Then something wild happens. The flaming sphere stops, hovering in mid-air as it slowly turns blue, before evaporating into a hissing cloud of steam.

The confused Rogue looks around, to find Niyì there waiting. Her eyes dart between him and us, and she holds out her hands, palms up as the fiery glow dims.

'I'm not here to fight you,' the Rogue says. 'We just want—'

She doesn't finish her sentence as Niyì sends a bolt of ice towards her. The Rogue bats it away with a flaming fist then pushes her arms out in front of her. A wall of heat blasts its way towards Niyì and he staggers to the ground. Before Hassan and I can react, the Rogue sprints past Niyì, racing down the corridor and away from us.

Hassan wastes no time getting to Niyì and pulls him up.

'How you dey?' he pants.

Niyì doesn't respond, but his eyes follow me as I pass them. I ignore him, my attention fixed on Adanna. She stirs as I approach, then opens her eyes. They widen at the sight of me. Niyì says nothing when he and Hassan reach us, but his face is thunderous.

'Are you okay?' I ask Adanna.

'I'm fine,' she groans, before sitting up. 'Where's the Rogue and what in solar's name are you doing here?'

Me? What is *she* doing here? In fact, what are all three of them doing fighting Rogues in hallways?

'I was worried about you,' I reply instead.

Nìyì jerks at my words. 'What? You think because you did well in Ìdánwò you don't have to follow the rules now?' he barks at me.

I don't understand why he's so angry. An answering spark ignites in me and I face him.

'I was just trying to help,' I snap back, and Nìyì's glare hardens. 'I'm sorry, okay. I thought Ada was in danger,' I add.

My voice cracks on the last word, and Nìyì pauses, his glare dimming ever so slightly. I look over at Hassan, wondering if he's upset with me too. I can't tell. He's staring down the hallway in the direction the Rogue escaped.

Adanna gets up slowly, then places a calming hand on Nìyì's arm. He shakes her off.

'She could have got herself or someone else killed. Dr Dòyìnbó makes these rules to keep us safe.'

I force myself to meet his angry eyes, but I'm not ready for the disappointment I see there. I can't say anything to defend myself because he's right. I shouldn't be here. I should have just stayed in my dorm. *But then, so should they!* Fury at the unfairness of Nìyì's reaction rises up in me. *Seriously, though, what are they doing here?*

Adanna's eyes dart between Nìyì and me and she winces as if our emotions hurt her ears. Nìyì frowns, but when he speaks this time, his voice is gentler. 'This isn't a game, Onyeka.'

'Indeed, it is not,' a deep voice says, startling the four of us. We turn to find Dr Dòyìnbó, flanked by two uniformed guards. 'Would someone like to explain what's going on?'

Niyì, Adanna and Hassan straighten, moving into a line. They're totally in sync with each other.

'We encountered the Rogues near the perimeter of the campus, but one got through,' Niyì answers. 'We were able to contain her, but she escaped.'

I gape at him. They were looking for the Rogues on purpose.

Why?

'You'd better do a sweep of the campus and I expect a full report,' Dr Dòyìnbó replies, and Niyì nods. 'That will be all. Onyeka, please stay.'

Hassan and Adanna turn to leave immediately, but Niyì hesitates, looking from me to Dr Dòyìnbó.

Dr Dòyìnbó's bushy brows lift. 'Is there a problem, Niyì?'

'No, sir.' With one last glance at us, Niyì walks away. The guards follow him.

My throat dries up as I'm left alone with Dr Dòyìnbó. His eyes bore into me.

'While Niyì, Adanna and Hassan have a reason to be out of their dorms, I'd like to hear why you're not where you should be.'

I have no explanation, so I say the only thing I have left.

'I'm sorry. I didn't mean to cause any trouble,' I say quietly. 'I was looking for Adanna. I thought she might be in danger . . .' My voice trails off as the weight of my mistake fully hits me.

'You did well in Ìdánwò,' Dr Dòyìnbó says gently, 'but you can't go jumping into things you don't understand.' He squeezes my shoulder. 'I'm glad you're unharmed,' he adds. 'Now, if there's nothing else, I suggest you head back to your dorm.'

A lump fills my throat. I hate that I let everybody down. Even worse, I hate this feeling of being shut out. I thought Niyì, Adanna and Hassan were my friends, but they're clearly keeping something from me. *I'm the odd one out again.*

A lonely ache shudders through my body, along with a need to connect with someone who truly cares about me.

'Have you heard from Mum recently?' I finally blurt out. 'I've tried calling her a million times, but it hasn't been going through.'

Dr Dòyìnbó's face changes, turning into something so full of regret, I flinch.

'What is it?' I whisper, already shaking from the weight of my dread.

'I was hoping to tell you at a more appropriate time . . .' Dr Dòyìnbó begins, then he stops and sighs. 'I'm sorry, but your mother is missing.'

My muscles tighten in instant rejection of his words. They can't be true. I won't let them be.

'I don't understand,' I say. 'She's coming back. She said she would come back.'

Dr Dòyìnbó shakes his head. 'She didn't check in for our last meeting and I haven't heard from her since.'

My heart drops so far into my belly, I'm not sure I'll ever be able to find it again. *So that's why she hasn't called me.* I thought it was because she had bad news about my father and was avoiding me. I was annoyed with her.

'You need to find her.' My voice breaks then and Dr Dòyìnbó places a gentle hand on my shoulder. Tears I didn't even know were there start to fall. 'You need to ... Please,' I end on a croak as I wipe my nose clumsily. 'I can't lose Mum. I can't.'

It's too much.

'I already have people on it,' Dr Dòyìnbó replies, his hold on my shoulder tightening. 'We haven't found anything yet, but we won't stop until we do.'

He stares into my eyes and the determination in his face calms me a little. I trust Dr Dòyìnbó. If anyone can find Mum, it's him.

'So what happens now?' I ask, my voice still wobbly. Do I stay at the academy? It's not as if I can go back to England now.

Dr Dòyìnbó's smile is full of understanding. 'We'll continue as before. I'm trying to locate your aunt, using the information your mother sent before she disappeared. I think Tópẹ́ would want us to continue the search for your father.'

I give him a tired nod. What even is the point of anything if Mum is missing?

'Perhaps you would benefit from a distraction this weekend,' Dr Dòyìnbó goes on. 'I think it's time you met Nchebe officially.'

I stare at him blankly.

Who's Nchebe?

CHAPTER TWENTY-FIVE

'When were you going to tell me your nausea was getting worse?' Adanna says, giving me the side-eye. 'Did you think I wouldn't notice?'

I stare at her. It's Saturday and we've been in HOME for the last twenty minutes, waiting for Hassan to arrive. Adanna woke me up early this morning and forced me to get ready, even though weekends are the only days we get to lie in. She'd practically dragged me here. I only let her because I was proper curious to finally find out what Adanna and the boys were doing taking down Rogues yesterday.

Instead, she's quizzing *me*.

I look away from her accusing eyes, the memory of my nausea suddenly fresh in my mind. It's definitely getting worse, but I hadn't told anyone. Not even Mum the last time we spoke a few weeks ago.

A sharp ache blasts through my chest and I push all thoughts of her out of my mind. I have to, otherwise I'll fall apart.

'I'm fine,' I finally reply.

Adanna crosses her arms and raises an eyebrow. 'Did you know you sound like a goose when you lie?'

'I do not,' I splutter.

'Okay, fine, you don't. But I still know when you're lying.'

She stares at me, daring me to deny it. Even without her Ike, I doubt I'd be able to anyway.

'Fine,' I say, giving in. 'The nausea is getting worse, and yesterday after Ìdánwò, I thought I was going to pass out.'

Adanna's eyes go wide. 'That doesn't sound good, Onyeka. I could smell it all over you too. You need to tell Dr Dòyìnbó.'

I back away. 'No way. If I tell him, he'll stop me from using my Ike.'

And that's the last thing I want. I still have a lot to learn, but I'm finally getting the hang of it. It's as if I've found the missing part of me.

'But it shouldn't be that bad,' says Adanna, cutting into my thoughts. 'Maybe it's because your Ike came so late.'

'What about you?' I quickly reply. 'You've always got a headache.'

Adanna screws up her face. 'We all get a bit sick if we use too much Ike, though Psionics get it worse. I think it's because our Ike requires so much of our mind, and I can't just turn mine off. Still, I've never felt the way you smelled yesterday.'

'I'm fine,' I insist again.

She throws me a sceptical look. 'I'm sure your mum would want you to say something if she were here.'

I wasn't expecting her to say that and her words slice through me like a sharpened knife. I suck in a small breath.

'Well, she's not,' I snap back. 'She's missing!'

Adanna stares at me, horrified, and I grimace. I hadn't told her yet. I don't know why. Maybe I thought saying the words out loud would make it feel too real.

'Look, it's okay … I'm okay,' I say, trying to sound convincing. 'Dr Dòyìnbó is looking for Mum, so there's nothing to worry about.'

Adanna frowns, but before she can say anything Hassan finally arrives. He's dressed in a pair of black joggers and a matching T-shirt.

'How far?' he says with a mischievous smile. 'Are you ready to meet Nchebe?' he continues, mimicking my English accent. Adanna's eyes roll so far up, I worry they're about to fall out.

Hassan's banter is contagious, and I smile back, ready to change the subject.

'So who *is* Nchebe?' I ask.

A look passes between them, and Hassan's grin grows even wider. Finally, I clock the truth.

'You guys?'

Hassan smacks a fist against his chest, a smug look dropping over his face. Adanna gives him a shove and he almost falls over. He lunges at her and she quickly jumps out of the way.

'Nchebe means "shield" in Igbo, and that's what we are,' she says, dodging Hassan again. 'Our job is to defend the academy from any Rogue attacks.' The grin on her face is a proud one. 'And when a new Solari's powers show for the first time, we find them before they can reveal themselves to the public or hurt anyone. Just like Niyì did with you.'

Niyì too?

I guess it makes sense, and it explains why they're always together. I'm kind of impressed and a little bit jealous too. I can't really picture them defending anyone though. *Besides, shouldn't Protectors be doing this job?*

'But you're my age,' I finally say, thoroughly confused.

Hassan disappears without any warning and Adanna turns in a circle, trying to find him.

'Each year, Dr Dòyìnbó recruits three kids from the top students in JSS1 to form Nchebe. The older Solari are preoccupied with graduating and becoming Protectors,' she says, totally distracted. 'Our age doesn't matter. Hassan and Niyì saved you from that Rogue, didn't they?'

'Trust me,' says Hassan, materializing behind her. 'We be di best.' He pulls the hood of Adanna's sweatshirt down over her face. Adanna shrieks, while he laughs.

I've never seen them like this before, but then again, I didn't know they were part of a super group either.

Adanna pushes her hood back up, a small frown on her face. 'Where's Niyì? He's never late.'

Hassan kisses his teeth. 'He no get watch?' Then he closes his eyes. 'DAMI, training protocol three,' he calls out.

Instantly the blue beams in the walls start to vibrate, then a huge wooden obstacle course materializes around us. In one impressive move, Hassan leaps onto a large platform, landing in a crouch. Suddenly, a log the size of a car springs out from nowhere, barrelling towards him. I gasp, leaning forward to warn him, but there's no need.

A yellowish dome of energy springs up around Hassan and the log bounces off harmlessly. My jaw drops. I didn't know he could do that. Then he's off again, moving around the course like a jaguar, dodging obstacle after obstacle with a speed and agility that make my head spin. A few times, I think he's timed things wrong, and I hold my breath, but he never once loses focus. He uses his Ike to both defend and manoeuvre himself through the course.

'Wow,' I tell him when he returns. He's covered in sweat and his breathing is heavy. 'I thought your Ike was invisibility.'

'Na, Allah give me energy fields,' Hassan replies.

Wow . . . his Ike is making energy fields?

'They can bend light, which is how he's able to turn invisible,' Adanna adds. 'He uses them like a cloaking shield.'

'That's so cool,' I say with a grin.

Hassan gives me a small bow and I can't help but giggle. Then a slow hand clap sends the three of us spinning towards the main doors.

'Impressive,' says Niyì. 'Now if you're all done playing?'

'Bros, you late o,' Hassan replies, moving towards him.

Niyì's face doesn't change. 'We have a new assignment.'

Adanna snaps to attention, and even Hassan, with all his jokes and banter, turns serious.

'There's been news of strange activity near Millennium Market and we need to check it out,' Niyì says, and my eyes widen. 'Dr Dòyìnbó thinks it might be a new Solari.'

'Why na?' Hassan asks with a groan. 'You know I no dey like crowds.'

'You could always just disappear,' Adanna drawls sweetly, earning herself a dirty look.

'I go make you disappear,' Hassan snipes back.

Adanna gives him a small shove, then turns back to Niyì. 'When do we leave?'

'In an hour,' he says. 'Dr Dòyìnbó is still confirming the details. We'll take the Gyrfalcon and the Beast. Hassan, you'll search from the air, while Ada, Onyeka and I cover the ground.'

I jerk at the sound of my name.

'Me?' I squeak.

'Since you like to tackle Rogues, finding this Solari should be easy,' says Niyì. I frown at the strange note in his voice, but his attention has already shifted back to Hassan and Adanna. 'You guys should go and get ready.'

They share a look before beating a hasty retreat, but I hang back, waiting until Niyì turns to look at me.

'Why am I coming along? I'm not Nchebe.'

'It seems Dr Dòyìnbó was impressed by your bravery yesterday,' he replies with a shrug, and I get the sense that 'bravery' isn't the word Niyì would use. 'He thinks since *you're* still so new to your powers, you might be useful in convincing the new Solari to come with us quietly.'

'Are you still angry with me?' I ask. We haven't spoken properly since the Rogue attack yesterday and it's been bothering me.

The question seems to catch him off guard, but he recovers quickly. 'No.'

My eyebrows lift. 'Then why are you being weird?'

Niyì looks away and an awkward silence settles between us. His jaw clenches, his right foot tapping an impatient beat.

What is going on?

'I said I was sorry,' I try again.

'I know.'

I roll my eyes at him. 'Then what's with the attitude?'

'Fine!' Niyì bursts out. 'I just . . . I don't understand why Dr Dòyìnbó insisted you come.' His hand lifts, rubbing the top of his head. 'We're not babysitters, and you're clearly not very good at following orders. New Solari are unpredictable; we can't afford any mess-ups like yesterday.'

A knot forms in my belly and I stare at him. 'You think I'm playing? That I like messing up?'

Niyì's eyes widen and his hand reaches out, clasping the top of my arm. 'No ... I didn't mean—'

'Forget it,' I say, pulling away.

'Onyeka,' he calls after me, but I ignore him.

The knot in my stomach hardens as I rush out of HOME. I can't believe he said that. I thought we were friends. Then another thought hits me and I come to a sudden stop.

Do Adanna and Hassan think I'll mess things up too?

My eyes sting with unshed tears and my hair whips behind me as I continue, pushing through a set of double doors.

'What was that about?'

Adanna's worried voice stops me. I swing round to find her waiting by a nearby wall.

'Niyì thinks I'm going to mess up his precious mission,' I reply shortly. Her eyes lower and I swallow. 'You think so too, don't you?'

Adanna shrugs. 'It is a bit strange that you're coming along.' My shoulders drop, and she steps closer. 'But you didn't mess up in Ìdánwò.'

I did when I ignored DAMI's instructions to stay in my room though. *What if I make another mistake?*

'Maybe Niyì's right,' I reply as my anger drains away.

Adanna rolls her eyes at me.

'You're absolutely right – you'll endanger all of us. You should definitely stay here where it's safe.'

Huh? I step back, almost hitting the wall behind me. 'Whose side are you on?'

'Mine, but I thought I'd tell you what you wanted to hear.' I open my mouth to reply, but nothing comes out. 'Look,' says Adanna with a sigh. 'You might mess up, and then again you might not. Why are you letting that walking freezer affect you either way?'

I laugh. I don't understand how Adanna gets away with insulting everyone the way she does. My laughter dies, she's right. It shouldn't matter what Niyì thinks if Dr Dòyìnbó wants me to go.

'Okay,' I say, straightening my shoulders. 'I'm not going to let him tell me what I can and can't do.'

'Good,' says Adanna with a grin. Then her face turns serious. 'I won't tell Dr Dòyìnbó, but if your nausea gets bad again, you have to say something, okay?'

'Yes,' I agree, glad she's not going to snitch on me.

CHAPTER
TWENTY-SIX

An hour later, I discover what the Beast is. It's a car. Scratch that – it's so much more than a car. It's a bizarre cross between an SUV and a monster truck, and it's totally covered in solar panels. The way it shines in the sun is both intimidating and seriously cool at the same time. The grill alone is almost my height, and when the doors open upwards instead of outwards, I nearly fall over.

There's no steering wheel either. DAMI is in charge.

Adanna jumps in first and starts talking to DAMI immediately. Hassan already took the Gyrfalcon and I'm left standing awkwardly with Niyì outside. I'm still not happy with him, so I climb in before he has a chance to say anything and find the latest CurlyUnicorn02 video on my Second Sight.

The Beast begins to move, pulling out of the campus, and for a while everyone is silent.

'We'll start by searching Millennium Market,' Niyì says, interrupting a really good product review. 'Hopefully the Solari will be there, but we can always widen the search if not.'

'How are you going to find one person in a whole market?' I ask. Mum never took me to markets back home because she was so scared I'd get lost.

'Second Sight is equipped with thermal scanners,' Niyì replies, and I give him a confused look. 'Because of the mutation, Solari have a core body temperature that's higher than normal,' he tells me. 'We just have to find a child with a matching heat signature.'

'They'll flash up purple in Second Sight if you activate it,' Adanna adds.

She turns back to the screen in the dashboard in front of her and I switch to my text messages. I'm a bit behind in replying to Cheyenne, so I fill her in on everything that happened yesterday. I haven't told her about Mum yet – it feels too hard. I focus instead on Niyì and his weird attitude.

A new message comes in and I smile.

He actually said that fam? Did you bop him one? Tell me you at least sent him flying with your hair!

'We're about to hit Abubakar Bridge,' Adanna calls out before I can think my reply. 'It's kind of cool,' she adds with a flash of dimples.

I look out of the window to find she's right. The bridge stretches from the mainland to Lagos Island like a metal cobweb. Totally enclosed by a glass shell lined with solar panels, the sun glints off the surface so it sparkles like a jewel.

'Rah,' I gasp.

'Told you,' Adanna replies. 'The shell powers up the road itself so vehicles can charge as they move along it.'

As the Beast glides across the bridge, I press my face against the window, watching the strange sights and sounds of Lagos Island beyond. The man-made harbours with their sparkling blue water are filled with expensive yachts and lined with pretty palm trees. I wind my window down and hot, salty air hits my nose.

As we whizz along the super highway, I'm struck by the way people and technology live side by side. There are automated drones everywhere. Some are cleaning and doing what looks like maintenance, while others follow people around, like robotic pets. I spot a motorized buggy taking a baby for a walk on the pavement, the mum walking next to it, talking on her phone.

But what surprises me most is the lack of noise. The wide lanes are filled instead with the quiet hum of electric cars and bikes. Above us, Hyperloop pods speed past.

'This can't all just be running on solar energy, can it?' I ask, amazed. 'It's like magic.'

'Superconductivity actually,' says Adanna in a distracted voice. Her head is buried in one of the screens embedded in the Beast. I remember then about the superconducting alloys she mentioned in Professor Sàlàkọ́'s class. 'They use room-temperature superconductors, which allow electricity to travel with zero resistance and maximum efficiency,' Adanna adds.

'Okay then,' I say, regretting that I asked.

I turn to look back out of my window and my jaw drops as I see Millennium Market for the first time.

'Woah,' I breathe.

The market stretches out for miles and up almost as far. Rising from the ground in tiered levels are towering structures masquerading as buildings, but not like any I've ever seen before. Each level is stacked on top of the other, like Lego pieces, and it's hard to tell where one begins and the other ends. Along the walls, colourful plant life crawls in a lazy tangle, weaving between the solar panels that seem to be everywhere.

Where AOS is all organized metal and concrete, Millennium Market is a messy labyrinth of recycled … everything. I see bits of old cars, loads of used plastic containers and so much else I can't even identify. But it all comes together to create something unique and colourful, like a mosaic.

Each structure is connected by flimsy-looking walkways and bridges made of wood and metal. They swing in the air and the people crossing them sway in sync, as if surfing through the sky.

At street level, shops line the narrow roads. Brightly clothed shoppers clash with the colourful patterned fabric hanging from almost every shop front and doorway. I'm amazed by the sheer number of bodies, crammed shoulder to shoulder, as electric scooters weave through the heaving mass.

The market feels alive. I can't think of any other way to describe it. A living, breathing thing, the people being the blood running through it.

The Beast comes to a smooth stop beside the pavement and the automated doors open. Adanna and Niyì climb out and I follow them into the hot air outside.

'Find a parking spot, DAMI,' Niyì says. 'We'll call if we need you.'

'*Understood*,' the AI replies, and the Beast glides away.

The sharp sound of haggling and bickering fills my ears – an odd shout or insult rising over the steady hum. The banter seems friendly with a ton of different languages swirling in the air. I pick out a few Yoruba words, but the rest I don't recognize.

'See her hair, Mummy. It's so pretty.'

I stiffen at the word 'Mummy' and turn to find a little girl with a thick halo of tight curls, grinning at me eagerly. Beside her stands an older woman with an apologetic look on her face. I'm wearing my hair in big, chunky twists today that cascade down my back, with the front pulled up. Adanna said it looked good, but it still feels weird to have my hair down on purpose, especially with so many eyes ready to stare.

'Erm . . . hi?' I reply, taken aback.

The girl's grin widens and Adanna steps forward, her expression serious.

'Hello. How can we help?'

The girl ignores Adanna, her attention fixed on me. 'I want to touch it. Can I touch your princess hair?'

I frown as the woman beside the child shakes her head sharply then turns to me. 'I'm so sorry,' she says.

'Please,' the little girl pleads. She stares at me with eager eyes. 'Will my hair look like yours when I'm big?'

I suck in a sharp breath. In London, people wanted to touch my hair all the time, but it always felt wrong. As if I were a pet or some sort of puzzle they were trying to solve. No one has ever said I look like a princess or that they want their hair to look like mine.

I take a step towards the girl and bend down. Her face breaks into a wide smile and small hands stroke the twists flowing down my back. She bursts into giggles and I can't help but smile back.

After a while, I release myself gently, and with a firm tug her mum pulls her away.

I stand up to find Adanna looking at me, a smirk on her face.

'That was cute,' she says.

I give her a small shove. 'Go away,' I mutter back, smiling.

Behind her, Niyì stares at me with a strange look on his face. I can't help but wonder what he's thinking.

'Let's go,' he finally says, before striding off.

We search for several hours, using our thermal scanners to check people as we pass. But there are too many shops, too many people and none of them are Solari. Even Hassan has trouble finding any unusual activity from the air.

'Are you sure we're in the right market?' Adanna asks.

Niyì throws her a look of irritation.

'Yes,' he barks. 'Dr Dòyìnbó sent us here. Do you think he got it wrong?'

Adanna narrows her eyes at him, but she stays silent. Her attention drifts to the people walking past and a tired look comes into her eyes. 'This isn't working,' she finally replies. 'It's too busy.'

'Do you have a better idea?' Niyì snaps back.

'Are your missions always like this?' I cut in, staring between them.

Niyì grins at me suddenly. 'It's worse when Hassan's here.' His face drops when I don't smile back at his joke. I still haven't forgotten what he said to me.

'We need to work out what to do now,' I say, before they really start bickering.

A new look comes over Niyì's face and he taps the side of his Second Sight frames.

'Hassan?'

'How far?' Hassan replies.

I smile as Hassan's voice echoes in my ears. *I didn't know Second Sight could do that.*

'The market is a no go,' Niyì says. 'Can you do a thermal sweep of the Eko industrial district?'

I look at Adanna. 'Why didn't we do a thermal sweep in the first place?'

'The Gyrfalcon has to fly really low to pick up anything,' she replies. 'There are too many people at the market and it would raise suspicion. There are just factories being built over that way. A scared Solari might be hiding in one.'

The scan seems to take for ever, then we hear Hassan's voice again.

'I don find am,' he says with satisfaction.

Niyì throws me and Adanna a triumphant look. 'Now we're getting somewhere.'

CHAPTER TWENTY-SEVEN

The row of half-finished buildings looms over us as the afternoon sun blazes above. About three kilometres from the market, they're set in the middle of a field of overgrown grass that's half my height. They look as if they've been abandoned. A jigsaw of scaffolding covers the concrete walls and the glass in the windows is missing, leaving only empty holes of darkness yawning back at us.

Hassan said the heat signature he picked up was coming from somewhere inside. We approached the buildings on foot so we wouldn't scare off the Solari if they were about. Adanna stayed with the Beast in case the Solari somehow gets past us. I wanted to stay too, but Niyì insisted I go with him. I think he's worried I'm going to do something stupid again.

'Stay here,' Niyì barks. 'I'm going to take a look inside.'

'But—' I begin.

'Look, it's much safer out here.'

I frown at his words. So he *is* trying to keep me out of trouble. Well, I didn't ask him to babysit me. Before I can argue, Niyì is already moving away. I stare at his back. *Is he seriously planning on leaving me here like a useless spare part?* Then he disappears, swallowed up by the entrance of the building closest to us.

I glance around, unsure what to do. I could just follow him, but somehow I don't think that plan will end well.

Suddenly, I hear a sound, and spin towards the building furthest from me. The glare of the sun is bright, forcing me to squint. But then I see her. A little girl, tucked into the shadows of the doorway.

She says nothing, just stares at me with eyes as big as the chibi character from my favourite anime.

'Hi,' I say, moving closer. 'I'm Onyeka.' She doesn't reply – even the blank expression on her face doesn't change. I step closer again. 'What's your name?'

She takes a step back and I freeze.

'I'm not going to hurt you,' I say.

Then she spins around and darts inside the building. I stand there for a moment, unsure. She could be the Solari we're looking for, but I can't be certain. I didn't get a chance to activate the thermal scanner before she ran. Niyì told me to stay put and now I don't know what to do. She'll be gone by the time he comes back, and who knows when we'll find her again. She's too young to be out here on her own and it's not safe.

The memory of the fear and confusion I felt the first time my powers showed up flashes through my mind and I make my decision. Despite what Niyì thinks, I'm not going to mess things up. I don't need his help either.

I enter the door-less entrance, moving quietly through the dimly lit space and into a large, humid room. A faint glow of light shimmers ahead and I move towards it, coming to a smaller room, lit only by a single exposed bulb hanging from the low ceiling. The place is gloomy and a damp smell hangs in the air, like washing that hasn't dried quickly enough.

Someone whimpers and I step towards the sound, looking for the little girl. I find her huddled in a corner and my stomach tightens. *She looks so lost.* I activate the thermal scanner and the child lights up in bright purple across my vision, just like Adanna said.

She is Solari!

As I move towards her, two things happen at once. The little girl looks up at me with a sly smile that makes me freeze. At the same time, the ground rumbles as something hot slams into my body, sending me flying forward. I wrap my arms around my head as I land in a heap.

I look up, disoriented. My heart starts to race, and I catch a glimpse of black boots before a hand wraps around my hair.

I cry out as pain flashes through my skull, but the hand holds firm as it lifts me up until I'm suspended in mid-air.

The smell of spicy cologne fills my nose and a deep voice calls out.

'I've got her.'

I kick furiously, but the man holding me is too fast, blocking my legs easily. Strong hands release my hair, grabbing hold of my arms instead.

'She doesn't look like much,' he says with a laugh.

I thrash, straining in his tight grasp. His arms feel like stone and my struggles make no impact. Dizziness overwhelms me and I gasp for air. I'm in serious trouble.

Two more men dressed in black burst into the room. Behind them is a girl, also wearing a black outfit. They all glow purple through my lenses. The girl turns towards me and her bright red eyes lock onto mine. I stiffen.

It's the Rogue! The one who attacked us in AOS. She lifts a hand towards the little girl, who dashes to her side.

'Good job, Şeun,' the red-eyed girl says. 'I wasn't sure if you could pull it off.'

Şeun smiles back at her and anger bubbles through my belly. The little girl was in on it too. She must be one of them. *Why didn't I listen to Niyì?*

He tried to warn me, but I let my pride push me right into a trap. I try to tap into the anger to activate my Ike, but there's too much going on and I can't focus.

'Let me go,' I call out, my voice hoarse with emotion. 'Now!'

No one is listening.

'We'd better go, Zahrah,' the man holding me says to the red-eyed Rogue. 'She's got a friend running around somewhere.'

Zahrah nods and the other two men start to move, the little girl tucked between them. The man holding me follows, dragging me along. They're almost at the door when an icy blue mist weaves its way into the room, casting a dense fog. Niyì steps through, sending a blast of icy shards straight at the man closest to him. The man drops to the floor and the little girl scurries into a corner.

'Onyeka!' Niyì calls. 'Are you okay?'

Before I can reply, the other man lunges at Niyì, but he's already moving. Niyì dodges and kicks out with his right leg and then the guy is on the floor too. Zahrah barrels towards him, but Niyì is faster. In one smooth movement, he tackles Zahrah, grabbing her by the neck.

'Who are you?' Niyì's growl is fierce and I'm reminded of the warrior I saw when I first met him.

'They're Rogues,' I shout, and the man's arm around me tightens painfully.

Zahrah says nothing and I see the moment Niyì recognizes her. Before he can say anything, five more men spill into the room, blocking the doorway.

'Great,' the man holding me says. 'We've got two now.'

In answer, Niyì squeezes Zahrah's neck even more tightly and she flinches.

'Let Onyeka go,' he demands.

I catch a faint glow from the corner of my eye and my head turns to the little girl. My heart stops when I see her. Her whole body is glowing orange, as if she's been lit from within. *As if she's powering up.*

'Niyì,' I call out to warn him, but it's a mistake. *She's just a distraction.* Niyì's eyes dart away from Zahrah and that split second is all she needs. In a blur of movement, she sends Niyì spinning and somehow he's now the one locked in her grip.

Niyì gasps as a big ball of fire blooms from Zahrah's hand, hovering close to his head.

'Use your Ike, Onyeka,' he yells.

CHAPTER TWENTY-EIGHT

I don't move. I'm paralyzed by the sight of Niyì, pinned beneath Zahrah's flames. *This is all my fault!*

I was so busy trying to prove a point that never even mattered, so desperate to show him I wasn't useless . . . that I belong. It's why I was so hurt by his words, because I thought I'd finally found my place at AOS.

This last thought focuses me. The memory of Niyì stopping the fireball before it hit me and Hassan blasts through my mind. He didn't abandon me then . . . I won't abandon him now.

With a suddenness that leaves me breathless, a wave of fury rushes through me. I grab on to it gratefully, using the memories to anchor it. The man holding me grunts as one of my chunky twists headbutts him in the face. He lets me go so he can cup his nose and I push him away. Another twist whistles through the air, hitting him in the chest, and he flies backwards.

At the same time, the rest of my hair whips out around the little girl and she gasps as it pulls her to my side like a lasso. *Since they've got Niyì, I can play dirty too.* The men surrounding us freeze as they see my Ike for the first time. Zahrah isn't so impressed; the ball of fire near Niyì's face burns even brighter.

The man who was holding me straightens, his face an angry mask. He pushes a hand out towards me and I freeze, unsure what he's about to do.

'Stand down!' Zahrah commands suddenly. The man gives her a belligerent look but drops his hand. 'You know you can't use your Ike,' she adds, then turns to me, her expression careful. 'Look, this is getting out of hand. You're not really going to hurt Ṣeun, and besides, you're outnumbered. So let's talk.'

A low growl of frustration leaves my lips. She's right, I don't want to hurt anybody, but I don't trust her either. Not with Niyì trapped and her goons surrounding us. Niyì's mouth opens in a soundless plea ... *Run.* I shake my head in silent reply. That's not even an option.

'What do you want?' I finally ask Zahrah, my voice hard.

'The serum, and you're going to lead us to it.'

I frown at her. 'What serum?'

'Don't act dumb,' Zahrah replies.

What is she talking about? My eyes drop back to Niyì, but there's a strange look on his face. He's about to do something. With a shout, he shifts, catching Zahrah off guard with one of Ms Bello's signature moves. I understand now why she insisted we learn to defend ourselves without using our Ike. Niyì wraps a hand round Zahrah's arm and a thin layer of ice spreads along it until the ball of fire fizzles out. She releases him with a howl.

'For solar's sake, Onyeka, run!' Niyì yells at me.

'Stop them,' Zahrah shouts, cradling her arm.

With Niyì free, I don't hesitate. I push the child away and sprint towards the door. Two guys charge at me, but before they reach me, my hair tears ahead in two twisting bolts, powered by my fury. The bolts slam into the men, sending them flying, and clearing a path out of the room.

Behind me I hear Niyì's footsteps and shouts of chaos and confusion. I don't stop, dashing through the hallway. I have no idea where I'm going and nothing looks familiar. I approach a closed door and my hair shoots out, battering through the solid wood before spiralling back into knots above my head. I turn round, but there's no sign of Niyì.

Where is he? He was right behind me!

But I don't have time to wonder as I leap through the hole in the door. The humid air hits me like a slap. It's so silent outside, with only the whisper of a faint breeze. A short set of steps leads me to the edge of the long grass enclosing the buildings and I stop, trying to get my bearings. The sound of footsteps has me moving again and I plunge into the sea of waving green.

The grass is so tall it hits my waist and I stumble, almost falling to the hard ground below. I pull myself up, fear pushing me forward. Sharp blades of grass slap at me as I sprint, and in my panic, I quickly lose all sense of direction. The only thought driving me on is safety, but I have no idea where that is any more.

There's a loud crash nearby, and I grind to a halt, searching for movement. *Maybe it's Niyì?* Then I hear it again. A thrashing of bodies to my left as *someone* weaves through the dense grass towards me. I take off running to my right, but even with all the training on the treadmills in AOS, I'm getting tired. I was never much of a runner.

The grass starts to thin and through it I can just about make out the edge of the field. I pick up my pace again, racing towards it, but skid to a halt at the sight of a narrow river blocking my path. A steep slope drops down into its muddy depths, just a few metres from where the long grass ends.

I hesitate, trying to think of a way across, when something shifts in the air, a sudden change in temperature. There's someone behind me. My hair whips up and I turn, ready to strike.

'Niyì?' I whisper, relieved.

His hands are raised and he's smiling, but the corners of his mouth are strained.

'Chill, Onyeka,' he says. 'Same side, remember?'

'Where were you?' I splutter through laboured breaths.

'Securing our exit,' he says. 'Think you could call that off?' He points to my hair and the dark strands waving high menacingly.

'I don't think I can right now.'

Niyì throws me a grin. 'Ask it nicely?' I stick out my tongue and his grin widens. I don't get a chance to answer as we hear the crashing of feet, closer now, and Niyì's grin drops.

'Let's go. Your friends are coming.'

'They're not my friends!' I snarl back.

But my words are lost beneath the roar of a powerful engine and a gust of wind that nearly knocks me off my feet. The Gyrfalcon materializes overhead, hovering in place. *Hassan has found us.*

The hatch opens, and from it a metal ladder descends, stopping within arm's reach.

'It's time to go,' Niyì says to me.

'But—'

The words stop in my throat as his hands circle my waist. He lifts me up and I reach for the first rung and start to climb. Just then, Zahrah breaks through the grass, her arm stretched towards us.

'Watch out,' Niyì yells, before throwing up a narrow wall

230

of ice. It's just in time, as a red-hot arc of fire leaps from Zahrah's hand, hitting the wall. Niyì spins, jumping onto the ladder as she rounds the wall ready to fire again.

The moment Niyì makes contact with the ladder, it jolts upwards, and the Gyrfalcon begins to rise. I look up, relieved to see the opening, when a hot blast smacks into the metal rung above me, close to my hand. Sparks fly from the impact.

I look back down to find Niyì dangling from one arm, his other hanging limply by his side. He's been hit!

'Keep moving,' he screams at me.

We're too far off the ground and I can barely hear him above the roar of the Gyrfalcon's engine. His grip slips as another strike ricochets overhead. *He won't make it if he falls.*

Another jolt of the ladder almost knocks me off balance and Niyì's hand comes away completely.

'No!' I yell as Niyì drops.

My hair chases the sound of my cry, clamping around his uninjured arm and halting his fall. I jerk from the sudden impact, bracing myself against the ladder. Like a winch, it winds him in towards me, and I pull him onto the rung above.

'Nice,' says Niyì with a grateful smile, but his face is grey, as if he's used too much Ike.

'Shut up and climb,' I reply, relief making my voice gruff.

He doesn't argue and we struggle up the remaining few metres towards the opening. Hassan's dark hands reach down through the hatch, pulling Niyì up. His hands reappear and I reach up to grasp them but a searing pain punches along every nerve in my body. My hands start to shake. *I'm going to be sick.*

I buckle, my head hitting the rung in front of me hard, and I slide back down the ladder. A painful jolt in my scalp stops my fall, and through blurry eyes I see my wiry strands wrapped around Hassan's hands.

The world begins to slow and the pain is agonizing as Hassan pulls me up the rest of the way. Though the Gyrfalcon's lights are bright, darkness dances along the edge of my vision. Something wet drips from my nose – I'm bleeding. Cold creeps into my body, making friends with the pain already there.

'Come on, Onyeka,' yells a familiar voice, but it sounds far away. Too far for me to identify.

As the darkness closes in, my last thought is of Mum. *Did the Rogues take her . . . and is that why they are after me too?*

CHAPTER TWENTY-NINE

I drift back to consciousness slowly. My eyes don't want to open so I reach out with my other senses. The sting of something attached to my hand. A soft pillow underneath my head. The steady beeping of medical equipment.

I'm in the med-suite at AOS!

With effort, I force one eye open. After a few seconds the other one decides to join in. I'm surrounded by a load of high-tech machines. The only thing I recognize is the IV drip beside my bed. The room itself is stark white and bare and the wall in front of me is covered with tons of graphs and other data. I reckon they must be readings from all the machines.

I pull myself up and nausea hits hard. My hand shakes as I lift it to my head and a memory teases me. I grab at it, trying to remember what happened.

We were attacked by Rogues!

The rest of my memories come racing back faster than Usain Bolt. The beeping of the monitor speeds up as I remember everything that happened.

Is Niyì okay?

I swallow. I don't even know how long I've been out of it. The sound of muffled voices pushes through my panic and I freeze. I slip back down in the bed and force myself to count until the beeping slows down. The Fibonacci sequence is comforting, even though I haven't used it in ages.

The voices get closer and I still can't make them out. I close my eyes just as the door opens. I'm not quite ready to face anyone.

'How long before she wakes up?' someone says. It's Adanna, but she sounds strange, as if she's holding back laughter.

'I'm not sure. Ordinarily I'd expect her to be awake by now,' replies Dr Dòyìnbó's deeper voice. 'Her vitals have stabilized.'

'Do you know why the Rogues were after her or what the serum they were looking for is?' It's Niyì this time and his voice is proper sharp. 'It was weird – I've never seen an adult Rogue before and suddenly there were eight of them.'

'Unfortunately we don't know.' I can practically feel Dr Dòyìnbó fidgeting with his tie. 'Nor have I been able to trace Onyeka's mother.'

My heart sinks at the news. I should just open my eyes so they know I'm awake. But something stops me.

'I'm concerned about '…' Dr Dòyìnbó's voice stops abruptly and I swear I can feel him staring at me through my closed lids.

Silence stretches … they're *all* looking at me now. *I'm going to have to fess up, aren't I?*

Then Dr Dòyìnbó's cheerful voice speaks again.

'Hello, Onyeka. It's good to have you back.'

Busted!

My eyes fly open and my gaze locks onto Dr Dòyìnbó's amused face. Beside him, Adanna's smirk tells me she knew I was awake all along. Hassan and Niyì just look down at me in silence, serious expressions on their faces. The steady beeping of the machine is the only sound in the room.

'Hi?' I croak through dry lips, finally finding my voice.

Niyì's face relaxes a bit then. 'How are you feeling?'

I frown at him. 'As if I fell out of a jet?'

'You almost did,' grumbles Adanna. 'You've been here for two days.'

Two days? No wonder I feel awful.

'How's your arm?' I ask Niyì.

He lifts the arm in question and waves it at me. 'It's fine. The burns were only superficial and the medibots took care of it easily.'

'You were very lucky, young lady,' Dr Dòyìnbó cuts in sternly, and I swallow. 'I wouldn't have let you near that mission if I'd known about the severity of your sickness.'

My eyes swing to Adanna and she stares back at me defiantly. I look away. I can't even be upset with her. It wasn't fair to make her keep my secret in the first place. Plus, she did say I should tell Dr Dòyìnbó.

'I'm sorry,' I whisper, hoping she knows I'm talking to her too.

Dr Dòyìnbó's face softens and he leans forward to take my hand, careful not to disturb the tube sticking out of it.

'I was concerned from the beginning that the late onset of your Ike could cause complications, but I never imagined it would be to this extent.'

'How we go cure her?' Hassan asks.

'I'm waiting for the answer to that very question,' Dr Dòyìnbó replies.

'Has it got anything to do with her aunt?' Adanna asks eagerly.

I sit up painfully. My aunt? *What's going on?*

Dr Dòyìnbó gives me a strange look. 'It might.' He pauses as his eyes get that faraway look of an incoming message on Second Sight. 'It seems the answer has just arrived.' Dr Dòyìnbó steps away from my bed. 'If you'll excuse me.'

When he leaves, the others go silent and just stare at me.

'Were you ever going to tell Hassan and me about your parents and aunt?' Niyì asks eventually.

I grimace. 'I'm sorry.'

Adanna smothers a grin, while Niyì glares at me.

'Why you no tell us first?' Hassan mutters.

'Oh, get over it already,' Adanna snaps back.

I open my mouth to tell him that's how I felt when I found out about Nchebe when Dr Dòyìnbó walks back into the room. And he's not alone. Behind him is a woman. She's tall and lean with the smoothest skin I've ever seen. Her thick ebony hair falls in a curtain of tiny plaits that reaches her waist. Coloured beads and shiny metal cuffs glint under the med-suite lights.

As she gets closer, I realize with shock that her eyes are two different colours. The right one shines a golden brown with shimmering flecks of green bleeding into it. The other eye is almost black. The effect is hypnotic. She smiles and it's my smile – the same one in the picture of my father.

'Dr Naomi?' I whisper.

The smile widens as she stops beside me. The power of it is electric and I feel it spread to the others in the room.

'Yes,' she says. Her voice is honey, smoke and spice all rolled together.

Just then, a loud and angry gurgle rumbles from my belly, and I grab it. Naomi's laugh flows over me, warm and thick like syrup. I look away, fully embarrassed. She gives my shoulder a comforting pat and the movement seems to jolt the others out of their awed fascination.

'Chai, you must be hungry,' Adanna says to me. 'I can get you some akara?'

I smile at her gratefully.

'Perhaps we should all go?' says Dr Dòyìnbó with a meaningful look at Nchebe, and they file out of the room.

'You have no idea how happy I am,' my aunt says when we're finally alone. 'To have found you again is wonderful.'

Her words have a strange choppy quality and I stare at her blankly. *Found me?* I didn't even know she was looking for me.

'You must have questions?' she adds.

'Loads,' I finally say with a shy smile. 'I don't even know what to call you.'

Her laugh flows again. 'Dr Naomi is fine. Aunt Naomi, if you'd prefer?' She's silent for a moment, waiting for my reaction. I don't think I'm ready to call her my aunt though, so I just nod. 'What do you want to know?' she asks.

'Everything,' I say.

Her laugh wraps around me like a warm, fluffy blanket and I relax into it.

'I guess I'd better start from the beginning,' she says. 'Your father and I are fraternal twins, and our Ike didn't appear until we were eight years old. Dr Dòyìnbó found us after Benjamin hypnotized our head teacher into thinking he was a chicken. The Academy of the Sun didn't exist at that point, but we became its first students five years later. Others soon joined, some even older than us, though back then Solari graduated at eighteen.'

I lean forward eagerly. 'What was my father like?'

'Annoying,' Dr Naomi says with a small laugh. 'We grew up on a small farm in Ijebu-Ode. That's in Ogun province. Benjamin liked books and knowledge. He had this way of studying something, as if he could see into the very heart of it. He used to drive our mother to distraction with all his questions.'

Dr Naomi shakes her head, as if she's remembering some of them. 'Everything changed after our Ike came. No one knew much about it in those days and our parents were confused and scared. It's why they agreed to let us go to AOS. And it's why Benjamin made it his life's mission to understand the genetic mutation. It was easier to follow him than be left behind.'

As she talks, her hands twist around themselves. 'We started working for the Upper Council five years after graduating. We were trying to find a way to minimize the uncomfortable effects of using Ike. Only Protectors are allowed to use their Ike after graduation, to reduce the risk of Solari being discovered. Our roles as scientists didn't require it anyway. However, Protectors were struggling, and the Councils needed a cure to allow them to do their jobs properly.'

'What *is* your Ike?' I ask, remembering what she said about hypnosis.

'Your father and I are mind benders. We can bend a

person's memories and will. We can make them do anything we wish if they're close enough.'

My eyes widen. That sounds incredible and a bit scary too. I bite my lip as another question occurs to me. 'Why don't I know about you?'

Dr Naomi looks away. 'Because I wrote the letter that sent you and Tópẹ́ into hiding. I imagine your mother felt it would be safer not to tell you anything about Nigeria, including me.'

I recoil from her words. 'Why did you want us gone?'

Dr Naomi sighs. 'Benjamin has always been on the secretive side. He came to me one night deeply disturbed and said if anything ever happened to him, I should get you and Tópẹ́ out of the country and shut down the lab.' She looks away. 'I thought it was an extreme reaction, but then he reminded me of the lengths the Councils have gone to in order to keep Solari a secret. I've always feared that he stumbled onto something the Councils wanted hidden. It's why I've been laying low and why I was so shocked when I found out you and your mother were back. She contacted me and then disappeared before we could meet.'

I fall back into the softness of the bed and close my eyes. Dr Naomi's story matches most of what Mum and Dr Dòyìnbó have already told me, yet I'm still no closer to finding out what happened to my father or why Mum is missing.

'Do you know what's wrong with me then?' I ask.

She nods. 'Our research suggested that Ike usually manifests early because young children are remarkably resilient and better able to cope with the stress it puts the body under. It's why we all experience some measure of discomfort from using our Ike. We always had concerns that a later manifestation would prove too much for the body to handle and cause too much damage at a cellular level.'

I frown at that. 'You're saying my Ike is damaging me?'

'Yes,' she says simply.

There's a tightness in my chest, but the rest of me feels strangely numb. I hadn't really let myself think about how serious my illness might be. I push a thick twist of hair off my face with a shaking hand. Dr Naomi watches me with a concerned expression.

'We were trying to find a way to reduce that damage when Benjamin disappeared. That's when I realized his paranoia might have been justified.'

'Do you know where my father is?' I ask eagerly.

Dr Naomi's expression turns sad. 'No.'

With that single word, the last of my hope dies. Just then, Dr Dòyìnbó returns, a steaming plate of akara balanced on the tray in his hands. Dr Naomi blinks, her bright eyes dimming slightly. She steps back and Dr Dòyìnbó places the tray in my lap. I look down at the crispy fritters, my appetite fully gone.

'I imagine you're up to speed now?' Dr Dòyìnbó asks.

I nod back tiredly.

'Good. I believe your father's lab might have some answers. Both to his disappearance and your sickness,' Dr Dòyìnbó continues.

'What do you mean?' I sit up quickly.

'All our research is still there.' Dr Naomi's hand settles over my own. 'Dr Dòyìnbó thinks there might be something in the lab that will help us, but I need your help to get back inside.'

My head lifts as a small flutter begins in my stomach. 'How can I help?'

'Benjamin was always strict about security. He created a dual key system to ensure no one could gain unauthorized access to our lab. I have one key and I gave your father's key to Tópé, along with the note. I told her to pass it on to you one day.'

Dr Naomi stretches her arm towards me and pulls up the sleeve of her blouse. Around her wrist is a slim gold chain, and hanging from it is a white cowrie shell, identical to the one that never leaves my neck. I gasp.

Dr Naomi leans forward. 'You've seen this before, haven't you?'

I nod back, unable to talk. Slowly I reach for my necklace and pull it out.

Dr Naomi's eyes close. When they open again, the difference in their colours seems even more noticeable.

She reaches towards the necklace, but pulls back at the last minute.

'Thank goodness,' she whispers. 'That shell is the key.'

'You'll want to leave soon, I take it,' Dr Dòyìnbó says and Dr Naomi nods.

'What's going on?' I ask. *Have I missed something?*

'Dr Dòyìnbó has made arrangements for us to return to the lab,' Dr Naomi tells me. 'We don't have much time before the damage to you becomes permanent or the Councils find out I'm back.'

Us? She can't be talking about me . . . can she?

'I'm going with you?' I ask.

'We don't have a choice,' says Dr Naomi softly. 'The keys are activated through DNA recognition and Benjamin changed his key to match your DNA.'

'Nchebe will be going as well to keep you both safe,' Dr Dòyìnbó insists. 'Onyeka is still weak and the Rogues could very well attack again. I won't put either of you at risk.'

Two pairs of eyes lock on me and I swallow hard. Everything is moving so quickly and my head is swimming. I latch on to the one thing that doesn't feel too scary. My aunt is here and she's going to help me.

CHAPTER THIRTY

Early the next morning, after Hassan's first prayers, the Gyrfalcon takes us to Lagos Island. We land beside a plain building near somewhere called Freedom Park. From the air it looked like some sort of warehouse, its metal walls and curved solar roof gleaming in the bright afternoon sun. Inside, we find aisle after aisle of shelves, each packed high with brown boxes of all sizes.

'Welcome to our top-secret laboratory,' says Dr Naomi, beaming widely.

Adanna looks at me, her brows raised, and I shrug back. *It fully looks like a warehouse.*

Dr Naomi takes us past the first three aisles. When we reach the fourth, she turns into it, and we follow in silence. Dr Naomi stops and faces the shelf, a secretive smile playing on her lips. Then she reaches underneath it and presses something. The shelf separates and I step back as a large rectangular hole in the ground appears. A staircase made of gleaming steel winds down inside it.

'Chai!' Hassan whispers.

Dr Naomi is grinning. 'I bet you weren't expecting that!'

My stomach tightens at the thought of what's waiting at the end of those stairs and why my father went to such lengths to hide it. There's something important down there. *I can feel it.*

Dr Naomi steps forward. 'Stay close.'

We descend with her leading the way. I'm still weak from the Rogue attack and it doesn't take me long to get tired. Finally, the stairs stop at the top of a wide corridor and by the time we reach a huge, grey door I'm breathing heavily. It looks old, and there's no handle or lock, just two small, oddly shaped grooves, several centimetres apart. I stare at them, confused.

'Have you got your key?' Dr Naomi asks. 'It only works if we're holding them.'

I move beside her and pull off my necklace. My gaze falls on the weird grooves again ... each the size and shape of a small shell.

Anticipation and excitement build in my stomach as Dr Naomi motions me closer to the groove on the right. She nods once and together we push the shells into their matching holes.

With a loud *whoosh*, the door opens, and Dr Naomi steps into the darkness beyond. I fasten the chain around my neck and follow, Nchebe close behind me. I hear a click and the darkness evaporates, a patchwork of fluorescent lights beaming down on us from the low ceiling.

The lab is huge, practically the size of the entire warehouse. Coming from the gloom of the stairway, it takes a moment for my eyes to adjust to the brightness. Everything smells stale and a heavy film of dust covers every surface. It's obvious no one has been in here for a very long time. The space is made up of smaller sections, each separated by glass walls that somehow make it feel as if it's still one big room.

'This is the main lab,' says Dr Naomi, striding towards the largest area.

Metal cabinets line the walls and two big worktables cut across the room. There are test tubes, microscopes, chemicals and tons of other equipment I don't recognize placed neatly on top. There's a load of old-looking tech too.

Dr Naomi heads straight to a workbench and soon the soft clicking of her fingers flying over a keyboard echoes across the room. It's as if she's forgotten we're even here. Niyì and Hassan move to the door of the main lab. I guess to keep watch. Adanna is practically skipping as she makes her way over to my aunt. I follow slowly.

'Have you isolated the affected gene, and do you know the pattern of inheritance for the mutation?' Adanna asks her.

I stare at Adanna, totally baffled. Dr Naomi looks up, surprised, then a slow smile spreads across her face.

'You study genetics at AOS?'

Adanna beams back. 'It's my hobby. I want to be a geneticist one day.'

Dr Naomi flashes Adanna an impressed look. 'Ike is caused by a mutation in gene SLRJ39. We call it the Solari gene.'

'I read about it in one of the reports in Dr Dòyìnbó's office,' says Adanna excitedly. Seeing my confusion, she picks up a model of DNA from the desk. 'DNA is like an instruction manual for our body to follow. If there's a typo or error anywhere in the instructions, things can change, causing a mutation.'

'That's right,' says Dr Naomi. 'Onyeka's father and I were studying the mutation in the Solari gene to find the cause of the sickness.'

They start talking more science stuff and I lose interest, moving towards the glass wall. A small room with a sofa and desk catches my attention.

'What's that?' I ask.

My aunt looks up at the sound of my voice, her eyes following my pointed finger.

'That's Benjamin's office,' she says. 'You can take a look, if you'd like?'

I don't remember walking the short distance to the office,

but somehow I'm standing in front of my father's desk. It's the closest I've ever felt to him and, because of that, it's the most beautiful place I've ever seen. It's also a dusty mess.

I have no idea what anything is, but curiosity has me lifting bottles of chemicals, the names of which I can barely pronounce. I come across a dusty picture frame and pick it up. Wiping the glass with my fingers, I find a photo of a smiling child. My chest tightens.

It's me.

I look about two, sitting on a trike outside a pale yellow bungalow. My blue-black hair surrounds my face in a thick cloud.

I spot another frame and I reach for it with shaky hands. This time it's a picture of Mum. I touch her face through the grimy glass, biting back the sob that wants to escape. Mum is out there somewhere and I don't even know if she's okay.

She's cradling a baby in the picture and the expression on her face as she looks into the camera lens is so happy. Behind her stands my father. The love and pride on his face as he stares down at Mum and me is almost too painful to look at.

The sob finally leaves my throat as I realize what I'm looking at. It's the answer to the question I've always been too scared to voice.

He loved us. He loved me.

My body trembles and my legs buckle – a reminder that I'm still weak. I grip the edge of the desk, trying to stay upright.

The second my fingers close around the wooden edge, it beeps, and I jump as a hidden compartment springs out.

Rah. My father really is paranoid.

Inside the compartment is a flat digital pad. It looks way older than the ones we use in AOS. I pick it up and an amber light spreads across my curled palm. With another beep, the pad springs to life and a blue beam flashes from the device into the air above it. Then the light shifts, moulding itself into the form of a human body – one that is immediately familiar.

A voice I thought I'd never hear erupts from a face I've only ever seen in pictures.

Welcome home, Onyeka.

My father's voice pierces through me, his face so lifelike and vivid.

'Guys,' I cry, my voice a wobbly mess. 'You'd better come quick.'

I bet this has all come as a bit of shock, huh?

I can't take my eyes off the hologram in front of me, and I lean forward, trying to take in every detail. It doesn't take long for Nchebe and Dr Naomi to spill into the office and four sets of eyes get really big.

'Woah!' Adanna whispers. 'That's why you smell like bananas.'

> If you're seeing this recording, I can only hope it's now safe for you and your mother to return to Nigeria. If you're there, Naomi, thank you for protecting my wife and child.

I look at Dr Naomi and her eyes are closed, her hand pressed to her mouth.

> I don't have very long to record this, but it's important you know the truth. The sickness is much worse than we believed. It's a degenerative disease linked to the use of Ike. The disease seems to peak when Solari reach their early twenties. If they continue to use their Ike past this point the disease will kill them. Protectors aren't just graduating, they're dying!

Niyì recoils, his face a tight, angry mask. Beside him, Hassan's mouth is open, as if he wants to say something, but no words come out. Adanna just looks shattered. There's so much pain and bitterness in my aunt's face that I look away.

> I was able to make a cure ... but there's a catch. If Solari take it, they will lose their Ike. It wasn't my intention, and perhaps with more time I could have fixed it.

I flinch as his words repeat in my mind. Over and over, like a tornado, sweeping everything else aside and leaving only panic. Solari can't lose their Ike. It's a part of us! And the idea that we might lose it so we can live seems wrong ... *Would it even be living?*

I'm sorry for not telling you, Naomi.

The hologram begins to flicker suddenly as if there's a glitch, and my father's last words become garbled.

But when I discovered the truth about ... realized I was ... danger ... didn't want to ... you at risk too.

I look at Adanna and she shrugs. 'It's been sitting here for a long time,' she says. 'It's probably corrupted or damaged.'

The hologram of my father continues, but it's getting harder to make any sense of what he's saying.

Do not trust ... plans to use Solari to ... If ... succeeds, everyone is ... danger! In ... pad ... find ... formula for ... serum and I've hidden ... of it. It's in ... where we used to play as ... Where I found the cowrie ...

His holographic body leans forward.

Find Gbénga … knows about … he can help …

The hologram flickers one last time and then begins to melt away like a fading mist. An ache settles in my chest. I'm losing him all over again. Everything in me wants to scream at him to come back and not leave me alone with this incredible burden. But there is only silence.

'None of this makes sense,' Adanna whispers. 'How can we have a disease?' Then her voice cracks. 'He said we're going to die if we keep using our Ike …'

I stare at her, unable to think of an answer, unable to do anything but try to breathe past the tightness in my chest.

CHAPTER
THIRTY-ONE

'Dear Lord,' Dr Naomi breathes. 'All this time we thought Solari were helping to defend Nigeria, when really they've been dying. No wonder the Councils are so secretive about what they do.'

'No way. I don't believe it,' Niyì says in a gruff voice. 'He must be wrong. We're not dying. We're training to be Protectors, for solar's sake.'

There's total silence in the room as we all try to process my father's words and what they mean for all of us. Niyì begins to pace, muttering to himself angrily. Hassan has sunk to the floor, his face a mask of fear. I want to give him a hug and tell him it's going to be all right, but I don't know if that's true any more. Adanna is so still, her face screwed up in pain. The air practically crackles with the amount of emotion flying about and I wonder how she can bear it.

Dr Naomi seems to be the only one of us still functioning. She steps closer to me and takes the pad, her hands not quite steady.

'Do you think it's all true?' I ask in a quiet voice.

'If Benjamin believed so, then it must be. He's the foremost expert on Solari after Dr Dòyìnbó,' she replies, fiddling with the pad. 'Give me a moment.' She turns away, moving towards my father's desk as her fingers fly over the screen.

'I knew it,' Adanna finally says through clenched teeth. 'I always suspected something wasn't right about the way we get sick.'

'I wonder how long the Councils have known,' I say.

'Does it matter?' Niyì snaps. 'It's bad enough that they knew and haven't told us.' He throws his hands up in frustration. 'Why let Protectors die? Why not just tell us about it so we can all choose for ourselves?'

'They care more about their army of Protectors, even if it means we suffer for it,' Adanna says bitterly. 'They're probably also scared we'd revolt if we found out. Would you want a bunch of angry Solari running loose?'

'I no wan lose my Ike,' says Hassan quietly. 'But I no wan die too.'

Niyì moves to him and clasps his shoulder. I look away, feeling helpless. Both options suck and it's not fair that we have to deal with either one.

'No one is dying,' Niyì says determinedly. 'We have to get

back to AOS. We have to warn Dr Dòyìnbó about what the Councils are up to.'

'What about the Rogues?'

'Seriously, Ada?' Niyì snaps. 'We don't have time for your obsession with the—'

'For solar's sake. Think, Niyì,' she interrupts. 'Who do you think Onyeka's dad was talking about when he said "Gbénga"?'

Niyì goes real quiet as we all realize Adanna is right. It has to be the same Gbénga who formed the Rogues.

'How else would the Rogue who attacked you have known about the serum?' Adanna continues. 'Onyeka's dad must have told Gbénga and he's been trying to get his hands on it since.'

'Nawa o,' Hassan says. 'Because of dis them dey attack AOS?'

Adanna nods. 'It's probably why they've been trying to get to Onyeka too. I'm guessing they think she knows where the serum is.'

'It doesn't matter anyway,' Niyì says, shaking his head. 'Our priority is to get back to AOS.'

He moves towards the door just as Dr Naomi steps away from the desk.

'We've got a bigger problem,' she says quietly, and Niyì stops cold at her tone. 'I've just looked through the pad. A lot of Benjamin's notes are corrupted, but according to what

I can access, Onyeka's disease has peaked early. It starts with intense nausea, then vomiting and eventually progresses to blackouts. That's why her symptoms have got so bad so quickly. Because she's continued using her Ike, the disease has progressed too far. She no longer has a choice.' Dr Naomi gives me a helpless look. 'If she doesn't take the serum . . .'

She doesn't need to finish her sentence. All eyes turn to me. I stare back blankly as Dr Naomi's words echo through my brain.

I have no choice . . . no choice.

'What's going to happen to me?' I whisper, my voice far from steady.

Dr Naomi looks at me with worried eyes. 'You'll lose control of your emotions first. Even with your anchor it will be a struggle to regulate them. Then your connection to your Ike will deteriorate, overwhelming your body with too much power until it burns itself out.'

I open my mouth to reply when a huge BANG echoes around the lab. Soldiers dressed in green camouflage uniforms burst through the doors, heading straight for us.

'Grab the girl with the big hair, the woman and any data you can find,' a deep voice growls.

My eyes widen as a big guy with a huge forehead steps forward and points at Dr Naomi and me. More soldiers than I can count surge towards us, clustering in a wide semicircle that blocks the only way out of the lab.

Hassan stares at them. 'Who be this?'

'It doesn't matter,' Niyì replies in a steely voice. 'They're in our way and they need to move.'

'Or what? You'll use your Ike on us?' the big man taunts. 'We can handle you.'

I stare at him. He's clearly not Solari. *So how does he know about Ike?* But no one else seems to have noticed.

'Let's see about that,' Niyì says, rushing forward with his hands raised, blue mist already drifting from them.

Hassan follows, but they don't get very far. The big guy pulls out a silver ball and tosses it at them. The ball disintegrates in mid-air, turning into a red net of solid energy. Before they can dodge it, the net lands on Niyì and Hassan, trapping them in place.

My gasp of horror is drowned out by the guy as he yells to the soldiers behind him.

'Get the others, and remember, we're not to hurt them.'

Adanna grabs my arm, pulling hard to get my attention. 'Stay here and don't you dare use your Ike,' she barks.

Before I can argue with her, she dashes towards the approaching soldiers with a wild yell. I catch a glimpse of her micro locs as she launches herself at the closest one. She takes him down easily, but there are too many of them. A long arm swings out, swatting Adanna away like a fly. The force of the blow sends her backwards and she cries out in pain.

'No,' I shout, as she crumples to the ground.

I don't even have to reach for my Ike – it's already responding. My hair whips into a defensive arc, like a halo of fury. But there's something else there with it – nausea rolls through my stomach and a bolt of pain shoots through my head. I almost gasp at the intensity, but I push through it. I have to.

A flash of hair whips through the air, hitting the first guy in the chest. He slams into the wall with a grunt, before sliding down in a helpless heap. I shift, my hair rippling as more soldiers stalk me like hungry wolves. Each one looks ready to pounce at any minute.

So I move first, swinging my hair like a fist, punching through three of them at once. Pain punches through my stomach too, like red-hot needles, as my body reminds me that I'm not supposed to be doing this. I quickly push that thought out of my mind.

More soldiers press forward, closing in on me fast. I spin away, my hair whirling around me like the blades of a helicopter. Grunts fill the air and I spin back to find the soldiers on the floor. Another wave of sickness washes over me and my legs almost give way. I'm getting tired, but the soldiers keep coming. *We're not going to make it out of here!*

'That's enough!' shouts Dr Naomi, her multicoloured eyes swirling with power. Every head in the room turns her way involuntarily, even mine, and I gawp as all movement stops. I didn't realize her Ike would be this epic.

She's a badass!

'SLEEP!'

Dr Naomi's voice cracks like thunder and only the soldiers surrounding us drop to the ground. I am properly impressed, and even Nchebe look dazed too. With way more effort than it normally takes, I use my Ike to pull my hair into four Bantu knots and then turn to my aunt.

But Dr Naomi looks about as good as I feel. Her body is trembling, and despite the air conditioning, her nose is shiny with sweat. I race over to her, grabbing her arm just before she falls to the ground.

'I thought you couldn't use Ike?' I ask her.

'Actually, I said I *don't* use it,' she replies with a tired smile. 'And I probably won't be able to again after that. I used too much.'

'We need to leave now!' Niyì yells, as Adanna frees him and Hassan from the net. 'There could be more of them on the way.'

The world begins to spin then, or perhaps it's just me and the world is fine. I lift a hand weakly towards Dr Naomi, and the next thing I know Adanna's pulling me along, a worried look on her face.

'Niyì,' she calls. 'Onyeka doesn't smell too good.'

Soon, we're at the entrance to the lab and I can barely keep upright. Hassan takes the shell from my neck and presses it into my hand so Dr Naomi and I can lock the door with both keys. Then Niyì places his hand on the door and ice spreads from his palm, covering the metal in a solid layer.

'That should hold them for a while,' he says.

Everything becomes fuzzy as the world begins to slow down.

'Stay with us, Onyeka,' Adanna yells, but I don't know how. There's too much pain, just like on the Gyrfalcon. Everything else drains out of me as my eyes drift shut.

CHAPTER THIRTY-TWO

'She still dey breathe?'

. . .

'Watch out with that force field, Hassan.'

. . .

'We can't go back to AOS – she needs the serum.'

. . .

Voices come at me, their words broken and disjointed. I struggle to make sense of any of it as I float back to consciousness. My whole body aches and I open my eyes carefully. We're back in the Gyrfalcon and I'm on a narrow bed, surrounded by beeping machines. It looks like a mini version of the med-suite. I look around and find Dr Naomi nose deep in my father's data pad. At the front of the jet, Nchebe are talking . . . well arguing, actually.

'We need the serum,' Adanna says, lifting her hands like she's said it a million times already.

'But if she use am, she go lose her Ike.'

Adanna shrugs. 'She'll lose her life if we don't cure her. She's running out of time.'

'We should contact Dr Dòyìnbó first,' insists Niyì.

Adanna rolls her eyes at him. 'Use your brain. What if the Councils are watching him? Do you want to put him and everyone else at the academy in danger?'

'Stop arguing,' I croak, wincing as the sound of my own voice screams through my head like an excited K-pop fan.

Four sets of eyes swing towards me and I'm quickly surrounded by my friends and aunt.

'How you dey feel?' Hassan asks me.

'As if I've been hit by the Beast,' I reply.

What else can I say? That I'm terrified I'm going to die or, worse, I'll lose my Ike and go back to being the lost and empty girl I was before I came to Nigeria? Okay, so that's not worse than dying, but it's still pretty bad. I don't say any of this, of course, but Adanna stares at me as if she knows it anyway.

'You know where the serum is, don't you, Dr Naomi?' I say, and she flashes me a startled look.

'Yes,' she replies, then her face turns hesitant. 'I've been looking at Benjamin's notes. He was smart to use CRISPR to make the changes to the Solari gene, but I can see where he went wrong.'

'Wetin be crisps?' Hassan asks.

Adanna nudges him. 'CRISPR not crisps. It's short for CRISPR-Cas technology. It uses a special protein found in bacteria and RNA, a molecule similar to DNA, to edit genes.'

'I dey sorry I ask,' Hassan says with a dazed look.

Dr Naomi's smile is strained. 'I need to recover as much of the corrupted data as possible and then analyse the serum to know for sure.' Dr Naomi shrugs. 'But I think I can fix it so it doesn't take away Ike.'

Hope swells in my chest. The thought of losing my Ike has been eating away at me since we found out about the serum.

Adanna reaches for the pad. 'I might be able to help with recovering the data.' Dr Naomi nods and hands it to her.

'So where is the serum then?' Niyì asks.

Dr Naomi grimaces. 'Onyeka's father hid it in Ogbunike. It's where we used to play as children and where we found our cowrie shells.'

'What is Ogbunike?' I ask.

'Chai!' says Hassan at the same time.

'It's an old system of caves. A heritage site in the eastern part of Nigeria,' Adanna replies, ignoring Hassan's horrified face.

Hassan shakes his head. 'Why cave na? You know I no like dark, smelly place.'

'But you have so much in common,' Adanna replies sweetly, earning herself a dirty look.

Niyì crosses his arms. 'We do not have permission for

this. We need to go back to AOS. Dr Dòyìnbó will know what to do.'

But what if he doesn't? What if this is our only shot to fix the serum so I can keep my Ike?

'The Councils are clearly after Dr Naomi and me. Who knows how long that frozen door will hold their minions,' I say quietly. Adanna's eyes meet mine and understanding settles between us.

'I want to give my aunt a chance,' I announce to Niyì. 'And since it's my life on the line, my vote beats yours.'

'I'm with Onyeka,' Adanna says, giving me an encouraging smile.

Hassan sighs, then nods. 'Me too.'

Niyì goes quiet, his face growing thoughtful. 'Nchebe work as a team,' he finally replies, then he nods at me. 'I trust you.'

I stiffen. That was totally not what I was expecting him to say. *He finally trusts me!* Even after what happened with the Rogue at AOS and then at Millennium Market.

Joy rushes through my body like a sugary drink. I'm practically buzzing with it, but it's too intense. Something is wrong. Then strange tears fill my eyes.

'That was such a nice thing to say,' I gasp as they begin to fall.

'Erm, Onyeka . . .' Adanna begins, but I don't let her finish, as emotions I can't contain flow out of me.

'No, seriously, you guys are so amazing,' I sob.

There are too many feelings and I don't know what to do with them. So, of course, my Ike comes out to play. Hassan shouts as a bolt of hair whips out, wrapping tightly around his ankle. His feet sweep out from under him, and the next second, he's dangling upside down in the middle of the jet. A short bark of laughter leaves Adanna's lips before she quickly clamps a hand over her mouth.

Hassan doesn't find it so funny. 'Abeg o, put me down.'

'I can't,' I say with a small hiccup.

'Na your hair. Tell am to stop.'

The hair he's complaining about is now swinging him up and down like a Hassan-sized yo-yo.

'Onyeka!' Adanna hollers at me, and my scalp prickles. 'You need to calm down.'

By now the strands round Hassan's ankle have begun to wander, moving up his leg like a curious child checking out a new toy.

'I don't know how,' I whisper urgently.

Adanna leans in close. 'Listen to me. You need to use your anchor. Focus on Cheyenne.'

I find a memory quickly of the two of us at Comic Con in our cosplay outfits, but then another one joins it – the memory of Hassan's hands wrapped around my hair as he saved me from falling from the Gyrfalcon.

'Have you found—?'

Before Adanna can finish, the hair holding Hassan up snaps back towards me and he drops to the ground in a tumbling heap. I start laughing then – an out of control giggle that I can't stop.

'What's going on? Why is she acting so weirdly?' Niyì says, a concerned look on his face.

'She's losing control of her emotions, like Onyeka's dad's notes warned us about,' Adanna says in a small voice. 'I can't believe I'm the only one who can hear them. They're so loud.' Adanna swallows, as if she's in pain.

'She needs her anchor,' Dr Naomi replies, moving closer to me.

Niyì frowns at her. 'What do you mean?'

'She needs to talk to Cheyenne,' Adanna cuts in. My eyes swing to her in surprise, and an encouraging smile lights up her face. 'It's okay, Onyeka. We're gonna fix this.'

Soon, Cheyenne's face pops up on the viewscreen, fox ears and all. She's not even looking into her camera properly, and I can tell she's distracted.

'What is it, Yeka? I'm in the middle of Battlestar Ninjas.'

'Oops,' I giggle again. Cheyenne fully loves that game and she hates being interrupted.

My high-pitched laugh gets Cheyenne's full attention and she finally clocks all of us, her eyes narrowing.

'What's wrong with Onyeka?'

'She needs you,' Adanna replies, before explaining

everything to Cheyenne. Soon they're bantering back and forth. And as happy as I am that they're getting on, it's me we're supposed to be fixing.

'Erm, hello,' I say with another giggle, but they ignore me.

'I love your T-shirt,' says Adanna, admiring the anime character on Cheyenne's top.

'Shut up, Adanna, and stick to the plan,' Niyì finally says.

Cheyenne grins. 'I knew he was cute.'

Niyì coughs, an embarrassed look coming over his face, and a startled laugh bursts from me. Adanna and Cheyenne share a look before they too burst into laughter and I'm reminded of how much fun Chey and I used to have. Then I'm no longer giggling.

'I think she's back,' Adanna replies with a smug look at Niyì.

'Yeah, she seems like Yeka again,' says Cheyenne with a laugh, and I can't help the smile that fills my face. Then her expression turns serious. 'Make sure you take care of my girl.'

'Our girl,' Adanna says with a smile, before signing off. A need to hug her fills me. 'Feeling better?' she asks me and I nod. 'Good. That should have bought us some time to find the serum before you lose control again.'

'DAMI,' Niyì calls out. 'Bring up a map of Ogbunike Caves.' A detailed map flashes up on the viewscreen and Niyì looks at me. 'We've got work to do.'

CHAPTER THIRTY-THREE

It takes us thirty minutes to get from Lagos to Anambra and we arrive late in the morning. We leave Dr Naomi, Adanna and the Gyrfalcon in an abandoned field, close to the Ogbunike Caves. Adanna stayed to help Dr Naomi recover the corrupted data on the pad, leaving Niyì, Hassan and me to search for the serum.

Niyì wanted me to stay behind, but I wasn't having any of it. It helped that Dr Naomi agreed. She said my father would have probably left clues and they might need me to figure them out. She even gave me her cowrie key, just in case.

The bush that leads to the caves is dense and broken branches poke at me. It takes way more energy than it should to push through them. I'm glad I put my hair up, though I had to do it the old way with my hands and a hairband.

Adanna told me the caves used to be a hiding spot during

the slave trade and times of local conflict. As we move further down the valley, I can't help but think about all the people who made this journey before me. The fear they must have felt as they ran and hid from people who wanted to harm them. The twisting green reeds and trees surrounding us now almost echo with remembered pain and sadness, and I shiver at the eerie feeling.

We soon find a narrow flight of stone steps. According to Niyì, there are 317 of them, and the sound of thrumming frogs and buzzing cicadas keeps us company as we descend towards the caves. I'm shaking with exhaustion by the time we get to the bottom of the final flight of steps. But the yawning, black mouth that greets us still manages to take my breath away. It's about five metres high and twice as wide with a thick moustache of plants and vines hanging from its lip.

I turn on the torchlight on my Second Sight, and as we enter the cave, a blast of humid air hits me. Soon I'm sweating like a cold drink left out on a hot summer's day. The inside of the main cave is massive, the jagged grey-brown walls sloping up to a high ceiling. Engraved into the walls are dozens of drawings and names in a weird patchwork of graffiti. My gaze is drawn to one that looks like a crocodile. My fingers brush over the rough edges in wonder. It's so detailed, the teeth look sharp enough to cut skin.

The faint sound of running water echoes through the

cave, and I swear I can almost hear the quiet groan of the rocks shifting around us. I remember from the map DAMI showed us, that there are a few tunnels weaving from this main opening, each leading in a different direction. What I don't know is which one we're meant to take.

A path worn by feet leads to an opening barely bigger than a human. Dr Naomi says she and my father liked to hide in the caves when they were little. Somehow, I can't imagine my father choosing the most obvious place to hide the serum. I scan the other tunnels; some are so small I doubt I'd even fit.

'Which way make we follow?' Hassan calls out.

The sound echoes through the chamber, bouncing off the hard rock.

Niyì's gaze swings to me. 'What do you think?'

I swallow . . . *I don't know!*

I move to the tunnel closest to me. It's narrow and low, and I crouch down, peering into the darkness beyond. The stench of it hits me like a fist. It's so strong it makes my eyes water. I rear back sharply, hoping the serum isn't in this tunnel.

'Well?' asks Niyì, his impatience pulsing around the cavern.

I ignore him, moving to another tunnel. This one is slightly wider than the last and I brace myself for the smell. But the air is clean, which surprises me. I focus my torchlight into the mouth of the hole and glimpse a narrow tunnel beyond.

I don't know what to do. Cheyenne's voice filters through

my mind then and I can almost hear her telling me that no one in their right mind would choose to go the smelly way . . . which makes it the perfect hiding place. But I can't be sure.

I search the wall around the opening, looking for something, anything that could help. Like the rest of the cave, the wall is covered in drawings and carvings, but nothing stands out. Then an idea hits me.

I follow my gut and quickly move back to the first tunnel. Niyì and Hassan watch me silently, their eyes following my every move. Prepared for the smell this time, I cover my nose with my hand and search the wall. A shallow etching catches my attention. *A cowrie shell.* My heart begins to race. My hand grasps my necklace and I feel as if my father is talking to me.

'Onyeka?' Niyì calls out.

'It's this one,' I squeal, excitement filling my voice.

'Are you sure?' Niyì says, coming up beside me.

'Positive.'

Hassan joins us and makes a gagging sound at the smell.

'You no serious,' he says, a horrified look on his face. 'Abeg, make we follow another way,' he pleads.

'Quit complaining and breathe through your mouth,' Niyì replies, stepping out ahead. 'I'll take the lead. Hassan, you cover the back.'

The opening is even narrower and darker than I thought and the night vision on my Second Sight kicks in. Ahead of me, Niyì squeezes through the opening, and as I follow, the tight space closes in on us. The tunnel continues to narrow, tightening until we're forced to scramble through sideways, with only the constant drip of water to guide the way.

Just when I think I've made a mistake, that I've led us into a dead end or, worse, a trap, I hear the splash of Niyì's feet hitting water. I soon see why as the tunnel widens out into a large underground cavern, half the size of the main chamber.

The ground beneath us is submerged in a pool of warm water that comes up to our ankles, making the floor slippery. My foot slides out from beneath me. I brace myself for the impact, but it doesn't come as an arm whips out, pulling me upright.

'Be careful,' says Niyì, his voice low. 'Which way now?'

He's not looking at me though. His gaze is on the three new tunnels stretching out ahead of us. This time I know what I'm looking for. I don't find anything by the first two, but just above the opening of the third, I find the cowrie etching.

This tunnel is wider than the last and we move at a faster pace. The smell of the air hits me first. It's fresher than before. Then a gentle breeze pushes through the tunnel, the coolness of it a nice relief.

'Wow!'

Niyì's gasp alerts me to a change, but it still doesn't prepare me for what I see. The chamber is vast. Twice the size of the one at the entrance of the cave, but it's the structure in the middle of the room that leaves me totally in awe.

A large stone pedestal rises a couple of metres from the ground, and on top of it rests a marble statue shaped like a cowrie shell lying on its back. The smooth roundness is carved in such perfect detail as it curves into a ridged mouth. A thick layer of dirt covers it, and I reach out, touching the shell with trembling fingers. The side of the shell closest to me isn't as smooth as I first thought and there's a single shallow groove etched into it . . . like the door in my father's lab. *But this one is meant just for me.*

It's totally unreal, like something out of the comic book Cheyenne made me. My father did *all* of this, to save the Solari . . . to save me. With everything that's already happened, this realization is the thing that sends me over the edge and my eyes fill with tears. I wipe them away quickly, pulling the cowrie shell necklace from my neck. Then I place it into the groove.

Nothing happens at first, then from the mouth of the marble shell a clear glass tube rises out on a raised platform. I reach for it with a shaky hand and hold it up to the light of my torch. The colourless liquid glistens harmlessly. Except it isn't.

I should be relieved. It's going to save me . . . but it could also take away an important part of who I am. I turn it over again, my hand sweaty now with fear. What if Dr Naomi isn't able to fix it? *What if I lose my Ike?* A tightness crawls up my throat and I force myself to swallow it down. The sting of an unknown and unwanted fate wraps around me, tightening like a net.

'Na dis be it?' Hassan asks in excitement, oblivious to my thoughts.

'Looks like it,' says Niyì, before I can reply. 'We should get going. The sooner we get it to Dr Naomi and Ada, the sooner they can get to work.'

I grab the shell necklace and put the serum in my pocket before following Niyì out of the cavern. Our journey out of the tunnels is much slower because Niyì insists we stop for Hassan to pray and for me to rest. And all the way I can't shake my worry about the serum. I want to be excited the way Hassan and Niyì are, but a strange fear holds me back. It doesn't help that the closer we get to the mouth of the cave, the worse my sickness gets, and by the time we reach it, I feel awful again.

Then a sudden sound of movement outside brings us to a stop. Niyì motions for silence. I frown at him. *What's wrong?*

'I have something of yours,' calls a voice I really hoped to never hear again.

I can already imagine the smirk on the guy's face and I don't even know his name. All I know is that he has a big forehead and likes trying to kidnap me. *How did he get out of the lab? How did he find us?*

'Run, Onyeka,' cries a different voice this time.

My chest tightens and it's suddenly difficult to breathe. *Please don't let it be her!*

But it is. It's Adanna.

CHAPTER THIRTY-FOUR

I jerk forward before I can stop myself, rage roaring inside me.

'Wait!' Niyì says, and the harsh sound of his voice pulls me up.

He looks at me, a warning in his eyes. I don't stop to wonder how he knows what I'm about to do.

'You can't use your Ike,' he growls.

But I'm already moving. I dash around him, sprinting to the edge of the cave's entrance. I duck down behind a small cluster of rocks, peering over the top so I can get a better view. Someone drops down beside me, and I turn to find Niyì crouched low, a scowl on his face. Our eyes meet before I turn again and poke my head up over the rock.

Just a few metres away, I spot the big man at the bottom of the steps we came down not too long ago. But it's the girl and woman next to him who grab my attention, surrounded by even more soldiers. *Where do these guys keep coming from and who are they?*

Adanna looks ready to hurt someone and Dr Naomi has a gag around her mouth. I guess they don't want her using her powers on them again. My Ike stirs in fury and I start to stand. Niyì's hand stops me, his head jerking towards the trees. I see them then, more soldiers, hiding in the dense, green leaves.

I slump back down. The question runs through my mind again. *How did they find us?* No one else knew we were coming here. We didn't even tell Dr Dòyìnbó, so the soldiers had to be tracking us. Something nudges at the back of my mind, but before I can grab it Hassan appears beside us.

'Dis our situation no good o,' he says.

I give him a look. *You think?*

'Come out slowly, and don't even think about using Ike,' the man yells at us. 'Unless you want your friends to get hurt.'

These guys fully didn't come to play this time. My eyes lock with Niyì's and Hassan's and a look of understanding passes between us. *We don't have a choice.* With a nod at me, Niyì stands and Hassan and I follow. The three of us shuffle out of the cave towards the soldiers.

'Onyeka, something smells wrong here,' Adanna shouts as we draw close. 'They knew how to disable DAMI's security protocols and—'

'Be quiet,' the man next to her growls.

'I told you we should have gone back to AOS,' Niyì hisses beside me. 'If we'd just told Dr Dòyìnbó, none of this would be happening.'

'You are very correct,' a new voice says.

One I never expected to hear ... not here. I look up and horror spreads through me as Dr Dòyìnbó walks down the steps and stops beside the big man.

His gaze moves to me and I flinch at the hardness in his face. Gone is the gentle man I've spent the last few months getting to know ... to trust. Suddenly, everything begins to make a horrible sort of sense. I want to throw up and it's not just because of the sickness.

'Hello, Onyeka,' Dr Dòyìnbó says with a small smile.

He nods to the big guy, who approaches me, searching until he finds the serum. He pulls it from my pocket and hands it over. Dr Dòyìnbó lifts the serum, peering into it with a frown.

'I don't understand what's happening,' says Adanna, staring at Dr Dòyìnbó blankly. 'None of this makes sense.'

I stare at the man I once trusted, the one I thought was looking out for Mum and me. My lips tighten as a new wound opens. His betrayal cuts even more deeply because I'd begun to think of the academy as my safe place. Now I'm forced to question everything about my time there, starting with the man at the very centre of it.

'He's in on it,' I snarl. 'He must be working for the Councils.'

Dr Dòyìnbó sniffs. 'The Councils have nothing to do with this. They've only ever been my puppets. Even after I left them, they still played into my plans.' He adjusts his bright yellow bow tie dramatically. *Have they always looked so silly?*

'Solari are no accident,' Dr Dòyìnbó continues. 'I've known from the very beginning that certain types of exposure to trarium would result in genetic mutation. After all, it happened to me.'

His words slam into me like a speeding train. *No way!* I activate the thermal scanner on my Second Sight and Dr Dòyìnbó lights up like a purple glow stick. *Wow.* I guess it never occurred to anyone to scan for Solari in a school full of them.

'So you be Solari too?' Hassan whispers, as we all begin to realize just how badly we've been played.

'The very first,' Dr Dòyìnbó replies. 'It was an accident. One of my experiments went wrong, exposing me to massive amounts of trarium. It's why my mutation is different and also why I'm immune to the disease that affects the rest of you.'

I shake my head, still confused. 'You planned all of this? Why would you want to create Solari?'

Dr Dòyìnbó looks at me with pity. 'The future. One that you will never know because I stopped it,' he continues. 'You have no idea the amount of poverty, religious conflict and poor governance Nigeria was destined for. But I do, because I've seen it all. That's my gift.' His lips curve into a mocking smile. 'When I was barely twenty-one, I saw my first vision of what Nigeria would become. I also saw that it would need a strong and powerful leader to stop it from happening, and I knew deep in my soul that I could be that man.' The smile turns bitter. 'But I was too young to be taken seriously as Laamu-EzeOba. So I used my solar cell technology and the influence it brought me to reshape this nation from behind the scenes. Now it's time for me to take my place as Nigeria's true leader and bring the rest of the world to heel.'

Adanna rolls her eyes. 'You think controlling people will end well?' she sneers. 'When has that ever worked out?'

'No one else has had an army of Solari behind them,' Dr Dòyìnbó snaps. 'Why do you think I allowed the trarium contamination to happen? AOS was merely a way to ensure I could train you so that when the time came, I could use Solari to realize my plans. But once the early graduates began to die, I discovered Solari couldn't use Ike and survive into adulthood. I had to postpone things until a cure could be found. But no more. I'm running out of time and Solari.'

'The Councils go stop you,' Hassan says. 'They no go let you win.'

Dr Dòyìnbó laughs harshly. 'You think the Councils will believe a bunch of children over me, the Father of Solar? By the time they discover the truth, it will be too late, and they too will fall in line, just like everybody else.'

Adanna stares at him defiantly. 'We won't let you use us that way.'

'Are you sure?' says Dr Dòyìnbó with a smirk. 'Who do you serve?' he bellows suddenly.

Adanna, Niyì and Hassan straighten instinctively, and a look of horror passes over Adanna's face.

'I've trained Solari to put serving Nigeria and winning above everything else,' Dr Dòyìnbó continues triumphantly. 'Well, I'm Nigeria now and your loyalty will be mine. Why do you think I created Ìdánwò and the house rankings?'

He's right. That's why the rankings have always seemed weird to me. It made Solari so competitive and so focused on being the best, even if it meant hurting others.

'What about the serum?' I ask, still confused about his intentions. 'What do you want with it?'

Dr Dòyìnbó looks at Dr Naomi with dislike and her eyes widen. She grunts, trying to speak around the gag in her mouth, but it's no use.

'Your brother had one simple task,' he says. 'I secretly recruited him to find a cure for the disease, but he got nosy and discovered my plans for Nigeria.' Dr Dòyìnbó nods at me, his expression harsh. 'When I discovered what your father had created, that his serum inadvertently removed Ike, I was livid. It's an unacceptable threat that jeopardizes my life's work.'

Adanna's eyes widen. 'You were scared that someone might use the serum to neutralize your precious army.'

Dr Dòyìnbó throws her a disgruntled look, and something clicks in my head.

'That's why you made my father disappear, isn't it?' I demand. 'Where is he?'

'He was trying to destroy everything I've worked to build, so he had to go,' Dr Dòyìnbó replies. 'My mistake was underestimating him. I didn't foresee him hiding the serum and using his Ike on himself to erase his memory of doing so. The minute I discovered he'd sent his whole family into hiding, I suspected he'd planned another way to access the serum and that you were the key. Luckily, my visions of the future allowed me to see that you and your mother would return once your Ike manifested. I've been waiting patiently ever since.'

I gawp at Dr Dòyìnbó. I can't believe my father wiped his own memory, just to keep us safe. Then I think about every Solari that has died while Dr Dòyìnbó waited for me, and my chest tightens.

'After your mother located your aunt, it was time for her to go too. I feared her paranoia about your safety would cause her to keep you locked away in AOS. I needed you and your aunt to meet and I also knew your desire to find your parents would lead me straight to the serum. And you did. I sent my soldiers to the lab to retrieve the serum's location from you, but you managed to evade them. Not that it matters now. Everything has worked out exactly the way it needed to.'

He gives me a triumphant smile and I want to throw up.

So that's how they knew where we were and how to overpower us. A heavy feeling settles in my belly as I realize how easy I made it for Dr Dòyìnbó. I was so willing to trust him that I never stood a chance, neither did my parents. My fingers curl into fists by my side.

'If you've hurt them, I'll make you sorry.'

Dr Dòyìnbó frowns as if offended. 'Don't worry, both your parents are safe . . . for now at least.'

My fingers loosen as relief fills me. I finally know what happened to my parents, but the fact that Dr Dòyìnbó has kept them captive this whole time fully makes my Ike boil. He's been lying from the very beginning. When he said he was my father's friend. When he told me he was looking for Mum. All of it . . . lies.

'You're the reason the Rogues left AOS, aren't you?' Adanna's voice is as cold as Niyì's ice. 'They've been fighting for their right to live this whole time, haven't they? You said it before – the Councils would never believe a group of children over you. You made sure of that, discrediting the Rogues by spreading lies about their intentions. I always knew there was more to their story. I just never thought you'd be at the centre of it.'

'Of course,' Dr Dòyìnbó replies with an impressed look. 'Gbénga left the academy all those years ago after he discovered the truth about the Protectors and my plans for

Nigeria, but he escaped before I could contain him. He's the one who told Benjamin after he sought Gbénga out. That's why I couldn't risk any more people making contact with the Rogues. It was a close call when they came for Onyeka at AOS. I thought sending her out with Nchebe would keep her safe. I never imagined they'd be bold enough to attack at Millennium Market though. My mistake – Gbénga was always a tricky one. It's why I had to make sure everyone believed he and the Rogues were the enemy.'

Niyì moves then. He's been silent this whole time, and when he finally speaks, his voice is a hoarse croak.

'You've been lying since the beginning,' he whispers, mirroring my thoughts. 'Pretending to care about us, when in reality you've been letting us die.' He swallows then, as if the words are hurting him.

Dr Dòyìnbó merely stares at him, as if Niyì is a puzzle he's trying to figure out.

'Answer me!' Niyì screams and his face crumples. 'AOS is the only home I have,' Niyì whispers.

His head drops and the tears slide freely down his face. I can't stand to see them.

'It can still be your home,' Dr Dòyìnbó finally replies.

His smile is so oily I want to scream at Niyì not to listen. How did I not notice before?

'Join me, my child,' Dr Dòyìnbó continues. 'Surely it is better to be a Protector, even for a short while, than to lose your Ike?' He reaches inside his blazer and pulls out a small jet syringe, then slots the serum inside it. He holds it out to Niyì and points towards me. 'All you have to do is prove your loyalty by destroying the serum. It seems only fair that I use it to take down Benjamin's daughter at the same time.'

I gasp as it dawns on me what Dr Dòyìnbó plans to do. His eyes, shining with malice, meet mine. 'I know how much your Ike means to you. But neither you nor your wretched family deserve it.'

Niyì's head lifts then and our eyes meet. I flinch at the devastation in them. For the first time, I see the scared, insecure boy who has been clinging to AOS for too long, desperate to become a Protector and prove his worth. It's the same way I've been clinging to the idea of finding my father . . . of reuniting my family.

Dr Dòyìnbó's betrayal must feel to Niyì like losing his parents all over again, just as I did. But Dr Dòyìnbó is wrong. Niyì already *is* a Protector. He's been protecting me from the very beginning.

Niyì turns back to our head teacher. 'I won't do it.'

Dr Dòyìnbó's lips lift in a sad smile. 'That's disappointing, but not entirely surprising.'

He nods and the big man grabs the syringe from him, pushing Niyì out of the way. Before I can do anything, it's heading for me, and I freeze. Everything slows downs as the metal tip of the syringe gets closer. The sun glints off it and it winks at me in a menacing way.

'Don't do this,' Adanna yells, and from the corner of my eye I see Hassan tackle the soldier closest to him.

It's no use though. They can't save me. Then, suddenly, something is between me and the syringe.

'Niyì, no!' I scream.

I lunge forward to try to stop it, but it's as if I'm moving through treacle. My stomach drops as the syringe hits Niyì's neck. His hand clamps around the man's arm, ice covering it. The big man's eyes widen as he watches it creep up his arm, then suddenly it stops, melting away as the serum in Niyì takes effect. With a soft groan, Niyì drops to the ground and time speeds up again.

'You fool!' Dr Dòyìnbó roars.

'Niyì,' I yell at the same time, dropping down beside him. His eyes flutter briefly, but they don't open.

CHAPTER THIRTY-FIVE

Something cracks inside me at the sight of Niyì so still and helpless. A greyish colouring begins to spread over his skin, and I cover my mouth with my hand to keep my sobs back. Heavy footsteps sound as Hassan drops down beside us.

'Niyì,' he yells, placing a hand on Niyì's chest.

The moment replays in my mind as I struggle to make sense of it. *How did everything go so wrong?*

'Look out,' Adanna screams.

I look up to see Dr Dòyìnbó's soldiers charging our way, another one of those metal balls whizzing through the air.

'Hassan,' I cry, but he's already moving. An energy field forms in his hands and the net from the ball bounces off harmlessly.

Then he leaps forward, using the energy field as a shield as he battles to protect us. The loud grunt of someone hitting the ground makes me jump and I spot Adanna standing over one guy, a look of satisfaction on her face. She gives me a nod, before tackling another with one of Ms Bello's signature moves. Even my aunt is fighting, despite being gagged. A soldier is on the ground, out cold in front of her.

I look back down at Niyì, reluctant to leave him. I can't believe it's come to this – forced to defend ourselves from the very person who swore to protect us. The same person trying to escape up the steps quietly. *Of course he's making a run for it!*

Rage unlike anything I've ever felt before fills me.

My body shakes with power as it pulses in an overwhelming wave. I want to rip into Dr Dòyìnbó for what he's done. As if it heard my wish, my Ike rises and my hair flashes out, ploughing through his soldiers until it reaches Dr Dòyìnbó and wraps around his arms. He whimpers as I lift him from the steps, but I'm beyond caring. He's taken everything from us and I've had enough.

I pull him towards me until he's within touching distance. My inky hair floats in front of his face and I let it drift across his frightened features. My hair moves downwards, thickening as it does, until it's wrapped completely around him. I let it tighten, in a slow squeeze. I'll make him pay for what he's done.

I unleash all my grief and anger. I want him to feel what I feel. But a part of me knows something is wrong. This rage isn't me. My Ike has taken over, feeding on my pain, and I'm too weak to stop it, my hair constricting even further around Dr Dòyìnbó.

'Onyeka, stop!'

Adanna's voice sounds so distant, and I push it even further away.

'No,' I growl.

'Yeka, this isn't you.'

The sound of Cheyenne's nickname for me coming from Adanna is like a bucket of cold water and I freeze under its hold. Up until this point, I've always had to look for a memory to anchor my emotions. As Adanna's words wash over me, the memories of Cheyenne come to find me instead, like faded photographs coming to life. The details are blurry, but the joy and love are clear and sharp.

Then new memories come. Laughing with Adanna as she braids my hair. Hassan teaching me Pidgin. Niyì telling me he trusted me. The memories combine into something bigger ... stronger. With each new memory, the overwhelming emotions retreat. I follow them as they lead me back to myself.

'Yeka?' Adanna whispers beside me. 'We need you.'

I turn to her. She brought me back!

Which must mean Cheyenne is no longer my only anchor. *How could I have missed it?*

I remember all the other times I drew on a memory of my

friends to anchor my Ike, without even realizing what I was doing and what it meant. In Ìdánwò with Adanna, at the factory with Niyì, in the Gyrfalcon with Hassan – they all brought me back to myself.

My hair loosens around Dr Dòyìnbó. I won't become like him. Besides, I need him to find my parents. My eyes meet Adanna's concerned gaze and another realization dawns on me. My family has grown. Niyì, Hassan and Adanna . . . they're my family now. Even Dr Naomi. No . . . Aunt Naomi. If I don't help them, we won't make it out of here. And I can't let that happen.

All this time, I thought the only way I would get to have the family I've wanted for so long was to bring my parents back together. But I'm surrounded by people who love and accept me exactly as I am. That's what really matters. That's what family is and where true power comes from.

I look at Dr Dòyìnbó with new eyes as he struggles against my hold. So many think of him as the father of Solari, but he has no real love for us. He'd happily let us die just so he can have power. He'd make us use our Ike to hurt others. But it doesn't have to be that way. We can choose who we want to be.

'We need you,' Adanna repeats gently. 'We've got bigger problems.'

She's right. Hassan and my aunt are struggling to deal with the soldiers bearing down on us. I let go of Dr Dòyìnbó and he drops to the ground with a loud grunt. I use my hair to pull a thick vine from a nearby tree, wrapping it tightly around his body.

Then I turn my attention to the wave of soldiers emerging from the dense bush surrounding us. I quickly lose count of how many there are, my focus shifting to the first wave heading towards us. My hair spreads out around me in a defensive shield. To my right, Hassan's yellow energy field forms, and on my other side, Adanna drops into a crouch, ready to kick some major minion butt.

'Stay with Niyì,' I tell Dr Naomi, and she nods.

A rush of power sizzles through my body. I relax into it, embracing the pull. I am the bow and my hair is a quiver of arrows, waiting to be released. The soldiers are getting close now.

Wait, I caution myself. *Just a little closer.*

When the soldiers are only a few metres away, I let my Ike go. Hundreds of strands punch through body after body, sending them flying backwards.

My Ike and I are one.

Suddenly, a row of metal balls whizz through the air in my direction, and I brace myself. But then they stop in mid-air and spin back the way they came, releasing instead on the bewildered soldiers beneath them.

I swivel just in time to see Adanna fly through the air in a roundhouse kick. Her foot finds its mark against a soldier that avoided the net. Our eyes meet for a second and she flashes me a dimpled grin, before she whirls back into the thick of it.

A movement to my right catches my attention and a cluster of soldiers go sprawling to the ground, downed by an unseen force. Hassan must be hard at work too.

Another wave of soldiers press forward and bolt after bolt of my hair whistles through the air, picking them off. A fresh batch dash towards me, but they're nothing against my Ike. My hair barrels through them, sending each one flying in a different direction.

'Na our only chance be dis,' Hassan yells, breathing hard. 'Make we leave here.'

His voice forces me to stop and I suck in a ragged breath. It turns into a gasp as I realize that Dr Dòyìnbó is missing. His soldiers litter the ground like fallen bowling pins, but he's nowhere to be found. I look up at the surrounding bush and everything is still. If he's run off, then it's unlikely any more of his soldiers will come after us. But we can't be sure.

'Which way?' I pant, with a worried glance at the steps that could lead us into another trap.

Dr Naomi points to the cave. 'There's a tunnel that goes all the way through to a river. I remember it from when I was a kid. We can stay there until it's safe to head back to the Gyrfalcon.'

'What about Niyì?' I ask. There's no way we can carry him through the caves.

Hassan throws me a tired smile. 'No worry, I fit do this.'

He throws out one of his energy fields and it surrounds Niyì, lifting him off the ground.

'Rah,' I whisper weakly, and his smile grows even wider.

Suddenly, all the pain I've been suppressing rushes back, and I throw up the contents of my stomach. Not that there's much there; I can't remember the last time I ate. Adanna holds my hair back as my body heaves. I don't even have the strength to put it up.

Finally, my body relaxes, and I begin to shake as a wave of exhaustion sets in. So does the fear. I stare at Niyì and something in my belly squeezes. What happens to him now? *What happens to all of us?*

I grit my teeth, forcing my body to move. We need to get to safety. For now, that's the Gyrfalcon. After that, I don't know. We can't go back to AOS and I'm no longer sure who we can trust.

Nowhere is safe for Solari. Not any more.

CHAPTER
THIRTY-SIX

Niyì wakes with a groan, and Adanna, Hassan and my aunt rush to his side immediately. I can't rush anywhere as I'm too nauseous to move from my foldaway bed. We're in the mini med-suite on the Gyrfalcon.

Niyì's bed is next to mine and I've been staring at his sleeping face for over half an hour, imagining what I'll say to him when he finally wakes up.

'You saved me.'

The words spill out of me in a whispered rush and the corners of his mouth pull up into a weak smile.

'You're Nchebe now.' He struggles to sit up. 'What happened?'

Hassan fills him in, right up to the point we escaped through the caves, then hid by the river for a few hours. When it seemed safe, we returned to the Gyrfalcon. Adanna immediately disabled DAMI so Dr Dòyìnbó couldn't track us any more.

'Who's flying the jet then?' Niyì croaks when Hassan finishes.

'The auto-pilot works without DAMI,' Adanna replies.

Niyì turns to Aunt Naomi. 'Can you still cure Onyeka?'

I blink at him. Even with everything that's happened, he's still trying to protect me.

'We're going to my farmhouse,' Aunt Naomi replies, which is news to me. 'It's where I've been hiding all these years. It has a lab and I can modify the serum using the data from Benjamin's digital pad, if Adanna can work her magic on it.'

'But the serum is gone,' Niyì says.

I look away, unable to meet his gaze as guilt skates along my skin. So is his Ike . . . because of me.

'Technically, it's inside you, but I can use some of your DNA instead and synthesize a new serum. It'll take longer, but we have no choice.' Aunt Naomi places a hand on Niyì's shoulder. 'I might even be able to get back your Ike. I'm not making any promises, but I'll do my best to undo this.'

'I'll help,' Adanna adds firmly.

Their eyes lock, a promise I don't understand passing between them.

'Where you dey think he go?'

Hassan's voice breaks the moment, and we all know who

he's talking about immediately. It's the thing I've been most worried about ever since Dr Dòyìnbó escaped.

Adanna snorts. 'The academy, probably. It's where he's most powerful and, as he said, nobody will believe us over him.'

The jet goes quiet, the atmosphere changing as fear creeps in. What makes it worse is that we all know Dr Dòyìnbó will come after us eventually. We know too much, and he's waited too long to give up his plans now. The thing is, this is so much bigger than us now, and we can't just do nothing.

I sit up with difficulty. 'We have to go back and warn everybody.'

'You're right,' says Niyì in a quiet voice, and my eyes swing to him in surprise. 'Dr Dòyìnbó is a danger to the whole country and no Solari will be safe until he's stopped.'

'Especially if he discovers we're trying to fix the serum,' Aunt Naomi adds with a shiver. 'If he gets his hands on it, he'll be able to fulfil his plan to use Solari as his personal soldiers for ever, like trapped animals.'

'Maybe we could get the Rogues to help us?' Adanna says suddenly.

All eyes turn towards her at the startling suggestion. Adanna shrugs.

'What?' she says. 'There must be a reason why Onyeka's dad contacted Gbénga all those years ago and he did say in his message that the Rogues would help us.'

She's right. We'll need as many allies as we can get to take

Dr Dòyìnbó down and free the Solari in AOS. But it's not just them, I have to save my parents too. Unless we confront Dr Dòyìnbó, I'll never get them back.

A stray braid curls around my face – my Ike is flowing freely. Fuelled by pain, but anchored by the love of the family surrounding me. But it's not complete without Mum, and every moment I lose getting to know my dad makes my Ike boil with a rage I can't do anything about.

Adanna comes to stand beside my bed.

'We'll find your parents,' she whispers.

'How did—?' I begin, but she just shakes her head.

'You always get that look on your face when you're thinking about them.' She points to my hair, swaying in mid-air. 'Plus, your hair's doing that.'

Hassan straightens then, his body flickering for a moment. 'I ready to do dis,' he says, a quiet determination on his face.

Niyì sits up fully. 'Me too!'

Aunt Naomi is silent for a moment, and I hold my breath when she shakes her head.

'We're going to need to go shopping first,' she says. 'I don't have much food at my place.'

I stare at her, and then suddenly we're all laughing.

'We'd better leave you two to rest,' Aunt Naomi says when we finally calm down.

She and Hassan move towards the front of the jet. I go to lie back down, but a hand on my arm stops me.

'Are you going to tell Chey what's happening, or am I?' Adanna says with a mischievous grin on her face.

I roll my eyes. Somehow, their earlier conversation seems to have helped them form a new bond. Which makes us a trio now, I guess. I don't mind though.

I grin back at her. 'Let's tell her together.'

AUTHOR'S
NOTE

I am a Black woman, a mother, an Afro hair care educator and an author. I list all these things because they're what brought me to this point; they're the reason you're able to read about Onyeka and her journey of self-discovery. There are many stories about children with superpowers, but very few from the viewpoint of a young Black girl. That choice was deliberate on my part. I love books and I love reading. I still remember my favourite books as a child and they, in part, shaped the way I view the world. Books taught me to dream beyond what seemed possible and to use my imagination. But they also taught me the very narrow view of what the world considers normal and acceptable, and it rarely ever looked like me.

As a child, I didn't exist in literature. When I became a mother, I found the problem was still very real when I struggled to find books for my children, featuring characters that looked like them. This was the basis of my decision to become an author and it very much shapes the kind of stories I write.

I hope that when you read this book, it acts as both a mirror and a window, allowing some of you to see yourselves reflected back and others to dive into the rich and beautiful world of my Nigerian heritage – one that is rarely seen, explored or celebrated in children's literature. From the Pidgin English that's a huge part of who Hassan is, to the delicious foods native to Nigeria. All of which you can learn more about in the glossary and language guide.

I know it may seem like Afro hair is a strangely specific thing to focus a whole book on, but for me, and many who look like me, our hair has never just been hair. Growing up, my hair always had negative associations attached to it. I always believed that there was something *wrong* with it that *had* to be *fixed*, either by aggressive and excessive styling, chemical treatments or just plain hiding. It's a belief that followed me right into adulthood, until I finally learned how to care for my hair and started helping others to do the same.

I've since realised that it is this belief that does the most damage. A lie we've all been fed and too many have swallowed, that Afro textured hair is somehow inferior because it doesn't conform to the Western standards of beauty. So, when the idea for a new story came to me, it centred squarely on the idea of a girl who discovers that the very hair she has been taught to think of as a flaw is, in actual fact, her greatest strength. Thus, *Onyeka and the Academy of the Sun* was born. It's a thrilling, action-packed story about identity, friendship and family. But, perhaps most importantly, it's a story about accepting and loving yourself as you are and stepping into the power that it gives you. A power that is already there ... waiting. All you have to do is claim it!

Tọlá Okogwu

GLOSSARY

Agege Bread   A popular soft, sweet white bread. It is named after the place in Lagos, where it was first sold.

Akara   A type of fritter made from beans and often eaten for breakfast. Also known as beanballs.

Batá Drum   A double-headed drum with one end narrower than the other. It is used by the Yoruba people during religious ceremonies.

Boli   Ripe plantain that has been grilled, roasted or broiled.

Dodo   Ripe plantain that has been sliced and deep fried in oil.

Efo Riro   A stew / soup commonly made with spinach, palm oil, stock fish, crayfish and red bell peppers. It is often accompanied by solids such as pounded yam or fufu.

Jollof Rice   A rice dish made with tomatoes, onions, bell peppers and various spices. Its origins are a hotly contested topic across West Africa.

Naija   Slang name for Nigeria.

Pepper Soup   A very spicy soup, packed with meat and flavour. Popularly sold at Nigerian relaxation spots and used as a remedy for a cold.

Pounded Yam   Boiled yam that has been mashed or 'pounded' into a soft, semi-solid state. A staple dish in Nigeria, it is often eaten with soups / stews such as efo riro. It can also be made using yam flour.

Puff Puff   A sweet snack made of leavened dough, deep fried in oil. Similar to a doughnut or beignet.

Suya   A popular street food of spicy meat (beef, chicken, offal etc.) roasted or grilled on skewers or whole.

Talking Drum   A small drum shaped like an hourglass. When struck in a specific way, it can mimic the tone and sound of human speech.

Zobo   A tangy, bright red drink made from dried hibiscus petals, fruits and sometimes flavoured with ginger and other spices.

NIGERIAN PIDGIN ENGLISH

Nigerian Pidgin English or 'Pidgin' is a language spoken widely across Nigeria and much of West Africa in various forms. It is a mix of English and local languages, which enables people who do not share a common language to communicate. It originates from the late 17th and 18th centuries, during the transatlantic slave trade. It was originally used by British slave merchants and local African traders and then spread to the rest of the West African colonies. Though not currently recognised as an official language, it is estimated that up to 75 million people in Nigeria use it today.

Common words:

Abeg	Please
Am	Replaces him or her in a sentence
Chai	An exclamation, used to express surprise, grief, disappointment or anger

Dey	'To be' or to be in the process of doing something
Dis	This
Fit	Suggests an ability to do something – 'can'
How Far?	What's up? / Hi
Make	Signifies that you are going to do something – 'let'
O	Usually used at the end of a sentence. An exclamation often used to reiterate a point, answer a call, or used to confer agreement
Wan	Meaning 'to do' or 'want to'
Wahala	Trouble / problem. Though depending on the context, it can also mean 'yes' or 'no problem' (as in 'no wahala')
Wetin	What

ACKNOWLEDGEMENTS

This book started out as a tiny grain of an idea, as so many things do. 'What if a girl discovered that the very thing she considers her greatest flaw is, in fact, her greatest strength?'

Along the way, this idea has grown, shifted, screamed and blossomed into the story you see today, and it would not have done so without the help of a great many people. So, buckle up, because the thank yous are here.

The first and most important thank you is to God, my source and the one without whom none of this would be possible.

To my husband, Goziam – my rock and best friend. Thank you for believing in me when I didn't, and for sacrificing so much, so I could find myself and this story.

My gorgeous daughters, Elizabeth and Rebekah (Onyekachi). Being your mother is the greatest honour of my life and I hope I make you proud.

To my parents for your unconditional support and faith. You've always made room for me to find my own path and I will forever be grateful.

To my siblings, Folu and Seye. Thanks for accepting me as I am.

To Lois and Naomi – the best hype-cousins a girl could ever ask for and to the rest of my family for the continuous love, support and free babysitting.

To my editors, Amina Youssef, Kate Prosswimmer and Melissa Gitari. Thank you for pushing me to write things I didn't think I could, and for understanding the heart of Onyeka. To Rachel Denwood and Ali Dougal, thank you for catching the vision so early and fighting for this book. Olivia Horrox, Dan Fricker, Jesse Green, David McDougall, Sophie Storr, Laura Hough, Dani Wilson, Maud Sepult, Amy Fletcher, Jane Pizzey, Dom Brendon and the rest of the Simon & Schuster team, thank you for championing Onyeka.

Thank you to my brilliant agent, Claire Wilson, for believing in this story when it was just a few hastily re-worked chapters, and for your never-ending patience and honesty. Thank you also to Safae El-Ouahabi and everyone at RCW.

To Brittany Jackson for the amazing cover illustration, thank you for bringing Onyeka and her hair to such glorious life.

Tomi and Rachel, thank you for welcoming me into your

tribe and for helping to shape this story from its earliest incarnation.

Jasmine, you are such an inspiration. They ain't ready!

To my Sweetratu, I couldn't ask for a better group of women to call my friends.

Thank you, Lauren, Mahsuda, Sam and Katie – for being a safe space in the infamous year that was 2020. I'd also like to thank the many friends that have supported me on my writing journey and the incredible writing community that has embraced me so warmly.

A special thank you to Lola Olajide, Rahima Begum, Kilani Latifat, Deborah Balogun, Phoebe Esin, Ijapari Onolaja, Adeline Gilbertson, Abi Daré and Femi Fadugba. This book would not be what it is without your incredible insight and help.

I am incredibly grateful to the Arts Council England for the Developing Your Creative Practice grant that birthed the first draft of this book.

A final thanks to you, the reader who chose this book out of the many wonderful stories out there. Thank you for coming on this journey with me and I hope to see you soon in the next chapter.

Tọlá Okogwu is a British-Nigerian author, journalist and hair care educator. Born in Lagos, Nigeria, but raised in London, England, she holds a bachelor of arts degree in journalism. Having spent several years exploring the world of blogging, hair care and freelance writing, she finally returned to her first love: fiction. She is the author of the Daddy Do My Hair? picture book series, as well as *Aziza's Secret Fairy Door* under the pen name Lola Morayo. *Onyeka and the Academy of the Sun* is her first middle-grade book. Tọlá now lives in Kent with her husband and two daughters. An avid reader and lover of music, she's also a sucker for melted cheese.

Learn more at tolaokogwu.com.

Read on for an exclusive scene from . . .

ONYEKA

AND THE RISE OF THE REBELS

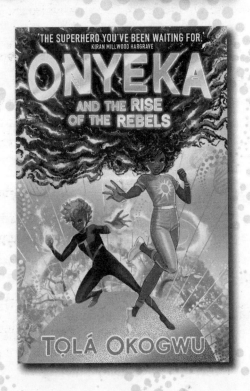

Adanna doesn't finish what she's saying as a loud siren blares through the lab. Aunt Naomi scrambles towards a small panel embedded in the wall. Her fingers fly as she types in a series of numbers.

'Someone's breached the perimeter defences,' she finally mutters.

We all stare at her. I didn't even know the farmhouse had perimeter defences.

'Who is it?' Niyì asks.

'I can't tell yet, but they're armed and fast,' Aunt Naomi replies, concern creeping into her voice.

'It has to be Dr Dòyìnbó,' Adanna whispers. 'Who else would be looking for us?'

Aunt Naomi's face looks strained. 'Well, whoever it is, they'll be here soon.'

'Wetin we dey do?' Hassan starts flickering in and out of view, and I feel my eyes go dizzy.

'The Gyrfalcon,' Niyì says in a firm voice. 'It's prepped and ready to go.'

Aunt Naomi grabs a bag from one of the cupboards and starts stuffing papers and other things I don't recognize into it.

'What are you doing?' I ask her. 'We don't have time for this.'

She doesn't stop. 'We can't just leave all this data here. It's too dangerous if it gets into the wrong hands.'

'She's right,' Adanna says from behind me. Then sparks light up the room as a computer next to her explodes.

'Chai!' Hassan squeaks. 'Wetin dey happen?'

'I'm frying the computer hard drives. It's not fool proof, but it's all we've got time for.'

Adanna closes her eyes and another hard drive explodes with a bang. Soon the lab looks like a fireworks display gone wrong. Wires fly across the room as Aunt Naomi's expensive equipment disintegrates. A big grin spreads over Adanna's face, but I feel a small pang of worry. I didn't know she liked blowing things up so much.

'We don't have time for you to destroy all of them,' Aunt Naomi shouts. 'We have to leave now. They'll be here soon.'

She leads the way out of the lab, and we rush through the hallway and back up the stairs. The kitchen looks just as it did at breakfast. Hassan and Niyì were supposed to clear everything away, but our plates still line the table top, pieces of cold yam and omelette congealing by the sink. Sunlight streams through the windows as we head for the glass doors at the back of the farmhouse. It's a straight path from there to the barn and the safety of the Gyrfalcon.

Even though we've all been waiting for the time to come, it's still hard to believe that Dr Dòyìnbó has finally found us. *We're not ready!*

Then there's a sudden loud bang and glass goes flying everywhere. Dense smoke fills the air.

'Get down,' Niyì screams as the remaining windows break with a crash.

I hit the floor, pulling Adanna down with me. The air fills with smoke, making it difficult to see . . . to even breathe. The intruders have arrived, and they've come prepared.

'Can you see anyone?' Adanna whispers urgently beside me.

I shake my head before I realize she can't see me through all the smoke.

'No,' I whisper back. 'We need to keep moving.'

'How? It's too smoky in here.'

She's right. But maybe I can help with that. Using the panic racing through me, I call up my Ike and anchor it quickly. I stand as my hair lifts around me, separating into two thick ropes. I let them rise into the air above my head and they start to spin, slowly at first, then building up speed until they whirl above my head like a giant fan.

The smoke begins to lift, sucked up by the vacuum created by my hair. Familiar furniture once again becomes visible. Soon I can see walls and shattered window frames where glass once sat. Then I spot a dark figure where the front door used to be. I don't hesitate and a bolt of hair whips out, knocking the figure aside like a bowling pin.

But they're not alone. More appear at the door and windows dressed in the same green camouflage uniform as the soldiers who attacked us in my father's lab. Their faces are blank, covered by thick, black breathing masks. I guess they thought they'd be storming a smoke-filled room . . . *#sorrynotsorry.*

Niyì, Hassan and Aunt Naomi are close to the back doors and they stand now, ready to face the soldiers. Adanna is up too, crouched in a defensive position. My eyes meet Niyì's. He's never had to fight without his Ike before. Even though Ms Bello taught us to defend ourselves without using it, we always knew we could call on it if we needed to.

If things get bad now, he won't have that safety net. I shake my head at him, hoping he listens and stays back. Niyì's face tightens and his stance shifts, falling into the strike position Ms Bello taught us. *I guess that's that.*

'The plan hasn't changed,' he calls out. 'We just have a new obstacle.'

His voice acts like a starter gun and the soldiers charge at us. I pull my hair back like a whip, ready to deal with the first person who even looks at me wrong. Everything slows down as a soldier nears and I feel anticipation rise in me. Then a sharp voice rings out.

'SLEEP!'

The soldier charging towards me freezes mid stride, his head cocked to the side in disbelief. Then he crumples to the ground like a puppet whose strings have been cut. He isn't the only one. Every other soldier falls too, hitting the ground in a collective thud that sounds like a slap.

'We don't have time for this,' Aunt Naomi says, breathing heavily.